D0204062

ELISHA'S BONES

A NOVEL

DON HOESEL

BETHANYHOUSE
MINNEAPOLIS, MINNESOTA

Elisha's Bones
Copyright © 2009
Don Hoesel

Cover design by John Hamilton Design

Scripture quotations are from the HOLY BIBLE, NEW INTERNATIONAL VERSION®. Copyright © 1973, 1978, 1984 by International Bible Society. Used by permission of Zondervan Publishing House. All rights reserved.

All rights reserved. No part of this publication may be reproduced, stored in a retrieval system, or transmitted in any form or by any means—electronic, mechanical, photocopying, recording, or otherwise—without the prior written permission of the publisher. The only exception is brief quotations in printed reviews.

Published by Bethany House Publishers
11400 Hampshire Avenue South
Bloomington, Minnesota 55438

Bethany House Publishers is a division of
Baker Publishing Group, Grand Rapids, Michigan.

Printed in the United States of America

Library of Congress Cataloging-in-Publication Data

Hoesel, Don.
Elisha's bones / Don Hoesel.
p. cm.
ISBN 978-0-7642-0560-6 (pbk.)
1. Archaeology teachers—Fiction. 2. Elisha (Biblical prophet)—Relics—Fiction. 3. Christian antiquities—Fiction. 4. Secret societies—Fiction. I. Title.

PS3608.04765E65 2009
813'.6—dc22

2008051034

For Dawn

Thank you for the last seventeen years.
This book wouldn't have happened without you.

BETHANY BAPTIST CHURCH
SEAL
VANCOUVER, B.C.

ELISHA'S BONES

Chapter 1

KV65, THE VALLEY OF THE KINGS, EGYPT, 2003

It's an indescribable sound when a piece of ancient stone finally gives. There's a subtle pop, like the top of an aspirin bottle coming off to reveal that annoying wad of cotton stuffed into the plastic innards. Except that, in this case, the sound is amplified by whatever magnitude is required to testify to two tons of rock wrenching away from symbiotic stone. I think what I hear is the instant equalization of air pressure—a force that can either ease or enhance whatever stresses time has built into the coupling. It's the moment when the whole event can result in either expectant silence, or in a violent redistribution of forces. And it all has to be in my imagination, because it's only a romantic notion to think that the mind could process the event in real time.

Several field technicians are trying to peer into the sarcophagus through the three-inch gap made available courtesy of the removal of the two-ton slab of red granite that hangs suspended on a precarious-looking pulley mechanism. I know the machine is rated for far greater than the stone's weight, but even that bit of professional knowledge doesn't alleviate the fear I would have about slipping my fingers into the crack. I place my hand against the stone and press against it to stop its lazy swing. At almost four thousand pounds, even an arc of a few millimeters would put a severe dent into someone's skull, and having worked with these young men and women for almost a month, I'm not certain that all of them are observant enough to stay out of striking distance.

It's stifling in here; lines of sweat run down my face and soak my collar. The burial chamber is less than six and a half meters long, and there are a dozen people in it and more machinery than should be allowed at a dig, purely on principle—not to mention the five bright fluorescent lights that make casting a shadow an impossibility. I know one of the supposed benefits of these lights is that they don't give off heat, but I'm not buying it, no matter what the brochure says.

I lean in, the stone stilled beneath my fingers, and I think that I can almost smell the cumin, thyme, and cinnamon that went into the preparation of the mummy, even through the probable two additional coffins encasing the reposing ancient. I glance around at the assembled junior members of the team, whom Jim has asked me to instruct as most of them pursue doctorates. I'm not much of a teacher—I could never hold down a professorship—yet I take pleasure in seeing the looks on the team's faces as they enjoy this unprecedented opportunity.

KV65 is one of those rare opportunities granted to someone in my profession—a find that makes careers, that puts one in every serious journal in the field for the next decade. True, this is Jim's baby, but he brought me in to handle the particulars, and that will yield almost as many peer accolades. It's virtually another Tutankhamen, even down to the post-Amarna dating.

Before I can call for a flashlight, at least four click on. The mingling beams push back the blackness of the sepulcher. Leaning in close, forgetting the earlier reluctance to place my body in harm's way, I let my eyes grow accustomed to the alternating splotches of light and shadow against the outer coffin until I can see a deep red that I recognize as ancient cypress. A few moments pass as I ponder why this is peculiar—why the sight of a wood that's perfectly appropriate for this region, and for the time period that saw this man interred, seems wrong. And when the answer waves its little hand, I find another of those teaching opportunities I so enjoy. I ignore it.

But one of my young acolytes will not see his education shortchanged.

"Dr. Hawthorne?" Brown asks. He's twenty-four, attached to the Smithsonian, earning a doctorate at Cornell, and might be the smartest person in this room. And I'm only slightly threatened by that. After all, the successful practice of archaeology involves more than knowledge; there's an equal measure of luck. And after watching Brown over the last few weeks, I'm inclined to think that's a commodity he has not stockpiled.

I straighten and motion for him to take a look, taking a step back as he crosses in front of me. I'm careful to avoid bumping his cast-encased arm.

"Interesting," he says after a moment.

"Yep." A quick glance around reveals that the other people in the room want in on the discussion, so I prompt post-grad Cornell. "Can you share with the rest of the class?"

"The outer coffin is just wood," Brown says. "There's no linen, no gold overlay. Nothing to indicate that this is anything but the burial chamber for a minor noble."

"Which is odd because...?"

"Everything we've seen to this point would indicate this is a royal tomb. It's almost spot-on Tutankhamen."

For as much as I dislike the whole teaching aspect of this assignment, at least I've caught on to one of the tricks practiced by genuine academics: allowing my most-qualified student to teach in my stead.

I'm as intrigued as is he by the incongruity of the barren outer coffin within a sepulcher—indeed an entire tomb—that is patterned after those of the pharaohs. And I have no immediate answer.

I wipe my brow, aware that I'm leaving a film of red dust under my hairline. Now that we've found something unexpected, I'm more bothered by the fact that Jim is not here. It's worse than Will's absence. At least my brother has a concrete reason for missing an event important enough to earn the presence of two *National Geographic* photographers. Jim wouldn't give me a reason that carried any kind of weight; he was merely insistent that the events of the morning proceed. Not that he had to do too much arm-twisting; were he here, I would still be the one walking the Scooby Gang through their paces. Even so, there's an unspoken rule that something of this magnitude should only take place under the watchful eye of the archaeologist of record. I shake my head, consoling myself with the thought that Jim's absence means the guys from *National Geographic* will have to put my face on the cover of their next issue.

I field a sudden urge to light a cigar and my hand moves to my breast pocket, but I let the impulse pass, the dust in the chamber making it hard enough to breathe.

Several members of the team are jockeying for position around the sepulcher, shining their small lights into the crack. For the few moments that I afford myself to watch them, I have to smile at their exuberance. I'm not much older than most of them, but at this moment they seem younger than I ever remember being.

Almost on their own, my eyes find Sarah. She's a Connecticut girl, with the superior and privileged vocal intonations to prove it. She's one of the few on the team who has halted her education with a graduate degree.

But I can tell that she loves the work. She is as attentive, detailed, and driven as any of the others working alongside her. And she's easy on the eyes. I've always been a sucker for a brunette, and Sarah has deep brown eyes to go with her lustrous locks.

As if she can sense my gaze, she looks up and, after a pause, gives me a small smile. That's another thing about northeastern women: a smile can convey a great deal.

I'm the first to look away, and Brown saves me from having to consider what that says about me.

"Dr. Hawthorne?"

The puzzlement in his voice has me at his side in an instant. I crouch and follow the beam of his flashlight as it passes back and forth over a portion of the outer coffin. All I can see is a slight curve, yet it's enough to hint that it's at least vaguely anthropoid. I'm about to ask Brown what I'm supposed to be seeing when the light flashes by a faded irregularity in the wood. I'm not certain how long it takes before I recognize the abnormality as script, but when the revelation comes, it adds another mystery to the tally.

"Coptic," I say, and Brown nods in my periphery.

The find draws me closer, until I'm breathing the stale air, squinting to make sense of the words carved into the wood. There is little that is new in excavations conducted in the Valley of the Kings; everything has a corollary. KV9 is what comes to mind, with its walls decorated with ancient graffiti in a mixture of Coptic and Lycian. But this isn't graffiti; this is something else entirely. For a brief moment Nag Hammadi passes through my mind, solely for the Coptic element, but I let the thought go before it can find purchase. Playing connect-the-dots without even the most basic evidentiary support is seldom productive.

The narrow opening and the inconstant lighting make it difficult to decipher much, but I engage in a round of serious squinting until I'm able to pull a few words from the darkness. And, in so doing, I feel a twinge of excitement creep up my spine even as a frown lodges on my face—which is what happens when the happiness of a new discovery is marred by the potential effects the find will have on the timeline of the larger work. I make a conscious decision to allow the former reaction to prevail, since the one phrase I can identify is so unusual. If I'm correct, it translates, albeit roughly, to *bones of the holy man*. I'd have to look at the whole of the text to verify the translation. What's more intriguing is how the writing could have appeared inside a sealed sarcophagus that, to this point, had borne every indication of having been preserved inviolate.

A kink in my back cuts my survey short and I stand and place an impatient hand on the lid of the sepulcher. I'm tempted to give it a push, a small nudge—just enough so that I can see what other surprises await me on the other side of the granite. What stops me—besides the ugly specter of archaeological protocol that mandates an incremental removal of the obstacle—is another, equally important, code which says that Jim should be present for this. I don't know his reasons for missing the opening, but I must give him the option to lead the team in investigating something so unexpected. And this isn't the kind of thing I can relay over the radio. I want to see his face when he hears the news—that whoever is interred in 65 might be some kind of Egyptian seer. I see the *National Geographic* guys loading film. I shake my head; Jim might wind up on the cover after all.

"Take a break, folks," I tell my plebes. The one who looks most disappointed is Brown, who was probably hoping I'd give the lid a prodigious shove. With a last glance around the burial chamber and one long look at Sarah, who has her perfect nose almost inserted into the crypt's crack, I turn and walk away.

The antechamber I enter gives me an immediate feeling of solitude, and it has the benefit of seeming some degrees cooler. Our team has already picked through this room, and we've begun a cursory study of the contents of the annex on its western side. I walk over and around chalk lines and tape, following in the path of countless footfalls through the eight-meter-long room. Leaving the antechamber, I step into a long and narrow corridor leading to the stairway that will take me topside.

I reach the stairs and start up, watching my footing on the roughhewn steps. The gloom starts to give way to natural light, and before long I am standing beneath a blazing Egyptian sun. The first thing I do is pull a cigar from my breast pocket, a Dominican. Once it's lit, I take a long and satisfying puff.

The Valley of the Kings sits in the shadow of al-Qurn and the peak, fittingly, has a pyramid shape. It's red and barren, and time-weathered in a way that makes it seem like the embodiment of age—the patriarch of the Theban Hills. In the bright sunlight of the valley, I see what the dust beneath the ground has done to my clothes. I attempt a few halfhearted brushes at my sleeves before giving up and starting for our camp. From around the other side of the hill come the sounds of my brother's team. I'm not really bothered by the fact that Will hasn't been around for the events temporarily halted somewhere beneath my feet. Had he not decided to stay the course with the bypass tunnel to the treasure room, it would have been going against form. When we were kids, Will would leave presents ignored beneath the Christmas tree if he'd opened one that caught his attention. It's a single-mindedness that can be maddening to everyone around him. I think he is scheduled to reach the tomb wall sometime this morning, and I try to set some mental Post-it Note as a reminder to be there when it happens.

Our camp consists of an RV and three pickups, which is a bit light for a dig of this size, but we're not out in the middle of nowhere. Most of the team is set up at a hotel in Luxor, where we also keep provision. As I cover the distance to the camp, though, I see another vehicle, a new BMW, parked next to one of the pickups.

I'm almost to the RV, ready to start up the steps, before I hear the voices coming from inside. On most occasions I wouldn't give it another thought; this is the command center, with people coming and going at all hours. What gives me pause now, beyond the unfamiliar car, is that the muffled noises I assume to be conversation sound decidedly unfriendly. Before I can make a decision about potential eavesdropping, the door swings open.

There is a moment when I think the first of the two men at the top of the stairs is going to fall on top of me as he brings himself to a sudden halt, unprepared to find another person blocking his exit, but that moment passes and he finds his balance. He is perhaps thirty-five, dark-haired, and too fair-skinned to call this place home. He wears a gray suit, and shoes that look far too expensive to be forced to endure this kind of environment. He stands there for as long as it takes to give me a single sour glance and then he's down the stairs. It's a strange passing—oddly close—because I haven't moved away from the bottom of the steps. Belatedly I step to the side, and as he walks through the space I've just vacated, he half turns and gives me a slight smile that sends a psychic shudder running up my spine.

Our inspector, courtesy of the Supreme Council of Antiquities, is the man following. Magdy descends the stairs and offers a polite nod when he reaches the bottom. He hurries after the other man, who has almost reached the BMW. When they drive off, I watch until I lose sight of the car behind one of the hills. I turn back to the RV and see Jim standing in the doorway.

"Trouble with Magdy?" I ask, even though it's obvious that something's amiss. The tension I've stumbled into is as palpable as a Scottish fog, even if it has dissipated with the men's departure. Jim's answer is a grunt and a step back to allow me into the RV. Only when we are both inside, and he has claimed a chair at the small table in the kitchen area, does he respond.

"The SCA is drafting orders for us to cease the project."

For one of the few times in recent memory, I am left speechless.

Jim gives me a wry smile. "That's essentially what I said. Only with a good deal more cursing." He chuckles and takes a sip of ice water.

"We spent months getting approval to excavate 65," I say, feeling a dull pain take hold along the base of my neck. "They can't make us pull up now."

Finessing an application through the SCA's Department of Foreign Archaeological Missions is a level of hell missing from Dante's book. Meticulousness and a genuine love for tedium are required skills for those trying to fight their way through the minutia of the application process. If even a single item is missing or incomplete, it can set a project back by months. That's the reason I know our potential ouster has nothing to do with a flaw in the application; I'd swear to the document's integrity right down to the molecular level.

And to the best of my knowledge, our inspector has been satisfied with the excavation and the subsequent preservation work, and with the timeliness of his pay.

I think Jim is allowing my indignation to suffice as his own, because I can almost see the anger leaching away from him. He leans back in his chair and starts drumming his fingers on the tabletop. "Technically, they can." Then he winks. "But if we file a protest with the director's office, we might gain a month or so before they force us out."

James Winfield, Professor Emeritus at the University of Canberra, is a throwback to the time when scholarly men met in quaint taverns and downed pints of dark beer while arguing points of philosophy, theology, and hard science. When I studied at his feet, I thought he looked like Oxford—at least the Oxford in my imagination. I've since been to Oxford, and I prefer my naïve fancies. He's also the man who taught me the value of a good cigar and the reason I associate refinement with the practice.

I can follow Jim's line of reasoning, can even be somewhat assuaged by it. What I can't understand is the reason behind the sudden removal of SCA support.

"Why?" is the only question I can muster.

Always a step ahead, Jim says, "Not why, but *who*."

"I don't follow."

"In one variation of the question, who within the SCA wants our project shut down?"

Running a hand through my dusty hair, I nod. But Jim's phrasing isn't lost on me.

"What's the other variation?"

"I would think that's obvious," Jim answers, forever the teacher. He waits until I track with him, which does not take long.

"Who was the other guy?" I ask, referring to the man accompanying our inspector. I have never seen a foreigner employed by the SCA, although it is not unheard of for them to bring in a foreign consultant. Too, KV65 is an important work site, and we've entertained more than the usual share of interested parties in the months we've been here. I'd just assumed our mystery man fit that category. Although, now that I think back on our near collision and the strange vibe I got from the guy, I reconsider—especially because Jim wouldn't have said anything had he not detected something odd about the man.

"I'm not sure," Jim answers. "It seemed obvious that his presence unnerved our beloved inspector. Magdy acted like a small insect in a large web."

That prompts a smile, if for no other reason than that an SCA inspector is the bane of an archaeologist's existence.

"What I do know," Jim adds, fingers drumming the tabletop, "is that he was one of my countrymen."

"A consultant?"

He lets my question hang there, and the look on his face suggests he is struggling to corral his thoughts. After a while, he shakes his head and looks up.

"Consultant is likely," he says, though his voice lacks conviction. He offers a dismissive wave. "I'm sure it's just a misunderstanding. A few phone calls and the whole business will be cleared up." Then he brightens as if only now remembering something. "How are things going below?"

While still reeling from the possibility of having to abandon KV65, I'm grateful for the redirection. Placing this other issue aside, I'm about to tell Jim what we've found when the RV makes a minor shift beneath my feet.

When the moment has ended, a silence fills the vacuum, and it seems almost as threatening as whatever set the vehicle to shaking. Jim and I lock eyes and then he is out of his chair and we are both heading toward the door. Our time in this country has given us ample experience with incidents of seismic activity; neither of us need to verbalize that what we just felt was something else.

My only thought is for the team I left down below, and the run across the hot sand is a blur. I'm two decades younger than Jim and so I leave him behind. By the time I reach the tomb entrance, the first of my team are exiting from the earth's darkened maw. The clinical part of me notes that the doorway is intact; there are no new fissures along the limestone and shale layers to indicate an earthquake. The plebes are coughing; they're covered in dust. One of the *National Geographic* guys is cradling a broken camera.

I see Brown come out. He's coughing but he gives me a small wave. "We're fine," he manages.

Despite his assurances, I do a head count. With everyone moving around, I have to do it twice before I'm reasonably sure that everyone's accounted for. And it is this relative assurance which makes me feel better about what I ask next.

"Is the sarcophagus okay?"

Brown, who is still hacking up dust, gives an emphatic nod. "It's fine. The structure held; everything's fine."

The fact that the team is all right, coupled with our good fortune of the tomb still being intact, elates me, and it takes a bit of the edge off of the urgency I'm feeling. When Jim reaches us, his breathing labored, he takes his own turn ascertaining the health of his charges and then runs a clinical eye over the dig site. The sun is directly overhead and there are no shadows in the valley, yet his eyes are hooded. Sweat beads on his forehead. He looks like a big-game hunter out on the savannah, surveying the vast terrain. Images like this are what I juxtapose against the more common mien of the academic that is his normal skin.

"What was it?" Jim asks.

The question gives me pause. I know it wasn't an earthquake, and Brown insists the tomb is intact, which precludes a cave-in. And what kind of cave-in would have been felt across the hundred yards separating the tomb from the RV anyway? Could it have been a whole subterranean cavern collapsing in upon itself?

"I don't know," I finally say.

I half acknowledge that one of the *National Geographic* cameras is snapping again, and I feel a bit like the emperor sans clothes. I'm hoping that this part will wind up on the cutting-room floor, but that's wishful thinking. More than likely, there will be an inset with a picture of my face, complete with poignant caption.

Jim doesn't say anything but I see him doing the same thing I am: ascertaining how an event we can't qualify has affected us. There's a very real hope that it hasn't. Our team and our site appear to be unhurt. This last thought hangs there, teasing me with something I can't quite put my finger on. I stand there, hands on hips, still catching my breath and squinting against the sun. I'm looking at the faces of these people I've come to know over the last few months, and it seems like a long time passes before it hits me that the face that should be most familiar is missing.

"Where's Will?"

The question falls on deaf ears. Most of them are milling about, content to let others determine what happens next. Jim is busy talking with Brown about the contents of the opened sarcophagus. The *National Geographic* guys are snapping away. It then occurs to me that neither of the two excavators assisting my brother is here, either. I smile and shake my head; it's just like Will to ignore the unanticipated movement of the very earth into which he's digging.

I don't realize I've left the group until I'm already halfway around the hill. I'm not sure what it is that makes me uneasy; I only register that I'm no longer smiling. That's when it hits me: I can't hear any noise coming from the auxiliary dig site.

I break into a jog and it's just as I'm about to round the last bend separating me from Will's team that I hear the first cries.

I now start to sprint, and as the last of the rock shifts out of my line of sight, I catch a first glimpse of Will's dig, with fear now my only reality. Where there should be straight grid lines and pin flags and a clean trench leading to an ancient wall interred in the earth, instead there is a chaos that looks like the aftermath of an explosion. The trench is gone, covered in with sand, dirt, and a large chunk of the adjoining hillside. Particles of sediment and pulverized rock hang like a haze in the air. I've stopped running, frozen by what I see. It's as if I'm experiencing all of this through a fog, and the only thing that seems to reach me is something sounding like an insistent buzzing. When the noise resolves into a man's weak voice, my eyes track to movement in the trench.

Urgency unlocks my legs, and I rush toward the man half buried in debris while at the same time reaching for the radio at my waist. I'm shouting something, but I can't decipher the garbled sounds of my own voice. Then the radio is on the ground and I'm on my knees, pawing at the dirt. It's Steve Connelly. The clinical part of me is trying to determine his condition as I work to free him; it's that part of my brain that I need to use right now, instead of the portion that knows Steve has been married for seven years and has two kids waiting for him back in Minnesota—the part that knows there were other people out here when this thing happened.

There is a flash of movement behind me and then there are several pairs of hands alongside mine, loosening the earth's hold on Steve. When we are able to pull him up, he's limp, but breathing. I let others move him away from the trench because it's becoming difficult to keep my irrational side in check. The activity behind me falls away as my eyes flit over the site. There is no movement, no flashes of color. There's a thin barrier between me and true panic, and I'm not sure how long it will stand up. The only thing I can tell myself is that I don't even know Will was down there.

Except that I know.

There's a shovel by the rebar that is the auxiliary dig's focal point. In what seems like slow motion, I walk over and pick it up, my eyes never leaving the trench. The first shovelful of dirt is like sand, and it runs off, spills over the side. I plunge the tool in a second time, then a third. I lose myself in the task, a growing urgency adding speed with each thrust. At some point, others frantically join me in the digging. I feel Jim there, although my eyes don't leave the worn surface of the shovel.

I don't know how long we dig, how much earth we move, or how many shovels take their turn. We're four feet down and it seems as if we've been digging a long time. I've stopped sweating. And then I hear something—a sound that doesn't originate amid the fevered exertion of at least a dozen men and women abandoning themselves to the work. It's a sound that seems to come from far away, a muffled voice. I stop. I stop for the first time. I listen. And I hear Will's voice, coming from below; he sounds so far away. With something close to a snarl I bring the shovel up and plunge it into the ground, and the abused implement breaks at the shaft.

Tossing the useless thing aside, I go to my knees, pawing at the red earth. "I'm coming Will!" I shout. My hands are bleeding, fingernails ripped away, but I don't feel any of it.

I catch sight of Sarah, who is now digging next to me. The privileged Connecticut girl, covered in grime, blood on her fingers, and tears streaming down her cheeks. Her eyes find mine and, in that instant, I know that haunted look will remain with me forever.

CHAPTER 2

EVANSTON UNIVERSITY, ELLEN, NORTH CAROLINA, PRESENT DAY

Merry Christmas," Duckey says as he slides a rectangular box wrapped in red foil across the table. His manicured fingers stay on the present for a few seconds, long enough to let me know that whatever is inside is something he would want for himself, even as the thousand-dollar watch peeking out from under his shirtsleeve assures me he probably already has several of whatever it is.

"Thanks, Ducks." I pick up the gift, a sticky film of syrup on the bottom, and shake it a little. I can hear something shifting around inside, but it is not heavy and does not seem breakable. "You want me to open it now?"

He waves off my question with his fork, then sinks the implement into a multilayered wedge of pancakes. "Your call. Just make sure you treat them with the care they deserve."

I consider doing the deed here, on the lacquered wooden table in the Student Union, but there is something that seems wrong about that, especially if I am right about what is inside.

With a nod of thanks I set the package to the side, careful to avoid the largest of the sticky spots, and reach for my coffee cup.

Jim Duckett, Dean of the Schools of Anthropology and Archaeology at Evanston University, finishes his pancakes and moves on to the last two sausage links on his plate. It still amazes me that he can eat like he does, at an age when the metabolisms of most men begin to slow and an extra layer of fat starts to build above the belt line. I'm convinced that no man should have a thirty-four waist at age forty-five. True, I wear the same size, but I'm still three years shy of forty. And I do eschew the elevator for the six flights of stairs in my apartment building.

"So you're staying here for the holiday break."

"Nowhere I'd rather be," I say.

Having exercised his privilege as dean to forgo the last week of the semester, Duckey and his brood will leave for Denver in the morning to visit his in-laws. The children will have two weeks of doting from their grandparents, and Duckey and the missus will haunt the ski slopes with guiltless abandon.

His plate empty, Duckey leans back in his chair and reaches for his breast pocket. It's a reflex. I see his fingers slide over the smooth metal of his cigar case and then fall away. We've been eating a late-afternoon meal, a breakfast-for-dinner thing, in this place—usually the same booth—a few times a week for the last two years, and he has never been able to break himself of the habit of reaching for an after-meal cigar. At least twice he's gotten as far as selecting one, clipping its end, and lighting up, with me watching in amused silence before the student manager of the grill could come over and remind him that "This is a no-smoking facility."

He watches me for a minute in silence, his appraiser's eye flitting over me and, apparently, finding something distasteful.

During this perusal, which I bear with stoic good nature—this being just the most recent of many such evaluations—I return his look with a smug smile. Around us, the sights and sounds of a semideserted student hangout run their courses.

"If you were anyone but you, I'd say you were itching for someone to ask you to spend the holidays with them," Duckey says. "But I know better. It wouldn't surprise me if you don't leave your apartment for days."

"I'll still have to check the mail."

"If you don't make it out of the building, it doesn't count."

"The life of a hermit is underrated."

"You're an odd human being."

"That may well be true, but I'll be the one walking around in my underwear and watching ESPN all day." I effect a faraway look and a blissful smile. "And I won't shower, and I'll eat frozen cookie dough right out of the wrapper, and I'll sleep in a fort made out of sheets."

"All right, Peter Pan, I won't feel sorry for you. But one of these days you're going to die in your apartment and no one will know until your stink drifts out from under the door. And I've smelled your place, so it may take some time for someone to notice the difference."

"You'll come looking for me when I don't show up for dinner."

"Don't count on it." Duckey looks at his watch—a luxury afforded by the books he's written. Some of them have even avoided the derision built into the peer review system, although I'd never give him the satisfaction of acknowledging that. "I've got to get going, Jack. We still have some packing to do and you know how the airport's going to be."

"Have a good trip, Ducks," I say. "And thanks." I gesture at the unopened present.

"You're welcome. See you in three."

After he's gone, retreating with the near-silent footfalls that are among the last vestiges of his CIA days, I finish my lukewarm coffee and then gather Duckey's tray as well as my own and deposit them on the grill counter on my way out. I'll miss Duckey, but he's right; I'll be content here by myself, cloistered with old books and good cigars. With that thought in mind, I begin tearing the red foil paper away from the present, until I see it's Cubans. Duckey orders the cigars from a shop in Spain and he slips me a box now and again, though usually they're the lower-end ones. But these are Hoyo de Monterrey Double Corona, arguably one of the best, and probably running somewhere near six hundred dollars. I stroke the gift lovingly as I step outside.

It is a good cold that hits my face and fills my nose as I traverse the uneven sidewalk between the university and my apartment building. Even though it's still Friday and there are officially two more days left in the semester, I feel an impending liberation—a freedom from any responsibilities more involved than watering my single plant. And since that's a cactus, I can even be forgiven that one duty. True, I will likely get to work grading four classes' worth of term papers sometime during my first week of vacation, when boredom comes calling, but for now I can enjoy the anticipation.

I hold my briefcase in one hand and cradle the present from Duckey in the other. It will be nice to relax with a book, to throw myself into some light reading. I have a new text that details the excavation of an ancient civilization on the Yucatan

Peninsula, which I've been looking forward to starting as soon as the semester ended.

Carter Village, my domicile, is composed of a single building, rising six stories above the sleepy college town of Ellen, North Carolina. Those six stories make it the highest structure for sixty-three miles in any direction, besting the Mendel Science Center by three floors. My apartment occupies the southeast corner of the fifth floor, and from one of my windows I can look down on the whole of the college campus, a comparatively small hamlet of learning in the center of a baser geography. There have been many nights in which I have stood at that window and looked down on the campus, its walkways lighted to keep the student body inviolate from the wild darkness, and wished a plague down on the entire thing: a single fell swoop of Old Testament wrath that would level the place and set the survivors to grappling with something pragmatic instead of academic. Of late, those instances happen with less frequency, and the jury's still out on whether or not that's a good thing.

I take the five weathered stone steps to the heavy oak door at the top and tug at one of the brass handles. I pass through, stopping at the mail station and retrieving three items from the small box: the water bill, a piece of junk mail advertising satellite television, and—my smile grows a bit wider—my *National Geographic*. I don't care how many serious texts I read, how deep erudition burrows into my skull, this magazine will always mean something special to me, even in an era when the glut of nature and science and history channels makes it anachronistic. In my opinion, no amount of video footage can provoke the imagination like a single brilliantly colored photo from this periodical. And there's always the sentimental element.

I will that thought away and, as I turn from my mailbox, Angie exits the stairwell, the door giving a loud creak.

"You're early," she says as she checks her mail.

"It's one of the benefits of not taking an interest in my students; I can get a grad student to teach a class and not feel guilty."

"Funny," she says, sliding her hand into the crook of my arm as she passes. "Come and have a cup of coffee with me."

I hesitate for only a moment. I always have time for a cup of coffee with a lovely woman.

Her apartment, although identical in layout, bears no resemblance to my own. My furnishings illustrate the interior design limitations of a single, broke college professor. Angie, on the other hand, has impeccable taste. Everything in her seven-hundred-square-foot abode is chic and complementary, and it has nothing to do with money. We bring home the same amount, give or take a few hundred dollars, and I know that a good portion of that has to go toward that new Mustang she washes and polishes every sunny Saturday morning.

I settle onto one of the two high-back stools at the breakfast nook, setting my mail and the cigars aside as Angie pours two cups of coffee from one of those faux-industrial coffeemakers.

"New shoes?" I ask.

"I bought them last month. You're just not very observant."

"I am about some things. Like your hair. You got it cut." She places a cup in front of me and I taste it, finding it strong. "And a few highlights?"

"Not bad, Professor."

Angie takes a seat on a stool across the island from me. She's wearing a white tank top that shows off her toned arms.

Angie's a runner, and a serious one. She wakes up at six every morning and does a circuit that takes her out of Ellen down Highway 31 and then back into town on State Road 77. It must be five miles and she hardly breaks a sweat. I know she hits some running paths on the other side of Baker Hill—my knowledge hard-earned after once making the mistake of agreeing to go with her one cold fall morning. I was new in the building, and she must have liked what she saw; and I certainly noticed her easy smile and long runner's legs. I figured I could work through the pain for a few mornings and see what kind of interest there was on both sides. She almost lost me a quarter mile into a tree-lined dirt trail that cut at some insane angle across the south side of Baker Hill. If she hadn't taken pity on me and cut her run short, I probably would have died. My body would have stayed on the path until some university student found me and poked me with a stick to make sure I was dead.

"I guess I just don't look at your feet. I've never been much of a foot guy."

"Wouldn't have pegged you for a hair guy, either."

She's right about that. I'm not a hair guy. I am, however, a detail guy—something of which Angie is quite aware. And my old profession was all about looking for clues; it's a required skill.

"Are you still staying here over the holidays?" Angie asks.

"When you've got a good thing going . . ."

Last year Angie asked me to go to Switzerland with her over Christmas. I think she felt sorry for me. The invitation was genuine, if a bit reluctant. I admit it would have been fun tooling around Europe with someone who could find a good time if it was hiding at a funeral, but I declined. A spur-of-the-moment trip to the Alps is not cheap. And seeing the relieved look on her face, even if she had tried her best to conceal it, told me I'd done the right thing.

"Are you going to invite me skiing again?" I ask.

"Not this year."

I'm almost pleased to hear her say that. Probably because the ski trip, the Mustang, the countless pairs of new shoes, and the fact that every piece of clothing she wears has been designed by someone famous for outfitting runway models, has begun to make me think that perhaps I'm not very good with money. If she can afford to do and to purchase all of these things, then she is either much better at handling money or she has a cash cow in her closet.

"I'm going to Australia," she says. "I got to thinking, what's the point of taking a winter break if you're going to spend it somewhere cold?"

My response is to raise my coffee cup and take a long drink, swallowing measured sips until the liquid begins to burn my throat. I wonder if she can see the irritation in my eyes. But then, knowing Angie, it would only make her enjoy her trip more. I'd love to go back to Australia. I wouldn't admit this to anyone but, regardless of the fact that I'm a professional with a string of enviable academic and career achievements to my credit, I've always wanted to pet a kangaroo.

"You do know that most shark attacks worldwide occur in the waters off of Australia, right?"

She sticks her tongue out at me and rises from the stool.

"What? Get eaten by a shark and miss out on more of these delightful chats? Besides," she adds with a conspiratorial wink, "if I don't come back, maybe they'll rent the apartment to a pretty co-ed."

I consider that for a moment, a manufactured smile on my face to let her know I might be enjoying the idea. But when I too stand, I return her wink. "You're all the woman I need, Angie."

I reach for the candy dish on the counter and pilfer a pair of bite-sized chocolate bars. I slip them into my pants pocket and start for the door.

"If you really think that, then you've got to get out more," she calls after me.

And she's probably right.

As I climb the steps I hear the hum of the elevator motor through the cinder-block wall. I know that elevator inspectors come out to certify the thing's safety but I have yet to chance it. I've just never had a good feeling about it, and I need the exercise anyway.

By the time I reach the third-floor landing, I'm breathing heavy and my left knee reminds me that I may need to look for an apartment closer to the ground. I'm sweating as I approach the fourth floor—not much, just a thin sheen on my forehead and an uncomfortable warmth beneath my heavy coat. It's almost anticlimactic when I reach my floor and push through the metal door, some vague sense of accomplishment on my person.

I am halfway down the hall, my feet silent on the dirty carpet, before I notice the man standing near my door. He wears a dark suit that is nicer than anything I own, and his hands are in his pockets. I get the feeling that he's been waiting for some time.

My feet slow and then stop, and I am standing in the middle of the hallway with a heavy briefcase in one hand, a box of expensive cigars and my mail in the other, and a curious feeling.

"Hello," I say.

The man rocks on his heels and smiles, although it's a strange expression, as if he is not used to it. It's enough to send a shiver up my back; déjà vu with substance. I can almost feel the sand under my shoes. Except that I know I've never seen him before.

"Good afternoon, Dr. Hawthorne," he says with the hint of an accent that suggests his roots are in northern dairy country.

I doubt it is a good thing that he knows my name. I'm not a paranoid person, but when someone in a dark suit is waiting for me outside of my apartment, and when that person also knows my name, and I see no balloons or television cameras signaling I've won a lottery, I get an uneasy feeling in my stomach. I conduct a mental inventory, searching for something I've done that could engender a visit from a law-enforcement official, because this guy is giving off a professional vibe, like Duckey might have before giving up government service for higher education. As far as I can tell, I'm clean. Except for . . .

"They're not directly from Cuba, if that makes any difference," I say, raising the cigar box for his inspection.

I see puzzlement flash across my visitor's face as he looks at the package, still half wrapped in red foil.

"Relax, Dr. Hawthorne," he says once he realizes what I'm proffering. "I'm not here about cigars."

I'm feeling a bit like a player in an odd film noir—the part in every such movie where two people meet in a place where shadows cover all but the parts of their faces below the nose, where a single bead of sweat runs down an actor's cheek, and where someone, invariably, pulls a gun. The only things missing in real life are concealing shadows—the hallway is actually quite bright—and the requisite sense of danger. And I'm reasonably confident no gun will come into play.

"Okay, I'll bite. Who are you, and why are you standing in front of my door?"

He chuckles at my directness and steps aside, allowing me access to my apartment.

"I'm sorry, Dr. Hawthorne. I know it's a bit unnerving to have someone waiting for you when you arrive home, but I missed you at your office earlier today."

I close the distance to the door and, after setting down my briefcase, retrieve my key from my pants pocket.

"You didn't answer my question," I say as I push the door open and stoop for my briefcase.

I see him nod and he gives another small chuckle.

"I guess I didn't." He offers a hand. "My name is Gregory Hardy, Dr. Hawthorne. And I have a business proposition for you."

Chapter 3

To the best of my recollection, this is my first time in a drawing room. When the butler—a detached but polite fellow with no discernible accent—brought me here, he said, "If you will wait in the drawing room, sir, Mr. Reese will be with you shortly." The way he said it, stretching out the words *drawing room* as if they identified a chamber of mystery, suggested what it might be like to gain entry to the Oval Office—a room with hundreds of years' worth of world-changing moments woven into the walls and carpet.

Mr. Reese's drawing room looks like nothing more than a small parlor, with expensive items and the signs of a tasteful decorator's hand, but a parlor nonetheless. It occurs to me that I've never known what a drawing room was and I'm a bit disappointed. Opposite the doorway are an active fireplace and a single burgundy chair half facing the hearth. There's a book on a fluted end table within arm's reach of anyone occupying the chair. To my right, two couches the same color as the chair fill out the room. They look new, as if they've never been sat on. Although there is a spare feel to the furnishings, I like the balance.

On two walls—the one to my left, and the one harboring the fireplace—are three paintings from the Impressionist school. I recognize two of them and I have no doubt that they are the genuine articles. It seems odd that if I were to view these same pieces in a museum, it would be from behind a velvet rope. Just because I can, I step up to the nearest painting and run my finger along its frame. I'm not bold enough to touch the painting itself. The artwork beneath my hand is probably valued close to one hundred thousand dollars, and I feel a reverence for the singular beauty of the piece. If this is any indicator of other treasures on the property, then Mr. Reese must have more money than God.

I turn away from the painting until I am facing the doorway and, once I register what I'm seeing, my breath catches in my throat. Above a high, narrow table that supports a few bottles of expensive brandy, hangs a large brass mirror that I immediately date as ninth century B.C. The light from the fire sends ripples over the polished metal surface and I see few imperfections on its face. The edges are gilded, the work of a master craftsman, with only small scratches and dents to mark its passage through the better part of three millennia. Like a moth to a flame, I cross the soft, dark carpet until I am mere inches from the artifact, until I can see my face looking out at me. I am beyond words; if the paintings evoked appreciation, this ancient mirror wrenches longing from deep within my soul.

"It's Hebrew."

"I know. Somewhere between 860 and 885 B.C." After another look, I turn from the mirror to meet the lord of this manor.

I've seen pictures of the man, although these are scarcer than photos of other men of similar means. Most of them have come from charity events; one documented a talk he gave at UNC. What strikes me most is that he looks frailer in the flesh.

"Very good, Dr. Hawthorne. By my guess, there are less

than fifty people in the world who could truly appreciate that mirror."

"And about that many who could afford it."

He laughs and it's a good-natured sound, if labored. He crosses the room and extends a hand that, in better light, reveals the accumulation of years in the wrinkles and liver spots. I'm six-one and Mr. Reese matches my height. It's possible he's even a little taller. But my guess is that I outweigh him by at least seventy-five pounds. This is a different human being than the one from the few pictures I remember, and I cannot help but believe that he is ill.

"It's a pleasure to meet you, Dr. Hawthorne," he says in a voice that's still strong. There's a spark in his eyes too, which defies whatever it is that is seeping the strength from him.

"Thank you, Mr. Reese. But please call me Jack."

"Only if you call me Gordon."

He releases my hand and gestures to the display of bottles.

"May I offer you a drink?"

I decline and Gordon drops ice into a tumbler and fills it with bourbon.

"I'm not supposed to drink anymore, but I have a great deal of good liquor in my home and it would be a shame to let it go to waste."

He gives me a wink and heads for the couch closest to the fireplace. I follow, a slight smile on my lips. This is a man I could like, despite the gaps in our economic and social positions. As he settles into the cushions, I take a seat on the couch opposite him. In the muted light of the room, the flickering flames of the hearth highlight the deep creases in his face.

"Thank you for coming down here on such short notice,

Jack. I know that your break from the university is a scant three weeks and the project I have for you may take some time." He speaks as if my acceptance of the job is a foregone conclusion.

"I didn't have much choice about coming, Gordon. It's not as if billionaires are breaking down my door to offer me jobs. If nothing else, I have to find out what you have in mind."

"Curiosity is the paramount character trait for those in your line of work," Gordon says with a chuckle.

"I won't argue that."

Gordon is silent for a moment, his eyes on the fire. Suddenly he turns to me, casting a thoughtful eye my way, and says, "You haven't done any fieldwork in almost five years. Why?"

It's a germane question, but not one for which I have a ready answer. There is the obvious one, of course—that Will's death drove me from my profession, along with the weeks of trying to get first the Egyptian government and then the American consular office to investigate it as something more than an accident, only to run into one wall after another. Even Jim counseled me to let the matter drop, despite the fact that there was an obvious blast pattern, and that the strange visit by the SCA minutes before the accident could not have been coincidence. As I consider these things, Gordon's eyes hold mine, convincing me that he already knows everything I'm thinking.

"I was tired," is my only response.

Gordon remains silent through the time it takes him to drain half of the glass. The fact that I've been less than forthcoming—even when we are both aware of the other's unobstructed view of the playing field—bothers me, but I remind myself that I do not know this man, and I owe him nothing—not even honesty. I don't have to validate public record.

"Are you well rested now?" he asks without a hint of judgment.

Despite what I have already told him, I've had a few offers during my time at the university. Some of them were unique enough ventures to tempt me into returning to a world outside of the staid confines of academia. In the end, I turned each of them down. I was not ready and, in truth, I'm not certain I am now. Perhaps Gordon Reese is catching me at the right time; maybe there's something in the wintry air that is making me antsy; or maybe I'm at some watershed moment in a long and undefined grieving process. Whatever it is, I'm here.

"That really depends on what you have to tell me, Gordon."

The expression on the billionaire's face indicates he appreciates my answer. He lapses into a thoughtful silence, his gaze back on the dancing flames, and I wait for him to speak. He brought me here for a reason, and he will tell me in his time.

"I trust you know your Old Testament," Gordon says.

I nod. "As well as most people do, I'd guess."

"A good deal more than most, I'd venture," he says, and a laugh shakes his thin frame. "It's practically an archaeological streetlamp. I wouldn't be surprised if half of all archaeologists, past and present, owe a good portion of their initial interest in the field to their childhood hearings of Old Testament tales."

I have to join him in his mirth because, in my case, his guess is spot-on. There's a decent chance that if I hadn't spent time during my formative years at the knees of my parents, listening to stories about ancient peoples and places, I might not have taken an interest in the study of civilizations arisen, fallen, and in some cases, passed from collective memory.

"I see I've come close to the truth?" Gordon asks.

I nod and give him his due. "It may have had some influence on my education, yes."

He grunts an acknowledgment and then shakes his head. "It amazes me how such a seminal work can be so neglected once one enters into serious study. It's quite odd, really."

I do not respond, principally because it seems such a childish thing to say coming from such a bright man. It's the equivalent of suggesting that a person earning his doctorate in English Literature should spend time studying children's books. While these books might have instilled in the doctoral candidate a love of reading, their usefulness has long been spent.

"I can tell by your expression that you do not agree with me?" There is no indictment in the question, but I sense a hint of sadness.

I let a few ticks pass in silence while I consider the question. I have no wish to offend this man, yet I have a feeling he would not be fooled by insincerity. I watch the flames dance over logs half consumed by their ravenous tendrils.

"The Bible does not teach a person the fundamentals of archaeology," I say. "While there are some interesting stories in there—some even corroborated by other documents and excavations—you can't use the book as some sort of treasure map."

"That is certainly true, Jack. However, the treasures are there, if one knows where to look."

We're getting to the crux of it now. I can feel the reason behind the meeting looming just outside the edge of the conversation. I do not answer. It is his story to unravel, his request to make.

"Second Kings," Gordon says. "Chapter thirteen, verses twenty and twenty-one."

Of course, I'm silent. I could no more quote the contents of those verses than I could recite pi to the thousandth place.

Gordon looks once again at the fire, and when he speaks he's quoting the biblical passage. " 'Elisha died and was buried. Now Moabite raiders used to enter the country every spring. Once while some Israelites were burying a man, suddenly they saw a band of raiders; so they threw the man's body into Elisha's tomb. When the body touched Elisha's bones, the man came to life and stood up on his feet.' "

From deep within my childhood experiences, I pull a memory that corresponds to what Gordon has just recited, although I remember hearing the passage in Old English. It sounds different spoken in contemporary language.

"Do you know, Jack, that there's no other mention of this event after these two verses? Imagine that: a dead man is tossed onto the bones of a prophet and he comes back to life. Today, that would be quite a story. The media would be all over it."

"As they would the fact that this same man made an axhead float in water, and that he summoned bears out of the woods to kill children who made fun of his receding hairline." It's coming back to me now—these fanciful Bible stories. I remember not liking Elisha very much. It seemed petulant to use the power of God to get even with taunting youths.

Gordon picks up on my thoughts and nods. "Yes, the Bible is full of what seem to us abuses of divine power. But I think the work is richer for it. There is a certain weight—a believability—that is granted to a book that shows its heroes in all of their insidious splendor."

Gordon's glass is empty and I'm beginning to wish I'd taken him up on the offer of a drink of my own. If nothing else, it would give me something to do during these pauses in the conversation.

"What's your interest in the story, Gordon?" Asking this question seems a better choice than engaging the man in a debate about the historicity of Scripture. That's not a discussion I'm prepared for, nor one I would want to participate in even if my thirteenth-century Incan stone ducks were all in a row.

"In a way, I've already mentioned it." He leans forward, pushing himself away from the embracing couch, closing the distance between us. Everything about his posture and his manner suggests conspiratorial excitement. "Tell me, what would happen if you and I were at lunch with the president and, halfway through dessert, he pulled out a gun and shot the waiter?"

It's an odd question considering the previous subject matter, and I'm left feeling stunned for a few seconds. Gordon, though, is waiting for an answer, so I take a stab at it.

"He'd be arrested and they'd haul him off to jail. President or no, you can't indiscriminately shoot people."

He looks irritated at my response and waves it off.

"My fault. You're using today as a frame of reference. Let's say that it's the 1960s and we're supping with Kennedy? What would happen then?"

I think I see now where he's going with this. "In that case, you and I would be whisked away and we'd never be heard from again. The waiter's death would be described as an accident, and anyone who saw anything would either be killed or cowed into silence."

"Ah, that's more like it. But the predominant characteristic of the event is that it would disappear from history, at least to the extent that something like that can be covered up. But there's always someone willing to talk, even if the history books are scrubbed clean. And that's where the absence of information attracts attention. It's the secrecy that draws people in, Jack. Tell people something, no matter how farfetched, and most will believe it. Tell them nothing—"

"And you've got a conspiracy," I finish.

"Right. It's the lack of information." Gordon's eyes bore into mine. "Just two verses, then nothing. Gone. Scrubbed from history—as much as could be done. But someone talked and so they couldn't erase it entirely. They minimized it."

A heavy silence settles over us, and it seems darker in the room. Gordon's face remains lit by the waning fire. It's difficult for me not to get caught up by his passion, his magnetism. What makes it easier to retain a clinical distance is my understanding of what Gordon has implied, and then what he wants from me. Gordon Reese thinks—believes—that the bones are real. Worse, he wants me to find them for him.

I consider my words, but no matter how I try to couch my terms, I cannot dilute what needs to be said.

"Mr. Reese, I think you're reaching. You can't use a silence of historical record to prove a conspiracy—especially not in a document as old as Second Kings." I feel odd even using the word *conspiracy*. "And if the story were true, who would try to cover it up? And why? Besides, there's no biblical precedent for hiding a miraculous event. Quite the contrary, in fact. Anything even remotely supernatural was documented with great care."

Gordon leans back, but not enough to signify disengagement.

"One of the interesting things about the story—the thing that sets it apart from many others in the Bible—is that there were so few witnesses. This was not Elijah on Mount Carmel, or the Ark of the Covenant smiting the Philistines with boils. This was a small group of men, alone in a cemetery. A much easier event to keep quiet."

"Except that they didn't keep it quiet. It's right there in black and white."

"Only to the extent that the Roswell crash is recorded in underground journals, or in the fashion that people whisper about the mysterious circumstances surrounding the death of Marilyn Monroe. No, Jack, it looks to me as if the writers of this section of the Scriptures—and remember, this was likely penned by a group of scholars during the Assyrian captivity—chose to treat this as legend, since they could not force it out of collective lore."

A part of my brain is now charting my exit from this place, and the prospect of a disappointing flight home. Yet another part—the purely academic—wants to discuss the theory, especially with one of the world's richest men. At least then, when I'm back at Evanston and telling the story to Duckey, I can share with him that I sat in Gordon Reese's drawing room and debated theoretical antiquities.

Before I can say anything, Gordon grips the armrest and pulls himself to his feet. As he struggles to get himself upright, I have a fear that he might fall over. But he regains his balance before I can react.

"It's a comfortable couch," he explains, "but if I sit too long, I can't get up." He takes slow and measured steps to the fireplace and removes the poker from its stand. With his back to me, he slides the mesh curtain aside and prods the spent logs with the implement until there's a cavity in the center and the flames find fresh purchase. The task done, he returns the poker to its stand but does not turn around.

"You didn't ask me to come here just because of two Bible verses," I say. Now that I think about it, it makes sense that a man like Gordon would have done his research before initiating this sort of project. He knows something, and this piques my interest.

"I've spent a good many years in this pursuit. It's only been recently, however, that my search has taken on a heightened sense of urgency." He places a hand on the mantel and turns so that he can see me. I realize, then, that I'm looking at a man who is not just ill. He's dying.

His eyes, though, are alive with flame—with purpose.

"You'd be surprised at what I've discovered, Jack."

I would have to be a fool not to realize why he's so interested in the remnants of a dead prophet. His own mortality is catching up with him and, like all men, he is searching for something to save him from his fate.

"Even if the bones are real," I say after a long pause, "and that's a big *if*—what makes you think they possess any kind of power?"

"Because the power of God does not fade over time, Dr. Hawthorne," he says, absolute certainty in his voice. "The bones are as alive with healing energy today as they were the day the Israelites tossed their friend's carcass on them."

It is a claim I cannot argue. How does one contest against another man's blind faith?

CHAPTER 4

I wake up with sweat on my face and a sick feeling in the pit of my stomach. I hate planes. I've always thought I have some inner-ear thing that brings me just south of ill on anything prone to unexpected movements. Planes, roller coasters, and big-city taxis all produce the feeling.

I look out the window but all I see is the thick cloud cover separating me from terra firma. My watch tells me it will be another hour before we start our descent into the Venezuelan capital—an hour to either sort through or ignore the mixed feelings I have about returning to a place I once knew well. On one hand, it feels good to be moving. For the first time in years I feel as if I've taken a step toward something. Still, there's a part of me that is not convinced this is a significant change in momentum. I tell myself that this job does not constitute a return to my pre-teaching profession. This is a short-term business deal, after which I will return to Evanston and go back to the serious matter of molding young minds and flirting with Angie. What belies that line of reasoning, though, is the tingle at the back of my neck that I only get when I'm excited about something. And when I'm eating Lemonheads. And I have to admit that I feel more energized than normal, especially considering that I've spent most of the day in cabs, airports, and planes of dubious mechanical soundness.

Through a break in the clouds I see the ocean as a patch of darker blue. I came near to growing up on boats, and the sea has been a comforting image for me for as long as I can remember. My dad was a nautical spirit trapped in the body of a skinny, bespectacled inventor. I don't know how many patents he held, but there was more than enough money for him to be able to launch the boat when the weather warmed, and then to keep my mom, brother, and me sailing the Florida Keys all summer. When I think about the man, I see him on the deck of some long-lined wooden beauty, wearing a contented smile. Through the eyes of a child, he seemed larger when azure blue seas surrounded us, when the wind caught the mainsail, and the bow sent spray over my face. It's that snapshot of my dad that I carry in my mind.

He's been gone for almost a decade, but I wonder what he would think about this trip. I can see him leaning back in the brown leather chair in his office, his index finger tapping the armrest. He would look at me for a while, then ask a simple question. Something like, "Are you sure you're doing this for the right reasons?" Reasons were important to the man. He was as concerned with motivations as he was with results. He was fond of saying that doing something extraordinary for the wrong reason was worse than doing nothing. Of course, he had firmly established opinions concerning what constituted a right reason. Everything he did was filtered through the lens of his religious upbringing. If the end result, as he saw it, did not mesh with his faith, then it shouldn't be done. That's it. No room for argument. If nothing else, knowing my father's conviction made me think long and hard before I answered any question he asked. I probably have him to thank for my interest in Greek philosophy, especially Aristotle's treatises on logic. In this case, provided my answer was satisfactory, a gleam would have appeared in his eyes as he imagined the possibilities for adventure that a trip like this promised. That's another one of the gifts my dad gave me: a sense of adventure, a need to explore. Mr. Reese called it curiosity.

The man snoring in the seat next to me shifts position and slumps closer and I can smell the salt and vinegar potato chips on his breath. An exploration of the man's culinary tastes is not the sort of adventure I have in mind and I give him a shove sufficient to send him invading the personal space of the unfortunate Korean gentleman in the aisle seat. The latter gives me a helpless look before shifting his shoulder so that the sleeping man is forced to perform some unconscious straightening maneuver or face the prospect of toppling over and testing the integrity of the seat belt. With a last hearty snort, the man achieves a precarious balance within the boundaries of the invisible walls rising up from his armrests. My Korean companion and I watch for a few seconds, avoiding each other's eyes, but ready for a resumption of the human Ping-Pong game that is international air travel.

I'm a bit surprised at the demographics of the flight, because—granting that it has been several years since my last trip to this part of the world—I cannot remember an instance prior to this one when the passenger profile was not ninety percent Latin American to ten percent white tourist. There are at least six American businessmen in the first-class section of the 767, along with a number of the wealthier tourists. I've also counted at least half a dozen Asians, a large number of North Americans of more modest means, a smattering of Europeans of dubious origin, and one young couple sitting in the row behind me who speak Arabic in quiet voices. I've grasped enough of the hushed conversation to know that they're recently married and have already been to Paris and New York. The flight reminds me that much has changed since I was here last, and that Venezuela—or at least Caracas—has made impressive progress toward becoming a modern city. This is a caution to remain alert, and to realize it might take some time to clear the cobwebs from a long-unused portion of my skill set.

I console myself with the knowledge that what I'm doing here amounts to little more than advanced library work—even if Gordon's research, exhaustive to the point of obsession, makes a compelling case. Maps, symbols, ancient texts—all of it seeming to form a blurry multimillennial snapshot of something with great significance. It's the most intriguing prospect I've ever been presented, regardless of the fact that it cannot possibly be true. Do I believe God exists? Sure. Do I believe the Bible is the arbiter of theological knowledge? There it gets a little hazy. The Bible contains hundreds of fantastical accounts presented to us as fact. But can a reasonable, modern man accept that the earth was created in six days, or that Jonah survived in the stomach of a large fish, or that Joshua stopped the sun from moving? And since these things are presented to us as truth, how can we determine what, in the Book, is factual? Do I believe that a prophet of God died and that his bones contain divine power? That these bones can bring people back from the dead? The simple answer to that question is no.

Nevertheless, Gordon's documents have brought me here, and it's up to me to either disprove or corroborate his theories. My belief is that I will catch my return flight having done the former, and I'm not sure if I can even hope for the other outcome. It's not the existence of the bones that I find troubling. Civilizations have been known to pass holy artifacts through the generations. Rather, what troubles me is the man's faith in the bones. The supernatural power he longs to find is a figment, and maybe it's the sympathetic part of me that thinks it would be better not to find the artifacts at all, rather than to deliver them to the man so that he can see his folly revealed.

My musings are interrupted when the plane's jostling sends my neighbor sliding into my personal space. After a deep sigh, I serve to the Korean and then sit back, a small smile on my face as I wait for his next move.

Caracas sits in the oblong bowl of an open valley floor, lush green mountains rising up along the north and east. It is like an old friend. After a long separation, and after the initial awkward phase, I can slip with ease into its eddies. It's a city teeming with industry and purpose, as well as a certain necessary aimlessness woven into the fabric of any place that lures throngs of people into close proximity. The feeling I have now, walking down Avenida Lecuña, is the same one I have when traversing Third Avenue in New York, or Beale Street in Memphis, or Merchant in Dublin. It's individuals, with their small stories, producing something larger than the sum of their parts, something buzzing with expectant energy. It's the cold fusion of urban life.

As the car-filled street grinds to a halt, save for the motorcycles that slip around and through the gridlock, I'm glad that I'm on foot. A half mile back I let the car go that Reese rented for me, so that I could beat the pavement and relearn the feel of the city. One thing I'd forgotten is how the streets rival those of San Francisco in their steepness. My calves start to burn as I make my way uphill.

I turn off Lecuña onto Bolivar, a street that reminds me of those accidental side streets in Europe, where a foreigner can eat and shop like a local and still remain steps away from streets designed to ease anxiety in the same manner a kindergarten hallway reassures children on the first day of school.

I pass three businesses that share a common weathered redbrick front. After the last doorway and before the long wall gives way to a narrow alley, followed by a similar arrangement of stores in off-white stucco, a darkened entrance appears, one absent of any identifying marks. A set of stone steps lead up to an unlighted corridor. I enter and start up the steps, trailed by the scent of wet rock and mold. Once I reach the top, the corridor forces me to the right, to a single windowless metal door coated with an old layer of thick brown paint. It's hardly the sort of setup most business owners concerned with foot traffic would prefer. But Romero has never been interested in mass-marketing his wares. He caters to an exclusive clientele, the kind with a lot of money, and the refinement to understand the quality of his products. Me? I'm neither refined nor have I ever been loaded enough to fit Romero's customer profile—at least until now, when I'm playing with someone else's money.

I grasp the door handle and give a sharp tug and it opens with a metallic creak that must be audible back on the sidewalk. The thing that hits me first is the smell. It's flowery—lilacs, I think. What it means is that Romero has a wealthy client who has expressed an appreciation for the flower. And for the money many of his regulars drop here, he does not mind going out of his way to tailor the shopping experience to their liking.

When I enter, I see my friend do the classic television double take and I smile at the surprise on his face and give him a little wink. I walk along the display of burial masks lining a portion of the street-side wall while I wait for the proprietor to finish with his customers. I imagine he's giving them the short sell now, just trying to get them out of the place. I run a finger along a well-preserved interment façade from Southeast Asia and wonder at the use of archaeology as interior design.

Most of his merchandise comes from this continent, with arrangements by period and by region. Past the burial masks is an assortment of Aztec and Toltec totems, their squat and grotesque bodies acting as scene markers for some events that can give me the willies if I really think about them. I like that he's left the shop as it has always been—free of clutter, decorative color, or unnecessary artwork. Instead, it is mostly white walls, gray carpet, and black metal lighting fixtures. The minimalism suggests a proprietor who has confidence in the product selling itself.

Out of the corner of my eye I see the old couple leaving, the man's hand in the small of the woman's back. Their body language suggests that Romero has made them quite a deal, and the buyer wants to get out before the seller realizes he has made a mistake.

I am still facing the burial-mask display when I feel Romero come up behind me.

"It looks like you just made those folks very happy," I say as the door shuts behind the couple.

"Curse you for showing up unannounced and forcing me to undervalue my merchandise."

"With the prices you charge, consider it a rebalancing of your karma."

And then there are strong hands pulling me around and into an affectionate, too-tight hug. When he pulls away, Romero's hands remain on my shoulders and he regards me with warm eyes. Romero Habilla is a large man, but still refined. I would almost call him elegant, except that word is appropriate for someone of slighter frame. He is a well-groomed bull.

"You don't visit for six years and you expect me to concentrate on a sale?" He claps my upper arm and looks me up and down. "You've gotten heavy."

My arm stings.

"One of the curses of academic life."

He turns but leaves a hand on my arm, directing me toward a doorway on the other side of the showroom.

"Yes, I heard you were teaching. At first I didn't believe it, but then I pulled up the Web page of your university and there's your picture." He squeezes my elbow and adds, "It's not a very good picture."

Romero's office is a mirror of the man in its understated sophistication. It is small and sparsely furnished but the few items in it are high-end. There is no true desk, but rather an immaculate teakwood table on which sits a dual-monitor computer, a phone, and a single notepad and pen. A comfortable-looking leather chair is behind the desk, and there are two smaller matching ones on the opposite side.

Romero leads me to one of the guest chairs and lowers himself into the other.

"It's good to see you," he says.

"It's nice to be back. A little strange, but nice."

"Yes, we're cosmopolitan now. Courting the world." He gives a dismissive wave. "It's veneer, my friend. The city is no different."

"That's not really what I mean."

He looks at me in silence for a moment before grunting and leaning forward.

"I'm sorry about Will. When Esperanza told me, I . . ."

He trails off and I give him a small smile—one that tells him I appreciate the sentiment. I think he feels guilty about not getting hold of me after it happened, but then I didn't make it easy for anyone to find me.

"My mom appreciated the flowers."

"It was the very least I could do. If I'd had more notice, I would have made the trip."

"Me too," I say, then wave off his questioning look. My body was there for my brother's funeral, but my mind was a world away. It's almost like trying to remember a dream. I see flashes of the people who filed into the church, the blue of the sky at the grave site, my mom in her black dress for the second time in four years. It's the scenes from the Valley of the Kings that are as vivid as the shots from a digital camera, and I've advanced frame by frame through them often enough that I see no reason to do it again, even for the purpose of commiserating with an old friend.

"Your store still looks like it belongs in one of those back alleys off of Red Square."

Romero takes the cue and plays along. "When you've got a good thing going."

I laugh at that, because it's just what I said to Angie a few days ago. Was it only a few days ago? "How's your sister?" I ask him.

It's the only sore spot between us and I immediately want to kick myself for mentioning her. But what choice do I have? I need to see her, or else my trip here will be handicapped by a factor of ten. Still, it bothers me to see Romero's face darken.

"What do you need?" he asks after a measured moment.

There is no hint of irritation in his voice—just an acceptance that something beyond the pleasure of his company has brought me here from North Carolina.

I shrug. "I'm not sure. It depends on what my subject-matter expert can tell me."

It hangs in the air between us while I watch his face. It darkens a shade more.

"You can't be serious."

"I am."

He lets out a long sigh—one that denotes a weighing of undesirable responses. Finally he says, "She may kill you."

"I wouldn't blame her."

Chapter 5

I've always appreciated that Romero did not sever ties with me when I left his sister. He would have had every right to, regardless of our long friendship and our mutually profitable trade partnership. I know his loyalties must be divided, that he has to weigh our history against the protectiveness any big brother would feel toward his sister. Still, I think there's a part of the man that may be frightened of his sibling, and it's that part which counseled me against what I am about to do.

That concern, though, didn't extend to coming with me. He walked me down the stairs and handed me a business card with her address scrawled in pencil on the back. He muttered something about waking slumbering monsters before clapping me on the back again and shoving me into a waiting cab.

Now that I'm here, I don't know how to proceed. I'm smart enough to know that the Bogart/Bacall thing doesn't work in real life. Bogey didn't have to deal with the screaming, the crying, the possible gunplay. But I've really got no choice. I'm certain that Reese knew about Esperanza when he approached me; he's a careful researcher. What it comes down to is that Espy knows more about Venezuelan history than anyone alive, and she's likely the only one who can help me make sense of Reese's documents.

Espy's office is in a new business park—so new that the

landscaping hasn't been completed. There are mounds of expectant dirt ready for shrubs and flowers, and stretches of flat earth prepared for sod. Romero said the university leased most of the office space before the developers even broke ground.

I pull open the glass door of the white faux-stone building that has the numbers 100–120 on a sign at the top of the second story. Inside, the place smells new, the commingling of factory chemicals and manufacturing odors that have yet to fade. The card in my pocket says 105. I follow the hall, glancing at the numbers above the doors, spotting the one I need too quickly. The door is open and I feel my heart start to beat faster as I approach an event that is as unpredictable as it is inevitable. Pausing just beyond the entrance, I chance a peek inside in some weak attempt to steel myself.

She's at her desk, leaning over a book, her reading glasses perched on the end of her nose. I smile as I see her lips move along to whatever she's reading. It's likely Russian, which is the only language I can remember giving her trouble enough that she had to sound out the characters.

I give the door a light rap with my knuckle.

When she looks up, and after her mind makes sense of this image from years ago, the transformation is both instantaneous and terrible. A veil of pure anger darkens her skin and I hear a sharp intake of breath that is a strangled, almost guttural sound. I barely have time to move out of the way of the book as it sails by in a flurry of pages past my right ear. The size of the tome and the velocity at which it connects with the wall behind me leaves no doubt that she meant to injure. Failing that, she lets loose with a string of curses in her native tongue—all of which sting far worse than the book would have.

I bear the diatribe with the understanding that I deserve

every bit of it and more, but hoping that the anger will peter out. I'm not much into self-flagellation, and if this trip yields nothing more than an opportunity for Esperanza to find some closure, then it will have been wasted.

As I take a step deeper into the room, Esperanza holds up a belaying hand.

"You've got to be out of your mind!" she says, forcing herself into English. Something occurs to her then. "Did my brother tell you where to find me?"

She brings her fist down on the desk and I jump back a little.

I've got nothing. I can lecture all day in front of college students—often while my mind is far away—and never have trouble articulating. Most times, though, I'm not scared to death.

"It's good to see you."

Even though it's how I feel, surprisingly enough, it's probably the worst response I could have selected from the menu. Her lips tighten and she leaves the chair, and I am certain that she means to do me the physical harm the book failed to accomplish. But she stays behind the desk, her hands on the brown solidity, and takes a deep breath. I can almost see the anger leaching from her, lowering from its dam-cresting strength, receding to something quieter and slower yet no less powerful.

"What do you want, Jack?"

That's what I wanted to hear. The pragmatist in me knows that when someone gives you the ball, you can command the situation. The simple fact that she has asked an open-ended question means I now have more leverage than I had when I entered the room. If I'm careful, I can control what happens from here.

The problem is that when the cabbie let me off, what I wanted was to show Esperanza the research, get her opinion, and be on my way. Now I'm not so sure. Things are more complicated when you're past the planning stage. Once you're involved in the real deal, it can be difficult to stay on script. I'm reminded of all the reasons why this woman once meant the world to me. A familiar longing is suffering through a surprise rebirth.

"I don't know," I answer, and it might be the first honest thing I've said in a long time.

"You're not serious."

"Oh, but I am."

"But you've got a PhD."

I think a curse toward Gordon Reese, back in the comparative safety of Dallas. But for him, I would be enjoying my vacation. It's all I can do to avoid backpedaling like some cartoon character, although the fleeting image of her chasing me around the desk almost brings a smile.

"If you want my help, you'll have to stand there like a man and let me take a punch. Otherwise, you and your research can walk right out that door."

I suppose I should be pleased I have her ear at all. In the brief time she gave me to state my case, I could see a flicker of interest.

I'm not frightened. She won't hit me until I tell her she can. That's the payoff for her: that I acquiesce to the assault. I suppose that's where the PhD rears its ugly head; she'll get more enjoyment having me stand here and take it than she would have received by nailing me with the book.

I don't suppose I have any real choice. "Fire away," I say with mock fearlessness.

Right before her small fist connects with my nose, I register two distinct thoughts. The first is the deep sadness in her eyes. The second is that I hadn't considered she would go for the face. The pain blinds me. Which leaves me wholly unprepared for the follow-up to my sternum, the one that knocks the breath from my lungs and sends me to one knee.

In the time it takes for oxygen to decide whether my damaged insides are safe enough to revisit, I feel as if I've been gasping for an eternity. Blood trickles from my nose and I harbor a passive-aggressive hope that the fluid will stain her carpet so as to leave some lasting proof of her brutality.

"You said one punch," I manage.

"I lied."

When I open my eyes, and after I see that there are several dark spots on the tan carpet, I look up to find her sitting on her desk, leaning back on her hands. There are a multitude of bright spots that dance over her, the kind associated with my own sublimated pain.

"Happy now?"

She tosses me a clean white rag and I take it and plug up the sieve that is my nose. I don't even make a pretense of mustering fictional dignity as I get my legs under me and push myself up. Perhaps Romero was right: a woman spurned is a woman best avoided. Still, I'm not sure what frightens me more—that an equally painful emotional deluge may be coming, or that I'm not prepared to run from one should it arrive.

Instead, she offers a satisfied smile and says, "You hungry?"

I pull the cloth away from my nose to see if the bleeding has stopped. I feel no fresh trickles of blood, but now the clotting fluid plugs my nostrils.

"I'm not sure. I just had a knuckle sandwich." It hurts to talk, and my voice sounds funny.

I've elicited a small chuckle from Esperanza. She hops off the desk and retrieves her purse from behind the chair.

"Let's go. You can buy."

And then she's out the door. After a last dab at my nose, I toss the bloody rag on her desk and follow. It's strange, but something in me feels happy about the whole physical violence thing. It's something I can understand, even appreciate. Some sort of cause and effect, yin and yang thing that my male brain can process. I won't delude myself into thinking that the rest of our reunion will be as amicable—as odd as it may seem to use that term—but, for now, I consider myself blessed.

Llamo's is a small, quiet restaurant that specializes in the premier dish in any Venezuelan restaurant: steak. I used to frequent this place, and it looks just the same as it did all those years ago. The walls are white, decorated with pictures of the owner's family. At least five generations smile on us, or cast somber looks our way, according to the prevailing generational mood.

Esperanza is working on a tuna salad sandwich and there's an untouched glass of white wine near her right hand. I might as well not even be here for the attention she's giving me. One of Gordon Reese's notebooks lies open on the table, and she is devouring each word with the same voraciousness with which she's downing her sandwich. I know her well enough to identify the expression in her eyes. It's a combination of intrigue and skepticism—the proper professional dyad. She turns a page, the sandwich held in her free hand, chewing a bite slowly. She grunts and turns another page.

"Your friend's done a lot of research."

"Yes, he has." When I was going through the notebooks back in Dallas, with Reese at my side to clarify the more obscure notes and references, I was impressed by the exhaustive nature of his records. If I were to grant him nothing else, I would at the very least have to give him acknowledgment in this area. I can remember digs I've conducted that haven't come close to this level of documentation.

"Have you corroborated any of this?"

I shrug. "I haven't found any references to Fraternidad de la Tierra, but some of the other names in the record appear to be genuine. It would take me months of Europe hopping just to verify all the players." What I don't mention, at least not yet, is the umbrella organization that Reese is certain exists—the one that orchestrates the passing of the bones from caretaker to caretaker.

She flips another page, then another, before closing the book. "What I want to know," she says after a long pause, "is where he got his first name."

I raise a puzzled eyebrow.

"Think about it," she says. She sets the rest of her sandwich down and reaches for the wineglass, which she drains with the same consideration someone in my part of the world might give a glass of ice tea. "He's got this thing going back twenty-five hundred years. But from what I can see, he only tracks the bones back to the thirteenth century—the Chevrier family, or paternal designation. Question is, how did he get from the cemetery to there? He has to have something he hasn't shown you yet."

I shrug. I'd wondered the same thing but hadn't considered it a deal breaker. If I can prove that his findings from the thirteenth century on are accurate, then I can feel good about pursuing the matter. What I need Esperanza for is to confirm the last portion of the record, the place where Elisha's bones seem to have dropped off the face of the earth: Fraternidad de la Tierra. The Brotherhood of Dirt.

She can read my mind.

"Fraternidad de la Tierra existed."

"Existed. As in, they no longer exist?"

"Definitely past tense. It was an organization that was active in the region during the latter part of the eighteenth century. Mostly merchants, a few political aspirants."

"So they weren't associated with a single family?"

"They were a guild. In the truest sense of the word. Membership crossed national and economic lines."

I take another bite of my steak. It's excellent. I've never had a bad meal here.

I'm more than excited. The way Espy is describing this group means they are one of those fringe peoples unknown to all but the most serious academics. The fact that they're integral to Gordon's research, and that she has verified their existence, means a great deal.

"When did they disappear?" I ask.

The last of the tuna salad sandwich disappears. "Not sure. From what I can remember, they were a nonentity before Bolivar came along."

"Why's that?"

It's her turn to shrug. "All pseudo-guilds dissolve over time. All it takes is for one branch to splinter because they think they're on the bad end of a business deal, or that some organization-wide decree doesn't favor them. Sometimes it's even because of political altruism." She raises her wineglass to one of the waiters lining the near wall. "All I know is that, by the start of this century, they were gone."

"Sounds like that bothers you."

"In a way, I guess it does." When I raise an eyebrow, she says, "I know I'm running the risk of oversimplifying here, but how many of the problems South America's experienced over the centuries are a direct result of the same sort of tribalism that kept Europe from unifying for so long? Something like a stronger version of this guild might have had some stabilizing influence."

"You've got the Catholic Church," I say, only half kidding.

"Funny."

Like me, Esperanza had a religious upbringing. But Latin American Catholicism is an entirely different animal from the staid Protestantism I know and love like a weird cousin at a family reunion. I think one would have to live among the Amish back in the States to understand how religion can so permeate a people group. I think what hides under the surface of both approaches, though, is fear. Fear of God. Fear of there being no God; fear of there being a God who is in a perpetual state of irritation; fear of discovering that your religion got it horribly wrong; fear of being afraid because that is assuredly a sin. The people here wrap themselves in what they fear most, like hunters who would dress themselves in the animal skins of fierce predators, while we pay distant homage to that same horrific thing from behind the three-inch safety glass of pious ceremony.

Esperanza stopped going to church when she went to Cambridge, and her mother didn't talk to her for two years. To hear Espy tell it, her mother attended Mass daily and lit candles for her daughter's soul. When I first met Marie Theresa, I was sure she blamed me for her daughter's rift from the faith, even if I had not met Espy until she was well into her third year at university. It took the older woman a long time to warm up to me, and I still think she crossed herself every once in a while behind my back. I was always finding garlic in my pocket, but that stopped after I ate a clove of it in front of the woman. She almost fainted.

Esperanza remains silent while I take another bite of the steak. When I've swallowed and chased it down with a few sips of water, she gives me a curious eyebrow.

"You're not buying this, are you?"

"The part about the bones having some kind of power? No. But could there be ancient remains that have been passed through millennia?" I shrug. "Stranger things have happened. Who's to say that in a thousand years people won't be wondering if Oliver Cromwell's head is hidden someplace? Or Mother Teresa's index finger?"

"Don't poke fun of a nun."

"Wouldn't think of it. But you can see what I'm saying. There are countless cultures that preserved the bodies of their holy men."

"Not the Israelites."

"That depends on the period. You're talking about thousands of years of history, two major captivities, a dozen occupations, and generations of ignorance about Levitical law. They would have handled their dead in lots of different ways, and there only needed to be a small window of time during which the Israelites had to preserve the bones. And it's possible they lost possession of them within a few years of removing them from the tomb."

"Your conspiracy."

"Not mine."

"It almost sounds as though you don't *want* to find anything."

I shake my head. "It's not that. I'm just not buying into the conspiracy—especially one like this. What would have been the point? Preserve sacred artifacts for thousands of years? Why? If you don't want the world to have them, just destroy them."

"Maybe they tried."

I hadn't thought of that, but then I don't believe in them to begin with, so there's no foul.

"So not only are they holy bones, they're also indestructible? Like Superman's?"

"You are so going to get hit by lightning."

"All I'm saying is that a list of family and organizational names isn't enough. Unless we find something of real substance, I'll have to go back and tell my employer there's nothing to be found."

Esperanza is silent as I finish the rest of my lunch. It takes two bites and then, almost before the fork is back on the table, quiet young men come to clear our plates and set steaming cups of strong coffee in front of us. Once the seamless interruption is over, she says, "I don't know what you expect to accomplish in three weeks. It's just three weeks, right? Then you have to be back in the classroom? Even if you forget about everything prior to the mention of Fraternidad de la Tierra, this is the kind of thing that would require months, if not years, of research." She sips at the coffee. "What do you want from me?"

I hate a direct question, which is defined as any kind that resists a muddled response, or my immeasurable charm. And more of them than I can remember seem to be aimed at me since my chat with Reese. They are forcing me to learn that I am a man sorely lacking in real answers.

"I'm assuming you want me to skip the obvious?"

"You mean that I'm the smartest Latin woman for five hundred miles in any direction? That I know more about Venezuelan history than anyone? That I speak more than a dozen languages? All true. But you had to have known coming out here that this is an extended research project—the kind you get a grant for so you can spend a lot of time in libraries, or making trips across the continent that will reveal nothing but that will give you the chance to write an update with a lot of big words justifying why you needed to make the trip and why you thought it was profitable, even if you didn't actually learn anything."

I remember that when I first met Esperanza, sharing the same study group in our first year Social Anthropology class, I thought her directness was one of her most endearing characteristics. Even when we went our separate ways, the excision was aided by her dislike of anything but frankness. It's funny how half a decade can change one's appreciation of another's qualities. If I'm honest with myself, I'm not sure what's going on in my head. There has to be some element of truth to what I thought when I sat with Reese a few days ago, that I'm at a watershed moment and ready to face some of the things I've avoided for years. Esperanza is certainly one of those things. But I'm nowhere near ready to spill my guts.

Seeing this, she picks up and peruses the bill, which she then slides across the table. "I'm assuming you've got this?"

"No, but Mr. Gordon Reese does." I pull a Reese Industries corporate card from my wallet. It has my name on it, and an expiration date of December 2012. It's nice to think that, after my assignment is over, Reese's accountants might forget about this card and let me charge my way to happiness for the next few years. As one of the waiters takes the bill and the card, I notice the look on my companion's face.

"That's who you're working for?" Her tone indicates that she doesn't quite believe me, yet among the derisive names I've earned over the years, *liar* isn't one of them, and she knows that.

The waiter returns then with the receipt, and I add a generous tip to the paper and slip the card back into my wallet.

When Esperanza stands, I follow, saying, "So, what now?"

"If you've only got three weeks, then we need to get started. And we're not going to learn anything about your mystery organization sitting here." With that, she heads for the door with a look in her eyes that I remember from those years ago. It's the one she gets when she's excited by something, and I know it's there because of Reese. Even a continent away, the man casts a shadow.

Chapter 6

The library of the Central University of Venezuela looks more modern than its older cousin back at Evanston. Lines of large windows render the main reading room bright and airy. It reminds me of a cafeteria. The commonality is that paper cuts hurt, regardless of which side of the equator one is on.

It's been three hours and I'm certain that every square millimeter of each of my fingers has at least one paper cut. A pile of books obscures most of the long table we're using, the majority of them spent of their usefulness. Espy is scouring a text from the 1930s, and with each rapid page flip, the frown on her face grows deeper. I have to admit, if only to myself, as my sore nose admonishes, that it's fulfilling to see her growing frustrated. Even though I'm relying on her, there exists a small portion of my psyche that wants some minor recompense for the assault back at her office. And she likely knows that, which would only serve to increase her irritation.

During the short drive here, Espy had slipped into silence, and I hadn't pressed. This has to have hit her hard, and I'm amazed at her equanimity—the strength of character that has her acting with civility. True, part of her temporary willingness to set aside the past is almost certainly a result of the mystery I've dangled in front of her; had I shown up on her doorstep without an intellectual carrot, it is likely she would have done a good deal more violence to my person.

She reaches for a water bottle, her eyes fixed on a page. I'm supposed to be helping, and I'm making something resembling an effort, but I'm out of my depth. She's admitted that this is like looking for a very large needle in a small haystack—difficult, but not impossible—and I do not bring much to the table. I'm passing the time watching her work, and becoming more amused every time I see her do something that reminds me of the time when we were together. Most of them are small things: the way she purses her lips when she's deep in thought; the way she absently brushes aside a strand of hair. The collection of mannerisms peculiar to a person. I'd forgotten how much she reminds me of her brother.

Even so, I can't escape the impression—even taking into account how long it's been since we've been in the same room—that there is something markedly different about her, something I can't put my finger on. It's almost as if she's wearing a metaphysical outfit with which I'm familiar, but she's accessorized with a new scarf. I ponder this analogy for a moment before returning my attention to the open book in front of me.

After a while, she closes her book and sets it aside. With a sigh, she reaches for another. It's substantial and I can't see the name for the faded spine. She opens it and flips through the chapters with the eye of one reconnecting with an old literary friend. I have no doubt that she's read most of the books on this table, but time would have relegated most of them to the position of third cousin at a family reunion—the one whose name is always just out of reach. The pages of this one give a satisfying crinkle as she turns them. I sink into my chair, giving up even the pretense of helping. I have nothing to do but watch her as she reads. I can think of worse things with which to occupy my time.

"Here it is."

I give a guilty start, banging my knee on the underside of the table. Ignoring Espy's smirk, I rise and cross to the other side of the table so that I can peer over her shoulder. Her finger rests on the name: Fraternidad de la Tierra, in bold font. The text is in Spanish. I reach around and move her hand so that I can read the entry. They've earned less than a half page in a large book, and the first two paragraphs are close to what Esperanza provided back at the restaurant.

"Not much here," I grouse.

"I remember there being a bit more to it," she offers, and I can see a sheepish smile in profile.

My eyes skip down the page until they alight on the material Espy didn't cover. The only thing I find interesting is that this passage provides, while not the origin of the name, an interesting bit of information about member allegiance to it. Every man who achieved guild membership underwent something akin to what I can only determine was an anti-baptism. Rather than undergoing an immersion in or sprinkling with water, initiates were buried to their necks in dirt and left alone for six hours. It seems that the Brotherhood placed some symbolic meaning in the power of the earth. I find myself trying to draw some correlation between the dust of the ground and the decay of human bone, knowing as I do so that I'm committing the academic sin of feeding a theory without any facts to support it.

I don't realize that I'm still holding Esperanza's hand until she pulls it away. With a small smile, I step back, the smell of her hair following me.

"Not a lot there," I say.

"No. Which is why I find it odd that they should figure prominently in the research."

I shrug because, to me, it seems quite the opposite. If they were a well-known organization, then any Tom, Dick, or Harry who fancied himself an academic could have picked them from the available records. Someone would have had to have done some serious research to select this group from among the relics of South American history, as evidenced by Espy's efforts.

"There's a picto-index here," Esperanza says, flipping back several pages. "There should be some kind of organizational crest represented."

I step to her side again as she moves through the pages, hitting the glossy ones that show the black-and-white photos. There are at least twenty pages of these, many with icons that I recognize without having to think about them. Toward the end she pauses, and her slender finger taps a tiny image at the bottom.

At first, I don't grasp what I'm seeing. It must be a full thirty seconds before I realize I'm not breathing. And I find that Esperanza has turned and she's looking at me with a curious expression.

"What is it?"

I don't answer. How can I put into words the amazement I'm feeling? Because I've seen this picture before. In fact, I've touched the ancient wall on which a duplicate of it is carved. And I know now where I have to go. And I also know that Esperanza was right about one thing: this project might take much longer than I thought.

Romero's store is closed and he, Esperanza, and I are the only ones in the place. The showroom lights are off and a heavy bar blocks the main entry. We're in his office, and Espy is sitting on her brother's table, the heel of her shoe bumping a slow rhythm on one of the slim wood legs. I'm leaning against the wall, my hands in my pockets, but I feel like I'm going to jump out of my skin. I know Espy feels the same way. The look in her eyes belies her relaxed posture. Romero is alternating between looking at me and studying the small picture in the book we brought from the library.

"You can't be serious."

I nod. It feels good to be right; smugness is an old shoe.

"This is from Quetzl-Quezo?"

I know what he's doing. He's working back through his memory, trying to see the rock carvings in the chamber below the subflooring. We took pictures with my brand-new camera and then spent weeks analyzing them, but at the time they resisted translation. If I had my files with me, I could pull up a duplicate of what is on the page in front of my friend. I have my laptop but, after five years of teaching, all it holds are tests, grades, and the promise of a satellite Internet connection. I might be able to get someone back at Evanston to scour my apartment for an old CD-ROM that may be buried under mountains of mail, magazines, and old research, but there's a strong possibility the pictures are lost for all time. The piece I submitted for peer review is long published in a second-rate magazine, and it has spent years alternating between obscurity or as the subject of erudite debates by esteemed but drunken archaeology professors on poker night.

It's rare that someone in my former profession discovers something like Quetzl-Quezo. In a field built on incremental discovery, where one researcher builds on the work of others, to find something that turns accepted theory on its head is like picking lottery numbers. It's the sort of dig that, with a little luck, can put one in history books. Without luck, though, finding an ancient temple of probable Mayan design somewhere it's not supposed to be can turn out to be a confounding riddle—and difficult to study when the dig isn't sanctioned by the Venezuelan government. Creeping around like criminals, surreptitiously ferrying gear into the jungle, paying the locals to keep quiet—all of these make it difficult to document an excavation. And few journals like to publish articles by young, trespassing archaeologists, because that's an easy way to find your reporters and photographers harassed at customs.

Nestled in the jungle in the mountainous north of the country, a stone's throw away from the Columbian border, Quetzl-Quezo is hundreds of miles from the most southerly advances of Mayan civilization. That, the stylistic differences between it and others situated in their proper places, and the fact that the markings on the inside are unlike any we'd seen have caused many of my peers to disqualify it as a Mayan structure. Instead, most believe it belonged to another people group—either indigenous to the region or on a migratory track. The latter might be correct; the former is almost certainly wrong. The fact is, none of the great ancient civilizations native to Central and South America had influence here. The Aztecs were farther north than the Mayans, the Incans clung to South America's western border, and even the short-lived Toltecs failed to venture this way. In my reckless youth I created a new classification for the structure: proto-Mayan. I'm older now, and I've learned that most of the theories espoused by the young are ridiculous, yet I've held on to this one. So Quetzl-Quezo is a moniker of the people who would settle farther north but already showing the discipline and skills necessary to carve a nation from the jungle.

It's always bothered me that we were never able to finish our work, and that no other team has been able to conduct a more thorough study of the site.

"This guild, then," Romero says. "This means they must have known about the temple at least two hundred years ago."

"Longer," I say. "Much longer."

"That's not a stretch," Esperanza adds. "We all know a lot of the really important things found over the last hundred years have been excavated in the backyards of natives. A lot of them look at us and wonder why we're wasting our time with something that's been part of their backdrop for as long as they can remember."

"So they either adopted the symbol from the temple . . ." Romero says.

"Or carved it there," Espy finishes.

"They had to have stumbled onto the temple and found the symbols," I say. "They're too old for it to have been the other way around."

"But that doesn't explain why they would have adopted an obscure ancient carving as a guild crest," Romero grumbles.

No one says anything for a time, but I know we are all thinking variations of the same thing. Mr. Reese's little project has just become both much more promising and more complicated. And it will involve more resources than I'd planned.

"I wish I'd brought a team," I say.

"We can put one together for you." Romero closes the book and leans back until the chair creaks. "They won't know the whys and hows, but they'll dig where you tell them, and they'll keep their mouths shut."

I've worked more than one site with just locals, so I'm comfortable enough with Romero's offer, although it would be nice to have someone else there who knows an effigy mound from an eolian deposit. Romero has worked alongside me more times than I can remember—before the revelation that brokering treasures required less work than finding them—but his days of traipsing all over the world in search of antiquities are long gone, and I will not ask him. He's a businessman now, with all of the concerns associated with the designation. He would come with me were I to ask him, which is why I don't.

"I'll need supplies, too."

"Anything you need, you've got."

"How long?"

"A day or two to gather your team, but we have all of the equipment in town."

Something in his expression more than suggests that he wants to forsake Caracas for a good dig. I understand. It's something that never quite leaves the blood. And Romero has turned enough dirt with me that he coughs dust. Dress a dirt jockey in nice clothes, teach him a few manners—in short, try to civilize him—and there's still that muted voice inside calling him back to sand and sweat and discovery. I'm more energized than I can remember feeling, like I'm waking from a long but restless sleep.

It's a feeling I wish I could pass on to my friend, and I'm disappointed for him. There is, however, a way he can help me and, while it will not bring the pleasure of real fieldwork, it gives him something to do.

"There is something you can do for me," I say. "Our research has the bones supposedly passing from the Chevrier family to Fraternidad de la Tierra. If we can find evidence that these two groups could have had contact with each other around the time of the supposed transfer, it would go a long way toward helping us to establish plausibility."

Romero is thoughtful; he knows what I am doing. He also knows I'm not throwing him a bone—that what I'm asking for would be helpful. "So you want me to research this?"

"It would help. I won't have access to anything while I'm at the site."

He nods, accepting the responsibility. And then I see something else in Romero's eyes—a troubled look that does not often roost there.

"I'm not sure you're fully aware of what you've gotten yourself into, my friend."

I don't have an immediate answer, principally because I know there is something behind the question to which I am not privy.

"Your little excursion has made you a popular man," the Venezuelan says. He leans forward in his chair; his posture suggests worry. "You were not gone thirty minutes before I had a visitor."

My initial response is a confused frown. I'm well aware that there are people in this country who would not be cordial were I to run into them, but I can think of no one who dislikes me enough that they would have designated resources adequate to monitor the airports—because that's the only way someone could have zeroed in on me in the few hours I've been in-country.

In response to my unasked question, Romero says, "He

was a foreigner. Perhaps South African; I've never been good with accents."

"What did he want?"

"To look at my merchandise."

I consider this for a moment and stop myself from asking the obvious questions. Most of Romero's clientele do not call this country home. They're a community connected by money and enlarged by recommendations at lavish parties. To find someone from the other side of the world interested in his wares, then, should not have caused him any concern. Even so, I will not question my friend's belief that this visit intimated something else.

"He purchased one pre-Columbian jade axe god pendant—for which I charged almost double my normal price—and then he left. And he paid in cash," Romero says.

"That's all?"

He nods.

"It was reconnaissance—fact-finding. Evidently he decided that asking questions would not have accomplished anything beyond causing suspicion. But I don't believe in coincidence, my friend; this man visited me because you came here."

Romero's words roll around in my head, and I'm left not knowing how to respond, because there are a great many thoughts vying for position amidst the gray matter. Chief among them is worry that I've entangled one of my oldest friends in something that might be more dangerous than I'd anticipated. Just beyond that, though, is an uneasy feeling that I don't have time to process, but I know it's connected to what happened in Egypt. The seamy underside of this business; the politics that had Will's death classified as an unfortunate accident, despite the fact that even someone with an untrained eye could see a blast pattern radiating from the trench. Dirt thrown upward. Guilt threatens to resurface; the self-directed accusation that I did not force a more thorough look into what happened at KV65 before retreating to Evanston.

I stop such thoughts at the threshold. I don't have the time for such self-indulgence right now.

"Then I guess I better do this as quickly as I can," I say.

Romero smiles. I think he knows what small battle I just fought with myself.

"Do you need a good historian?"

I'm not sure who is more surprised by Esperanza's question—me, her, or Romero. His eyes are wider than they were when Espy and I walked into his store together. I know he thought there was a small chance she would kill me, and a very good chance that she would inflict some type of injury on my person. He'd never entertained the thought that our meeting would end with the two of us eating a nice lunch and then traversing the city together. Sometimes Romero can miss subtleties. The body language in the room is tense, the silences half pained. Espy and I both know that there are things we need to deal with. She won't let me forget it. For now, though, I'm glad she's invited herself.

"I could use one."

"En serio?" Romero asks, his eyes still wide.

"Sí," I say, hoping my smile masks the sick feeling roosting in my stomach.

CHAPTER 7

The Andes are immense and verdant—as if color were a tool, focusing all of the world's mass into a landmark spanning seven countries, towering over national lines. In Venezuela the Andes split into two ranges: the Sierra de Perijá that run the border between Venezuela and Colombia, and the Cordillera Mérida that spread out along the east coast of Lake Maracaibo. It's this latter range we're crossing, on the way to San Cristóbal.

I'm amazed that we got everything into the small plane—a plane vibrating with the violence of a wet dog shaking the rain from its fur. For a while I thought we might have to leave a good portion of our equipment behind and pick up as much as we could when we reach our destination. But the pilot, a man named Raphael, directed the loading of our gear with an expertise born of years with this or similar planes. It's cramped quarters, with eight people wedged into whatever free space there is, and I'm growing more aware that bathing frequency is a subjective value, but I'm buoyed by a sense of purpose and, if truth be served, of being in charge of a team again. They don't look like much, but I have faith in Romero. He wouldn't provide me with subpar performers. At least three of them speak some English, and all of them took to loading the plane with an urgency that speaks of their pleasure at having a job. I know they will work hard when we arrive at the dig site, and yet I'm glad that Esperanza will be around for conversation and as a sounding board. There are other reasons too, but I'm still working through those.

She's in the back of the plane, in easy conversation with the laborers. I can't hear what they're saying over the engine noise, but she's laughing, and one of the men looks pleased at having amused her. I've always thought that Esperanza was the sort who could fit right in at a construction site anywhere in the world, unfazed by crude language or innuendo. She can take care of herself, and keep a smile doing it.

I sense that we're descending. Raphael gives me a thumbs-up and I notice the plane isn't shaking like before. Our pilot speaks decent English. He looks to be about fifty and has the hands of a farmer, someone who is used to hard work. His eyes squint even when the sun is not on them, like they are fixed that way.

He asks if I want a drink. I don't and tell him so and then watch as he pulls a flask from a compartment between us. I don't know what's in it but he seems to appreciate it as he takes a long draw. He offers it toward me and I again decline. Maybe I should be nervous about watching him drink as we get closer to landing, but I'm not. There's some understanding here that this is Raphael's world, his plane. His hands are steady. And it's not my first inebriated ferrying.

San Cristóbal slides into view from out of nowhere as Raphael guides the plane over another ridge. The small city occupies a valley, like many hubs of human activity in this mountainous region. Had we not flown directly over the place, I might have missed it entirely. Looking down, I take in the city's buildings, streets, its muted whiteness.

Raphael is concentrating now and I see the sliver of land on which he plans to drop the Cessna. I watch his hands as he works the controls, noting the confidence on his face, and I feel at ease as I watch San Cristóbal grow larger. In what seems just a few seconds later, we touch down and Raphael hits the brakes.

The next several minutes are a happy blur as I slip back into a role that is almost free of cobwebs. And I've got Espy to help with the particulars, such as working with the crew and coordinating the equipment transport. As I stand back, chatting with Raphael, I watch Espy, amazed at how much she resembles her brother in the way she manages the men.

We have two SUVs, both of which will be loaded down with equipment. I'm not sure what we'll need, which is why we're packing heavy. I'd thought about a backhoe, a dozer, and a few other pieces of earthmoving equipment, but that would have meant a larger team and a lot more time than I've got. I chuckle at that; Esperanza is right in that it's looking less likely I'll make it back to Evanston for the start of the new semester. Still, I'm not yet ready to give up on the original plan. For all that I'm enjoying myself, I'm not prepared to dismiss my role as educator. I have a whole life, stunted though it may be, waiting for me back in North Carolina, complete with friends, a paycheck, and my much-abused cactus. It might not seem like much, but it's what I've got. And I kind of miss my cactus.

As the last of our gear is off-loaded, I say good-bye to Raphael. I paid him on the front end with my magic card—the same one that bought our equipment. I'd joked with Romero that it was the first time I could remember having paid for supplies he procured for me. He'd frowned and then made a notation on the invoice.

"What now?" Esperanza asks, suddenly appearing at my side. "You want to find someplace to eat before we head out?"

"I'd rather not. The less time we spend here, the better."

I feel uneasy out on the tarmac, as if eyes are watching me. One of the gentlemen who would not be pleased to see me resides in San Cristóbal, and my chances of avoiding an unfortunate meeting are slimmer if we don't linger.

"If the men are hungry, have them break into the rations. We can restock in Rubio."

Before long we have the trucks leaving the city, turning onto a road that winds up and around the mountains. Esperanza is driving one vehicle, while one of the hired hands pilots the other.

The airport is situated near the outskirts of the city and so I don't see much of it before both the mountains and the jungle, in a way that's uniquely South American, swallow us up.

"Have you ever been to Rubio?"

"No," she says. "My cousin is stationed at the army base near there and he says it's not much to look at."

"It's a nice little town. Quiet."

"Like Ellen, North Carolina?"

"Ouch."

She shrugs. "Sorry. I saw an opportunity and I took it."

"Are you going to do that for the whole time we're out here?"

"I'm not sure. Depends on how much of a jerk you are."

"I can always ride in the other truck."

She doesn't offer a response and I get the feeling the banter is a bit more than she can take right now. For all that she is making light of it, this has to be hard on her.

If I didn't know better, I would think her mood was affecting her driving. It seems to me that she's approaching reckless mode. These mountain roads are narrow and there are no guardrails. And with blind curves being the norm, as she navigates our way around each one, often the SUV is hugging the wrong side of the road. I stare ahead, cringing at the prospect of another vehicle careening toward us from the opposite direction. No amount of time spent in this region can make me more comfortable about the driving.

I glance behind me at the two men in the backseat. One looks like he's sleeping, his hat pulled down over his eyes. The other watches the jungle passing beyond the window. If he has heard or understood our exchange, he gives no sign of it. I take a cue from his friend and pull my own hat down, settling back against the seat. It's a good hour to Rubio and I haven't slept in a while. If I don't conserve energy when I can, weariness will find me when I can least afford it. I have a sudden fear of Esperanza catching me in some heated exchange when I can barely keep my eyes open. The thought frightens me enough that, as I drift off to a bumpy sleep, I give serious consideration to changing trucks once we reach Rubio.

El Oso Durmiente, the sign says. The Sleeping Bear. It's one of several brown brick buildings in this section of Rubio. Tin-roofed homes dot the outer ring of the town—single-family dwellings of dirt and clay. Most of the houses closer to the center of town are a stucco of some sort, many of them painted in a collection of bright and garish colors.

As I get out of the SUV, I try to steady my legs. Toward the end of the ride—that last little whip around the mountain—Esperanza punched it. I think that even the guys in the back were nervous. I reach for one of Duckey's cigars and clip off its end, then hold a match to it until it catches. Espy makes a face and walks inside. The others follow while I linger, leaning against the truck and regaining my equilibrium. A thought hits me and I pull out my cell phone and hit one of the speed-dial options.

"Hello?"

"Hey, Ducks."

"That you, Jack?" There's a burst of static. "I'm not getting a great signal."

"It's me. I'm just here enjoying one of the fine cigars you gave me. Thanks, by the way."

"Don't mention it. How's your vacation? No, don't answer. Let me guess. It's about one P.M. in your part of the world, so I'm betting you're in the recliner, in your underwear, and you're eating a bowl of Honeycomb." A pause. "And you smell horrible."

"I'll give you the part about the smell, so you're not completely wrong."

"Okay, so you broke into Angie's. Sort of an interapartment vacation."

"Strike two, my friend."

"Listen, Jack, my brain's on idle for the next several days, so don't toy with me. It pains me to have to unsheathe my razor wit."

I can hear family-type noises coming from Duckey's side of the connection and, even though most of them are lost in the static, they are happy sounds. I smile into my phone.

"I'm in Venezuela, Ducks. Merry Christmas."

The phone is ringing less than five seconds after I hang up. As I step into the eatery, I'm feeling quite pleased with myself.

It's dark inside, which is a defining characteristic of all even mildly disreputable establishments. It is late afternoon, maybe an hour past the end of siesta, and the bar is sparsely populated. Two old men sit at a table in the far corner, nursing bottles of Maltin and smoking Marlboros. They look up as I enter. The dark is a comforting grayness that mixes with smells both familiar and odd.

My crew has gone to the teakwood bar, where the man on the other side—a large, serious-looking local whose face rings a bell—raises an eyebrow as I join them. Almost before I have claimed a seat, he supplies me with a Maltin. I pull out my wallet and extract several bolivars, going on the hunch that Reese's credit card won't see much use here. When I place the money on the bar, I see the bartender eyeing me with more than cursory interest. He knows he's seen me before. There's a sixth sense that all good bartenders have: they never forget a face. But he grabs the money without a word and then disappears into the kitchen.

"What were you doing out there?" Esperanza asks. She has a glass of ice water in front of her and stands with one shoe resting on the brass foot rail.

"I called a friend."

She nods and looks away. In a minute the bartender emerges from the back, his arms and hands laden with plates.

"I ordered for you," Espy says.

The food inventory yields two pizzas, a large basket of tortilla chips, a platter of burgers, and one order of nachos, which the unsmiling ogre of a man places in front of me.

"Thanks," I say, belatedly hoping that both the bartender and Esperanza infer the expansive nature of the sentiment.

"Don't thank me. You're paying for it."

There's a general silence as we eat. Romero's men are content to enjoy the free food and let either Esperanza or myself direct them. Espy and I, though, exist in some odd détente in which the past is sublimated but still very real. There is something forced in the dialogue, even in the way we stand.

It reminds me of the last time I spoke with her all those years ago. It was just before I left for Egypt. I thought I would be gone for at least a year. After that, who knew where my job would take me? It was a conscious choice to leave Espy behind—to make pursuing peer accolades my primary goal. Oh, I threw other reasons out there too, but the crux of it was the insatiable pride of youth.

The last of the nachos disappear and I'm stuffed and riding the carbohydrate high that will eventually send me into a semicatatonic state. That's probably why the sudden feel of cold metal against my neck does not provoke the reaction normally associated with mortal danger, save for the shiver that travels the length of my spine.

"You owe me money."

It's certainly possible. I owe a lot of people money. It's one of my many faults. Practicing archaeologists, even successful ones, don't make a great deal. Grants barely cover the costs associated with an excavation. Still, I pride myself in seldom owing money to more than one person in any single geographical area.

"Hello, Henry," I say.

It's taken Esperanza and the rest of the crew a few seconds to sort out what's happening. Espy looks past me and I can tell that she sees the gun positioned just behind my left ear. I give her a wink, just to keep her calm. The others remain still. This isn't their argument.

"By my recollection, you still owe me seventy-five dollars."

Esperanza's reaction is one for the ages. There is a morphing of emotions on her face, taking her from the initial nervousness, to confusion, on through anger, and, finally, disgust.

"Seventy-five dollars?" she snaps. "You skipped out on seventy-five dollars?"

"And eighty-three cents," Henry adds.

I shrug, and the gun tickles my neck. "Let's be reasonable," I say. I take a napkin from a stainless-steel container and wipe cheese off my fingers. I turn then and find myself looking down the barrel of a .357.

Eduardo "Henry" Sanchez may well be the ugliest man I've ever met. He stands maybe five-seven, carries around close to 230 pounds, and has a nose that looks as if it's been affixed to his right cheek with clear tape.

I met Henry during the initial study and excavation of the temple. It was midmorning and I was busy unearthing what would turn out to be a cooking pot, manufactured circa 1992 by the Able Steel Works in Able, Pennsylvania. Henry, one of the locals investigating the unprecedented activity, fell into a fresh hole. When I found him, he looked like a turtle on its back. He wouldn't let me help him until he'd exhausted himself trying to get out on his own. Over the next several weeks, as he spent more time at the work site, I surmised that he made most of his money working with various smuggling operations, running drugs through San Cristóbal. He had a nice house, a new car, and a lovely family, and I had dinner with them a time or two. When working in a foreign land, it's wise to cultivate good relations with the indigenous people.

"I was a little short of funds at the time," I try, with my most magnanimous smile.

Henry uses the gun to scratch his leg, then the side of his face.

"You hurt me, Jack."

"That's kind of his thing," Esperanza says.

It's nice that the two of them are discovering a camaraderie based on mutual disappointment, but there's still the matter of the gun. I'm reasonably confident that Henry won't shoot me—intentionally. But the way he's waving the thing around, gesturing, scratching, makes me nervous.

"I'm good for the money, Henry."

Both he and Esperanza laugh at the same time.

"I trusted you once, Jack. I'm going to need the money now."

I know it must be a matter of principle for him. Seventy-five dollars is hardly worth the hassle, even in a poor country. And I didn't mean to stiff him. We'd been chased out of the site by the government, who'd finally caught wind of our activities, but I'd paid off enough of the right people so they let us leave instead of tossing us into prison. On our way back to San Cristóbal, I'd brought the team here to let off a little steam. Most of them were young and on their first assignments. Some of them weren't even being paid, except with degree credits. I'd come up light in the wallet when all was said and done, and Henry had floated me the balance, unaware that we were on our way out.

I raise my hands in helplessness. "I'm not carrying that kind of cash on me, Henry. So unless you can take a credit card, there's not a lot I can do for you."

I think I'm off the hook. While Henry looks like a mean sort, the odds are in my favor that he won't shoot me.

"We can take a credit card," says an oddly high-pitched voice from behind me. "We just got a machine."

I turn around and the bartender is pointing at the technology in question, a proud smile on his face. The machine sits next to the manual cash register. I must have missed seeing it earlier.

"How about we run it through for a hundred and fifty? Cover your lunch, too?" He holds out a large hand that is incongruous with a voice which sounds as if it should belong to a cartoon character.

I know when I'm beat. I pull Mr. Reese's card from my wallet and hand it over. There's a part of me that wishes I could be in the same room with his accountant when the charges come through.

As I watch the man swipe the card and punch in the numbers, I try to ignore Esperanza's satisfied smile.

Chapter 8

The first thought to enter my mind as we drive the trucks out of the jungle and into the small clearing is that if age could be a physical property, it would be the crumbling limestone walls of this temple. Quetzl-Quezo, or what's left of it, is something set apart from the timeline, as if it died before the world began, and everything else has grown up around it.

It was once the tallest structure for hundreds of miles in any direction, the only one that could be seen rising above the trees. It doubtless gleamed under the assault of the hot sun; to the people who saw it from afar, it might have seemed to glow.

I feel now as I did when I first saw it, when whispered rumors among my colleagues hinted at its presence and drove me to find it first. It felt like holy land. It demanded reverence. It was—it is—beautiful.

It looks much like the Ruins of Palenque, but in miniature; and Palenque was not built when this structure was crumbling. There is no roof comb, no corbelled arch, and only three sets of steps, and yet many other elements are so clearly Mayan that it seems absurd to me that anyone could believe anything else. I dated the ruins to 800 B.C., a full two hundred years before the construction of anything like it on the Yucatan Peninsula. That tells me it is an extraordinary fledgling attempt at pre-Classic Mayan architecture. The builders didn't get it quite right, but they took much of what they learned here and applied it to the later, larger work.

Esperanza sits next to me in the truck's front passenger seat, and I glance over to see how she's taking this. She hasn't done a lot of fieldwork. Books, rather than shovels and scrapers, are her tools. I'm rewarded to see her eyes wide, her mouth open just a bit. I think she's barely breathing.

I cut the engine and step out onto grass, into the humid and bug-filled air. Another door opens behind me and the two men who rode with us emerge from the air-conditioning. I look at them and see much of what I saw in Esperanza's expression, and something else: fear. These are city boys, as modernized as any American, and they're not prepared for such a tangible connection to their ancient history.

"¡Dios yudanos!" one of them, I think his name is Antonio, says.

"God help us, indeed," I answer.

The other SUV pulls up next to ours and, after a few moments, the rest of the team joins us. Even Esperanza gets out and walks to the front of the vehicle, standing near the ticking engine.

Quetzl-Quezo sits in the middle of a man-made clearing. When we, the experts, swarmed the ruins, we cut and pulled down hundreds of trees with the heavy equipment we brought with us down the trail we'd beaten through the jungle—the same path we followed today, inching along, driving through overgrowth, clearing a path by hand when necessary. There are several mounds of earth piled in haphazard fashion around the site, like giant prairie-dog holes. They're the places that showed the greatest potential for harboring old tools, cooking implements, and bones.

At the base of each temple wall is a pile of crumbled limestone further eroded into smaller rocks and dust. I've long harbored an irritation that limestone is abundant in the region, making it the most logical building material. It's a comparatively soft rock that does not bear up beneath the ravages of time.

I take a step and stop at Esperanza's side. She is quiet for several beats until, without taking her eyes off the temple, she says, "Thanks."

I know what she means and nod.

I turn to the crew, who are milling about behind us. One of them is kicking at loose pebbles. Another seems fascinated by a small lizard clinging to one of the saplings that's fighting to reclaim the site. Clearly the magic of the moment has run its course.

"Let's start unloading. Set the tents up over there," I say, pointing to an arbitrary spot while making it look as if I have a compelling reason why that piece of earth is better than any other. Using the same method I pick another spot and add, "I want the tools stacked there."

With them occupied, I take hold of Esperanza's elbow. "Want to take a look inside?"

"More than anything."

"Don't get too excited. Most buildings like this are more impressive on the outside, where you can appreciate the scale."

"Thanks for the pep talk."

"And you have to remember the steps," I say, gesturing to the three ascending levels leading up to the temple entrance. "There are fifty-two of them. And if we're going to do this right, we'll have to go up and down several times a day." Even as I'm saying it, happy to be irritating Espy, I'm reminded of my own bum knee and how much I dislike climbing stairs.

"I'm pretty sure I can keep up." She disengages her elbow and starts for the steps, using the trail of weathered two-by-eights that straddle pits and small ravines. I'm right behind her, my boots thudding on the old wood.

We're halfway up before she starts to lose steam. The steps are tall but have a short tread length, which makes ascending them difficult. And while I doubt she's noticed, the cut of the stones changes slightly in either direction. Later on I'll tell her how the builders intentionally designed the nonuniform steps to produce echoes in musical notes.

When finally we reach the top—out of breath, with sweat beading on my forehead—I turn around so that I'm looking back over the clearing, at the five men cutting paths between the trucks and the two sites I chose, and at the jungle that closes into a solid wall of green along a defined line of demarcation. It's easy to understand how a Mayan priest would have felt, standing here above everything. It makes me wonder, again, why this temple is a freestanding structure. Why are there no plazas around it? Where are the evidences of dwellings, of industry? What exactly would a priest have looked down upon?

"It's dark in here."

I turn and see Esperanza peering into the single chamber that tops the pyramid.

"A lot of the later structures are open to the sky." I pull a miniature flashlight from the front pocket of my jeans.

I click on the light and step into the doorway, playing the beam over the interior. It's empty, save for the stone ceremonial table in the center. It's where the priests would have performed the ritual sacrifices integral to their religion.

"It's so small," Esperanza says, following me as I step deeper inside.

"We're at the top of a pyramid. What did you expect?"

I know where she's coming from. All of the labor involved in building something this large just to support a single fifteen-by-fifteen-foot room?

Turning back to the door, I direct the light over the lintel and the carvings in the stucco that decorate it. It's the only ornate part of the chamber—further evidence to support the time period in which I have placed its construction.

"Up until about 1950, experts believed these pyramids to be solid," I say. "That the whole structure supported a single room. A Mexican archaeologist discovered a hidden entrance into the substructure in the temple pyramid of Pacal at Palenque."

I see a spark of interest in Esperanza's eyes, displacing her disappointment. I think she'd been expecting something more elaborate, more ornate. Most people do.

Circling the ceremonial table, my feet echoing on stone, I search for the entrance to the larger chamber below us.

"Crap."

"What?"

A portion of the ceiling has given way, creating a barrier to the access panel. I aim the light up until I see the gaps in the ceiling, and the lines that suggest another round of falling rock is inevitable.

"I hate limestone," I say.

It is almost noon and we've been at it for the better part of six hours. There's a lot more debris than I'd first estimated. In fact, I find it difficult to believe that the sections of felled ceiling could account for all the rock blocking the entrance. It almost looks as if someone has brought in additional material just to make this more difficult. It's like something Duckey would do just to irritate me.

From my vantage point on the steps, the second tier, I sip from a water bottle and watch a swarm of bugs that seem to hang in the air in front of me like a small cloud. I'm covered with insect repellent but have still suffered a few nibbles from the more adventurous of the little monsters.

It's taking a while to clear the entrance because I've been adamant about using the proper methods. Even though I've already been inside, I can't bring myself to ignore the rules. It's unlikely, but I may have missed something the first time through—something that might be contaminated or destroyed by hasty work. Too, I suppose I'm milking my first time back.

The ringing of my cell phone brings me back from my musings. I pull the thing from my pocket and check the incoming number. It's not Duckey. He's called several times since I hung up on him in Rubio, and I have yet to answer. I'm enjoying the fact that I've got something on him—that I've driven a splinter into his vacation. I'll call him again before the twenty-fifth, so he can enjoy Christmas unencumbered. But for now I'm taking pleasure in messing with my boss's head.

"Hello, Gordon," I answer with a forced cheerfulness. I never liked having to give periodic accounts to the backers when I was out in the field, and I find that five years of separation have not made this part of the dance any more palatable. Still, it is his money.

"Hello, Jack," returns Reese. "How are things progressing?"

It's interesting how a few days can change the appropriateness of that question. Before Espy and I connected Gordon's research to Quetzl-Quezo, I would have assured him that I would have an answer for him soon. Now the query has no appropriate response. To do this by the book will take years, and while I know my benefactor is not paying me to conduct this as I would a normal dig, I can't think that I will have any useful data soon. Even if I discover something here, it will be another piece to a larger puzzle.

"We're making some progress, Gordon. But I'm not sure how quickly I'm going to have anything for you."

There is a silence that lasts perhaps a half beat, then he says, "You've reopened Quetzl-Quezo."

I suppose I shouldn't be surprised that he knows. I *am* using his credit card, and if viewing his research has taught me anything, it's that he's smart enough to look at the growing list of items flooding into his accounting department to determine what I'm doing. And I'd bet anything he's familiar with all the documentation from the original excavation.

"I found something I think merits investigation," I say. "I'm not sure how long it will take, but I think it's important enough to warrant the time and expense."

I can almost see him waving away concern for the cost. He probably has wine that is worth more than what I've spent so far.

"You're the expert, Jack," he says with a chuckle. "I wonder, though, if this means that you will not make it back for the start of your semester?"

"I'm not sure I can answer that. It's still my plan to be there, but I can't project how long it will take to finish things here." And that's assuming that things end here, tied up with a nice little bow. But I can't think about where I'll be in two weeks; I can't do that and devote my full energies to this project. I know I will need to make that determination soon, yet I can put it off for a little while longer.

"Of course, I understand. But I'm hoping that it will not be long before you find something of value." A pause, then, "I'm counting on you, Dr. Hawthorne."

From any other person I've spoken with, those words would be a simple admonition for an increased pace of operation. From this man, though, they carry the weight of desperation—only because I would not have expected them from him.

I'm still pondering this after I've ended the call, and as I hear footfalls coming down behind me—softer sounds than those made by clunky work boots. And even as she has been working as hard as any of the men, there is still a slight smell of flowers that precedes her.

"We're finished." She sits down next to me on the step and reaches for my water bottle. She almost drains it before handing it back. "Are you all right?"

"Just fine."

She nods and swats at a bug that has left the swarm and come too close.

"Then why are you sitting out here by yourself?"

"I'm resting."

"You mean you're thinking."

"Almost the same thing."

She wraps her arms around her knees and looks out over the clearing. "What do you think we'll find in there?"

"I know what we're going to find."

"Yeah, I was wondering about that. You've already been here; you excavated this place. If there's nothing else, and if you've already seen this carving you're so interested in, then why go through all the trouble?"

I smile, because she must have thought this through before we left Caracas. She could have asked me then—asked why I would waste so much of the limited time I have to pursue what seems like a fool's errand. She wanted to come here as much as I did.

"There are two reasons. The first is that we have nothing else to go on. We have two representations of an obscure symbol; one of them is in a book, and the other is inside this temple. The second reason is that we didn't finish our work here before your government drove us out. Who knows what we missed the first time?"

"So you're telling me that you wanted to bring half a dozen people and what looks like the entire contents of an army surplus store to the middle of the jungle because you couldn't think of anything else to do?"

Granted, the way she says it makes it sound absurd. But my question stands: What better course of action did we have?

"It makes all the sense in the world. It's probable that this guild of yours has been here—and not just at the site, but down in the burial chamber. With that established, then they either did a bit of carving down there, or they lifted one of the symbols they saw. And either one of those choices brings up a slew of others. One of the interesting ones I'm considering is whether or not the Brotherhood of Dirt was around a lot earlier than that 1659 Spanish placement you gave me."

She looks unconvinced.

"At this point I'm considering the involvement of another organization—some entity that has monitored the bones' passage from one group or family to another. Think about it," I add at her frown. "How does the handoff occur? Who chooses the next family or organization to guard the bones? There has to be some larger organization involved, someone or something bigger than any of these individual groups."

"You're really getting into this conspiracy thing. I thought you weren't buying it."

"I don't. But I work for Reese, and he believes it. And since it's his money, I have to follow his lead. If I do that—if I take a step down the road that says the bones exist, that they receive passage from one group to another—then I have to pursue it in a way that makes sense to me. Without some umbrella organization overhead, I think the theory falls apart."

Behind us I can hear the men moving down the steps. I wave as they pass. They're laughing and covered in dust from head to toe. They look like ghosts. I watch them as they navigate the narrow steps with their large work boots, then cross the plank trail. They head for the trucks where there's a cooler filled with sandwiches.

"I think they have the right idea," I say.

Esperanza doesn't join them but stays at my side, letting the silence pass between us. The sounds of the men's lunchtime camaraderie drifts up from the flatland below.

"I'm sorry about Will."

It's the first time she's mentioned my brother. For obvious reasons she didn't make it to the funeral. Even though she knew him well, my relationship with her had ended just before Will and I went to Egypt; the wound between us was still too raw for her to make the trip.

"Yeah, thanks."

It appears she's going to say something else but she doesn't, as if she can't find the right words to ask what she wants to know. It's human nature to want details. Will didn't die right away.

But she doesn't go down that road. Instead, she offers a sad smile and says, "You're angrier than you were when we were together."

I give her a look meant to convey that I don't understand.

"You hide it, but I know you better than just about anyone on the planet. You're angry about Will, and I don't blame you for it. But it's five years later."

"You're right. It's been five years. So how well do you think you know me anymore?" I sound like a petulant child.

The Espy I knew years ago would have been baited into anger. Instead, she fixes me with a pointed look. "Are you angry at God?" she asks.

"Since when do you talk about God?" I snap, feeling more vulnerable than I would have thought possible.

"Since about a year after you left me." It's not meant to be an accusation, though it comes across as one. "When I realized that God isn't just a convenient concept around which to base a religion. When I found out that He's real."

My best weapon at this point is silence and I make use of it. I'm not sure I could come up with the words I would need to describe how I could hear Will underneath a ton of dirt and rock. How I could hear the faint banging of a shovel coming up through the ground. Most of the images and sounds from that day are still vivid, even after more than five years. But two stand out. One was a plea, the only clear thing I heard Will say while he waited for rescue. We'd removed at least two-thirds of the debris so his words were clear when he shouted, once, for God to save him. God may be real, as Espy claims, but He must have been busy that day, because my other most clear recollection is Will's lifeless eyes when we pulled him from the hole.

"I'm hungry," I say, and then I start down the steps.

CHAPTER 9

"Careful now."

I've got the crowbar wedged beneath the thick limestone slab, and Antonio and Ruben are in similar positions.

"If I didn't know better, I'd say someone glued this thing shut."

I'm putting my back into it, which I will regret later. But after a few very long seconds, we're rewarded with a satisfying pop and the slab lifts. Two others place metal shims in the gap in case we lose our grip. We wriggle the stone to the side with a combination of pulling and pushing until we've cleared a space large enough to slip past. When I feel the slab is in a good spot—that it won't find some strange angle and topple into the hole—I release my hold and collapse onto the ground.

"You're out of shape," Esperanza says, then points to my fellow workers. While they're all breathing heavy, they appear to have emerged from the strenuous activity in much better form.

"I'm a college professor, not an athlete," I say, but her chiding gets me off my backside. I reach for my flashlight and direct its beam down into the hole. Cool, stale air wafts up, along with a smell I remember from the last time: mold. There's a lot of it here, because the rocks that make up the pyramid structure were not mortared, nor do they fit together as snugly as they do at other Mayan sites, so water has seeped in over the centuries.

The two-by-three-foot hole goes down three meters and ends in a narrow passage. At the end of this corridor, which runs the length of the second tier of steps, is a staircase that cuts down toward the bottom center of the pyramid and the burial chamber. Or what would have been a burial chamber at Palenque and other similar sites. Here we find an empty room—save for three dead rats, possibly killed by the dark mold covering the walls and a good portion of the floor, and the skeletal remains of a bird.

"It stinks," Esperanza says. She's knelt down next to me to peer into the hole.

"It's their ventilation system. They're still using the original contractor grade."

She hits me on the shoulder and I almost drop the flashlight.

"You would have been the one going back down the steps to get me another one," I say.

I straighten and look around. Our five intrepid workers are standing farther away from the rectangular opening than is warranted. And I think I caught Antonio at the tail end of crossing himself. I chuckle. They imagine some mysterious chamber of horrors beneath our feet, one full of traps and skeletons lifted straight from the movies. I don't correct them. Sometimes fear can be a good thing. It releases a whole set of interesting chemicals into the blood that heighten awareness and improve performance. I won't take that away from them. Besides, they'll only be disappointed when they discover what it's really like down there. Just to test my theory, I give them the choice.

"Anyone who wants to stay up here can, but you're all welcome to come down."

They share looks that speak of genuine nervousness, but then, almost as a single unit, they step forward.

I fetch a coiled rope ladder from near the doorway and secure the ties around the ceremonial table, tugging the knot hard to make sure it stays. I toss the ladder through the opening and it disappears into the darkness. The five Venezuelan men watch with wide eyes as it disappears.

I'm not as young as I once was and what I told Esperanza is true: I'm no athlete. So it is with some trepidation that I slide into the hole, my feet searching for a rung, and try to keep the sway of the ladder from upending me. After the swinging of the ladder becomes less pronounced, I lean back, smile at the others, and lower myself into the darkness.

I'm seven rungs down when a train hits me.

My chest seizes, and my breath comes in ragged gasps, as if I'm sucking oxygen through a clogged filter. The darkness surrounding me is now a physical thing—an insidious creature running cold hands over my naked skin. It is only two meters to the bottom but I cling to the ladder, even as the coarse rope burns my hands. I can't move.

I hear something above me that I recognize as a voice but I can't make sense of the words. There's a pounding in my ears that sounds like roaring surf beating against rocks. That louder sound, blocking out all else, is fear speaking to me, and I've never before heard its full voice.

It seems like hours that I hang there, my mind caught in a dark place, before I can will a rational thought to find any purchase. I know I need to regulate my breathing so I can organize my thoughts. I try breathing through my mouth, exhaling slowly. I repeat the process several times until a portion of the oppressive darkness lifts and I can make out the vague shape of the smooth rock surface before me.

I'm beginning to feel intense pain in my hands and it forces me to move down the ladder. In just a few seconds I reach solid ground and I fumble to pull out and turn on the flashlight. The beam that spills out over the corridor walls is the most beautiful thing I've ever seen, and I release a small sob of gratitude even as I wonder what just happened to me.

Esperanza is soon by my side, up close and pulling me away from the rope ladder that has started to dance as one of the others begins to descend.

"What was that?" she asks me in a harsh whisper.

"What do you mean?"

"You hung there for almost a minute, and you wouldn't answer me." She grabs my arm and leans closer, but with the flashlight trained down the tunnel she can't see my face. "Are you all right?"

Did she say I hung there for only a minute? It seemed much longer—as if half my life had passed by.

"I'm fine," I answer, hoping my voice sounds steady. "It's just been a long time since I've climbed down a rope ladder. My knee's acting up."

She probably would have said more, but now the others are behind us and it's getting crowded in here.

"Let's go," I say. I start down the passage, the light revealing nothing but bare stone. I'm embarrassed by whatever it was that happened to me back there. At least it wasn't as obvious as it could have been. Claustrophobia comes to mind, because whatever it was only took hold of me once I'd entered the hole. Yet I've never experienced something like that, and I've spent a good portion of my adult life in cramped places beneath the earth. Of course, it's been five years. I start to feel the cold fingers of fear touching my elbow and I push those thoughts away.

We've reached the end of the passage, and a narrow set of stairs follows the wall line to the left before turning and angling back toward the pyramid's center. I turn and review the crew, who are huddled close together, drawn by the light. I realize I'm not up to my pre-professorship form because I'm the only one with a light. Had I been thinking clearly, I would have outfitted everyone with lights, rope, and water. I console myself that I could find my way out of here in complete darkness. There is, after all, only one path you can take.

"Everyone all right back there?" I ask.

Heads nod all around, except Antonio who crosses himself again.

"Está bien, Antonio. Es como bajar a tu sótano para cambiar un fusible." *It's all right, Antonio. Just like going down into your basement to change a fuse.*

This gets nervous laughter from the others. I turn and start down the stairs—which are even narrower than the corridor—with the light aimed near my feet so I don't miss a step. The others will have to keep their hands on the walls and feel their way down. In six steps we're moving to the left and descending at a steeper angle. At the bottom, I see the entrance into the burial chamber and I'm thrilled that we didn't reseal it after leaving last time.

As we enter the large room, there's a bit of ambient lighting that comes through small gaps between the stones. It's not enough to see by but it supplements the illumination from the flashlight. The mold is worse than it was when we first broke through all those years ago. Then, we were meticulous in clearing it away, mindful of what might exist beneath it. And we'd been rewarded with strange carvings in the limestone as well as etchings in the lintel above the entrance.

I pull a pair of gloves from the pack hanging at my waist and I start to wipe the mold away. It takes a few minutes before I've cleared off a small center portion of a carving—the image of an antlered animal. There are three circles above its hindquarters, with two straight lines beneath its primitive hooves. There's no resemblance to what would become the Mayan written language. Neither is there anything that marks it as a precursor to the Epi-Olmec script that might have taken root in this region.

"I've never seen anything like it," Esperanza says.

That's not what I want to hear. She's my subject-matter expert. If anyone can help me make sense of these things, it will be her.

"We'll have to clear away the rest of the mold before we do anything else." With one last look around, I start back up toward the open air, trying to keep my mood from souring.

We've been working for two days, and the guys need a break.

When we pull into town, it's seven-thirty at night and Rubio is winding down from work and settling into the serious business of relaxation. I debate a few places in my head but choose to stay with a known quantity. That way, if the crew wanders off, they stand a better chance of finding their way back to the trucks. I pull up to The Sleeping Bear, the other SUV following suit, and all but Esperanza and I are out of the trucks and dispersing before I can say anything to them about when to meet back here.

It's busier inside than it was when we first arrived in town, and I get a nicer greeting from the bartender. His lip curls into something resembling a smile, rather than fixing me with that blank look that leaves you wondering if he's going to serve you or eat you.

Espy and I select a table, and a young woman in a white ruffled skirt takes our order. There's music playing from a jukebox in the corner, and several people are already dancing even though the night is young. I watch Esperanza as her eyes move over the crowd and I can see that she's enjoying herself. While she pays homage to books and academic research, she would never look askance on the dynamic social qualities of her people. She can dance with the best of them.

By the time our food arrives, I'm feeling more relaxed, the stress leached away. I even nod to Henry, whom I see up at the bar. It's not until I am several bites into my meal that my dinner date says a word, and it's not at all what I'm expecting. She utters a curse as she looks over my shoulder.

I hear scuffling near the door and I turn just in time to see three men in green uniforms push their way into the busy tavern. One of them delivers a shove to an inebriated patron and it sends the man sprawling over a chair. After a quick canvass of the room, all three sets of eyes train on me.

Two of them are armed with AK-47s, which they raise as the men approach our table. I take exception to the fact that both are pointed at me and that Esperanza is presumed innocent.

"You are conducting an illegal operation in the government-protected ruins," a man with the stripes of a colonel says.

There is an army base to the west of Rubio just a few miles

away. When we were here last time, we would often see off-duty soldiers frequenting the businesses here. They didn't bother us, and they seemed to get along well with the townsfolk. Rubio is almost an army town; their commerce depends on the soldiers.

"I think there's been a misunderstanding, Colonel," I say, leaving my hands in plain sight on the table. It's not that I think the young men in the uniforms are trigger-happy, but misunderstandings are best avoided. "I'm authorized to work in the area. I have the necessary papers from Central University of Venezuela's School of Anthropology."

The colonel frowns. He had obviously not been prepared for a rebuttal.

"If you were cleared to work here, why wasn't I informed?" the man snaps. "Where are your papers?"

"Let me get them." I raise my left hand from the table and, while maintaining eye contact with the colonel, slip it into my pack. I pull out my passport, a dated authorization form from the university, and an addendum extending the duration of the dig from the dates on the original form. That last is a nice touch, and I'd complimented Romero. It keeps things from looking too clean. Something like an addendum adds legitimacy to the enterprise.

The colonel takes these from me and looks them over with a sharp eye, but everything is in order. The people Romero works with are the best at what they do. In fact, the first time I met Romero, when Espy introduced us, it was to have him forge documents to allow me to take antiquities out of the country. He's only gotten better at his craft.

"I still wasn't notified that you would be here, Dr. Hawthorne," the man says.

The other two, sensing the change in circumstances, and acting on Espy's smile, lower their weapons. And now they're paying more attention to the lovely woman at the table than they are to me.

"I'm sorry no one told you, Colonel. I would have stopped by and introduced myself but, as you can see, we're not authorized for an extended stay and I'd like to get as much done as I can."

This appeases him, although he still seems troubled about being kept in the dark.

"Colonel, how about I buy you and your men a drink? That way your trip into town won't be wasted." It's as these words escape my lips that I see a ghost. Beyond the colonel, in a seat near the door, is a man in jeans and an off-white shirt. He wears a hat, pulled down low so as to almost cover his eyes. Before I can get a better look, or jump out of my chair, the colonel leans in, obstructing my view.

"That's very generous of you, Dr. Hawthorne," he says. And by the time he leans back, the other man is gone, the door swinging shut behind him.

Later, after I've put a few drinks for the colonel and his men on my card and have resumed eating my dinner, Esperanza says, "You know he's going to call Caracas when he gets back to the base, right?"

"I wouldn't think much of him if he didn't."

She raises an eyebrow. "That doesn't worry you?"

"Have a little trust in your big brother."

Back at the university, there's a form corresponding to the one I have in my pack. A clerk will pull the file and confirm for the colonel that one Dr. Jack Hawthorne is approved to conduct an academic exercise in the area of Rubio.

Still, the confrontation has me unsettled. Obviously someone told him that we were here. It might have been Henry. He's nursed his grudge for years, and my recent recompense may not have satisfied him. What bothers me more, though, is the possibility that my mind is playing tricks on me. Can it really be true that the man I just saw is the Australian who visited Jim at KV65? His is the face I've attached to the whole event—the person who vanished like smoke just minutes before the ground swallowed my brother. A clinical part of my brain understands—has understood since that day—that I'm reaching, that a malevolent look does not make someone a killer, or mean that something insidious is behind what happened. Add to this, however, that there was a rush to close the investigation, that no one would even consider the notion that it wasn't an accident. Or that even Jim seemed reluctant to pursue the matter, despite that the man I thought I knew would not have backed down from anyone.

I have no choice but to push these thoughts aside. It's far-fetched, because it would mean that whatever took place in Egypt is somehow linked to my current job, and that is improbable. The more likely explanation is that the man at the door bore a resemblance to the Australian. The colonel's visit is a more immediate concern, and a warning that we shouldn't overstay our welcome. Romero, thankfully, has bought us some time, so I determine to enjoy myself. The steak is good, the music upbeat, and my date is the loveliest woman in the room. For the time being, I content myself with these simpler things.

Esperanza runs her hands along the wall carvings, moving

from one to the other. There are a total of eleven distinct images or scenes. Among the odder things about them are their stylistic differences. When my team first uncovered the images, it was as if we'd discovered a repository of pictorial samples from several civilizations, and with no similarities save for a single symbol that gives them a thematic link. In each of the eleven carvings, never in the same spot, there's an oblong disc inset with a squiggle resembling an *S*, each instance deftly worked into the larger image. I'd thought at the time that if we could identify that piece, everything else would fall into place.

The picture from the book, the crest for Fraternidad de la Tierra, is the first in the line, or the last, depending upon which end one starts. She is at that one now, and she's smiling as her fingers trace the image. I know what she's feeling, because I've been there. She's at that point where academic knowledge becomes empirical. Something has jumped off the page and she can touch it, experience it.

What I'm feeling, though, is a sense of futility. I'd been hoping that seeing them would trigger something. Pieces would fall into place and I would be able to make a connection between them—something that would lead us to some course of action.

"Do you recognize any of them?" I ask her.

Esperanza steps away from the wall until she can see all three carvings on it. She spends several seconds focusing on each before turning to the next wall, then the next. After reviewing the last one, the only wall with two images rather than three, she says, "That one there, the one with the deer, it looks familiar. I'm not sure where I've seen it, but it rings a bell. And maybe that one." She points at a circle on the opposite wall—insets that make it look almost like a smiley face, with the ever-present oblong disc serving as an eye.

"That's all?"

She nods, then starts snapping pictures. Esperanza is the quintessential researcher. Even though she can't decipher them at the moment, once she gets back to her books and her computer, she stands a better chance of cracking whatever code exists here than anyone on the planet. Still, it doesn't help me right now and I know the fault is mine. I'm the one who is unequipped to make sense of the meaning behind the carvings. There is something important here, I'm sure of it. And it's likely tied to the small symbol found in each of the carvings.

"What do we do now?" Espy asks once she's finished taking pictures.

"Great question. I'm open to suggestions."

She is silent as we both regard the limestone puzzles. Then I see her eyes travel down the wall, to the floor of the burial chamber.

"Is Mayan architecture always above ground?"

"Almost always."

She taps the stone with the heel of her boot. "But this is pre-Mayan, right? Not everything here fits the schematic?"

I don't answer her right away, because what she's proposing would do irreversible damage to the pyramid. And there is little chance that she's right. Still, what other choice is there? Right now the only alternative is to return to Caracas, which would be tantamount to throwing in the towel. I'm not prepared to do that. At least Espy's plan will keep us here for a while, plus give me some time to think. The problem is that time is becoming a scarce commodity, especially with the specter of military intervention hanging over our heads. Beyond that, soon I'll have to make a decision regarding my future as an academic, and I've jumbled things up sufficiently that the decision is no longer as clear as it once was.

We all have masks on, purchased from a hardware store in Rubio, and I still feel as if I have dust coating my insides. I know my team feels the same way because they're all taking more frequent breaks, navigating the winding stairs and the free-swinging ladder to the open air above. But what we've found keeps me pressing on, despite the fact that our lack of protocol means I'm likely destroying valuable material, that there will be things lost to science. There's a second floor beneath the first, of the same period, one produced on top of the other. It's unprecedented in Mayan architecture and, while I keep telling myself that this isn't a true Mayan structure, the reminder holds little weight. I'm feverish with excitement, my mind parsing the possibilities. This is a level, a sophistication, of temple development that doesn't match the antiquity of the structure, as if they borrowed the idea from somewhere else.

The real payoff is that we've found etchings—just the barest hint of them, a few dark lines peeking out from beneath the last row of stones we pulled up. Once we get the next row removed, I'll have a better idea what we're dealing with. We're working in the western corner of the structure, which is a bit surprising because carving out that point of the compass for special significance is a quintessentially Egyptian characteristic. Even so, there's much here that doesn't match the accepted South American schematic, so I won't put any undue emphasis on this inconsistency.

Several minutes pass as we raise the last of the stones. Antonio and another man from the crew are levering a chipped three-by-three paver off to the side. I'm right there, not waiting for the dust to clear before I'm on my knees with a brush, moving dirt that's been undisturbed for longer than most people can fathom. I ignore the tickle in my throat, my burning eyes. The two men find a place for the stone and let it fall, and the sound reverberates through the chamber. The silence that follows is full of something. I feel it, and apparently so does Espy, who has appeared at my side. Even the men feel it; they're hovering just behind, anxious to see what their labor has unearthed.

It seems to take forever before the dust settles and I can start to make out more of the markings on the subfloor as they resolve themselves into . . . I'm not aware of having dropped the brush, yet it's no longer in my hand. It takes me a while to wrap my brain around what I see, during which I'm unable to speak. Espy places a hand on my shoulder. She sees it too, even if she may not fully understand the significance.

"It's impossible," I breathe.

"This is Egyptian, isn't it?" she says.

"Coptic. It's a form of demotic Egyptian rendered from the Greek alphabet. It was in use from the first century through the seventeenth." I'm talking fast, trying to make sense of this singular find. It shakes the foundation of everything I thought I knew about South and Central American cultural development—not the least of which is that no record of any kind indicates contact between the Americas and peoples from the other side of the ocean at the time this temple was built.

Espy digests the information and, since she knows more about the timeline for this part of the world than I could ever hope to, she now understands the importance of this find. "We shouldn't see something like this for at least another thousand years."

While she's coming to grips with that, I'm wrestling with another possibility: that my original dating for the construction of this temple was off by more than five hundred years. Coptic did not exist as a written language until the first century. If people from North Africa somehow migrated here during that period, it would place the construction of the temple during the late pre-Mayan period—with places like Palenque already well developed. Yet it lacks much of the refinement displayed there, and in Tikal, and at other locations.

Espy's mind is traveling the same path. "If people from Egypt arrived here in the first century, what do you think their reaction would have been to this side of the world's equivalent of the pyramids?"

"They would have recognized the similarities, a kinship."

"And they might have learned how to build one?"

I don't answer, but I lift my eyes away from the text and take in the whole of the chamber. Espy's right; it's the only thing that makes sense. Egyptians were not just here during the construction of Quetzl-Quezo, they were its builders.

I focus on the writing. The letters are not quite right. In the first part of the text, there are places in which the curves are too wide, where one character or another is not fully formed. It indicates that this is early Coptic, scribed at a time when the language was still absent of defined boundaries. I read it twice to make sure I've got it right. What's strange is that the latter text is obviously from a later time period and not just because of the use of a more advanced alphabet.

"What does it say?" Espy prompts.

"The first part reads, 'Come from the four winds and breathe into these that they may live.' " I look up and meet Esperanza's hopeful gaze, and I offer a smile. It's too close to be chance, yet it's not spot-on. "It's from Ezekiel: the Valley of the Dry Bones. Metaphorically speaking, it's a related text, but it's far removed from anything to do with Elisha."

Espy's not buying it. She knows the odds. There is a look on her face that I've shared on more than one occasion, when the things I've read about have taken form. She has a first-timer's glow and, despite myself, it's one that I share.

"You said the 'first part.' Well, what does the rest of it say?"

"It says I shouldn't be so hard on myself for having such a difficult time dating this place."

Actually, the rest of the inscription translates to a single word: *Lalibela*. And, to me, it's a much more exciting find than the biblical text it accompanies. Because I can catch a plane in Caracas and be walking the streets of Lalibela by tomorrow. It's the ancient equivalent of a Post-it Note—an arrow pointing back across the ocean. The thing that makes it especially intriguing is that the city didn't get its name until the eleventh century. And while I've been playing fast and loose with the dating, I would stake my dusty credentials on the fact that these two sections of text were recorded at least a millennium apart.

I sense the substantial weight of a long-lived conspiracy threatening to rest on my shoulders. For the first time since starting this project, I'm approaching the place where I'm willing to believe there's something here, and that it spans a vast timeline. And the thing that tells me that five years of teaching has changed me is that I'm almost frightened by the prospect.

I resist the urge to allow this foreboding to mar the pleasure I feel at having discovered a Mayan-style temple, built by

Egyptians, sporting a road map to Ethiopia, and hidden in a South American jungle. The disparate parts, by themselves, would keep me writing papers for the rest of my life—if I were still doing that sort of thing.

I'm about to tell Espy what the last part says when something wraps its burly arms around my mental faculties. All of a sudden, what we've found—the Egyptian connection, the Ethiopian city name, something—is coaxing a related item up through the clutter of other things begging for my attention. When it finally surfaces, I react with a start—one violent enough to send the rest of my team jumping back. It's the knowledge that there now exists a connection between this project and KV65, and a dramatic improvement in the odds that the man at the bar was in fact the vanishing Australian. Unbidden, the glimpse of text I saw scrawled on the inner coffin in 65 comes to me: *bones of the holy man.* It hits me like a medicine ball in the stomach, this translation of an intangible phrase into something with prophetic weight. It was the only phrase I saw before the SCA closed the dig. And here it was sitting in front of me the whole time, only I lacked the necessary background to see it.

Before I can say anything to Espy, I hear the sounds of someone coming through the passage from the surface. A quick count reveals that my entire crew is present with me, that the magical moment has them all foregoing the dust-free air topside. But I don't allow the ramifications of this puzzle to manifest until I see a stranger enter the chamber, the fluorescent lighting revealing a man in clothing unsuited to the environs. I recognize him; he's the man who introduced me to Gordon Reese.

"Good afternoon, Dr. Hawthorne," Gregory Hardy says, brushing the dust from his clothes, wearing a smile that is not quite a smile.

Chapter 10

I'm thinking about my cactus, trying to remember when I watered it last. Was it two days before I left for Venezuela, or two weeks? It might seem like a small thing but I'd hate to get home and find it dead.

The road passes beneath us as I guide the SUV through the mountains. Antonio has the other truck on my bumper. I'm going too slowly for him, but he'll have to live with it. I'm not as adventurous in my driving as he is.

Beside me, Esperanza sits silent, brooding. I've done my best to keep the mood light but, despite the fact that we've found something of real significance, she's in one of those dark moods I remember from our old days together. And she's not even the one wrestling with her future. It's me who will have to study what we've discovered and either return to the Reese mansion and tell a dying man that I can't follow this thing further, or make the decision to invest my foreseeable future in the pursuit of relics that may or may not exist. Of course, it's not as simple as that—knowing what I now know.

Espy's astute enough to know that something else is going on. She can tell that I'm rattled. Hardy's arrival has made it simpler to explain away my newfound irritability, but the fact is that knowing the man I saw at the bar in Rubio is the same man from the KV65 dig has brought me to a different place, one that's still too painful to visit.

Gordon Reese's little project now has larger, more dangerous parameters. It's not what I signed on for, even if the intrigue of an Egyptian connection makes it perhaps the most important discovery of the century. Truth be told, I'm worried where this will lead.

Just below these misgivings is a simmering anger that now has a focus. I'm not used to the feeling, and I don't much care for it, even as I realize that it might be a good thing. And the wound isn't raw enough to cancel out the fact that there's a part of me that wants to keep on task, to dig into this thing and figure out how all the pieces fall into place—and where my mystery man fits.

Hardy's arrival complicates matters. He's in his own vehicle, trailing the second truck. It irritates me that Reese has sent his pet to keep an eye on things. I force myself to remember that my employer has invested a great deal of money, and that sending someone to ensure the proper use of that money is within his rights. In fact, it's not much different than the inspectors utilized by the SCA. Still, it's irksome. It's this sort of miscalculation that does not fit with what I know of the billionaire. It's a desperate gesture, and while I can suspect his reasons for wanting to hasten the recovery of the artifacts, why would he sabotage his best hope for success?

With that in mind, I pull out my cell phone and thumb the display. Duckey's message count is now at six, and it gives me some perverse pleasure to know I've vexed him.

"What are you doing in Venezuela?" It comes out loud through the earpiece—enough so that I draw the phone away, losing the next sentence.

I wait for a break before repositioning the phone. "Hey, Ducks."

I hear the intake of a long breath on the top half of the world, followed by a calmer voice.

"Merry Christmas."

"Feliz Navidad."

"Venezuela?"

"Didn't you tell me to get out of the apartment?"

"What are you doing in Venezuela, Jack?"

"Actually, I'm thinking about leaving. It doesn't quite have that holiday spirit."

I can almost hear him grinding his teeth.

"You hate planes. You seldom plan anything. And you don't have any friends except for me and Angie. So forgive me for being surprised."

This is new territory. It's one thing to trade barbs in familiar surroundings, where everything is wedged between the siren songs of classes and department meetings. Duckey's trying to make sense of my global position, to force it to mesh with what he knows about me. I feel a measure of sympathy.

"I need a favor, Ducks."

"Of course you do." As he says it, I can hear relief in his tone. It seems I'm always in need of a favor, and Duckey's good at handing them out. It's a familiar role and he knows how to handle this portion of the conversation. "What is it this time? Out of money and need plane fare home?"

"There aren't a lot of casinos in this part of the world so, no, I'm good."

"Couldn't be that simple, eh?"

"Ducks, I need you to find out everything you can about Gordon Reese."

It's one of the few times I've rendered my department head speechless, and I've said some odd things over the years. In the ensuing silence I can hear sounds in the background and I can almost see Duckey sitting in someone's kitchen, wearing a flannel shirt and jeans, surrounded by three generations of family. I've never felt more separated from another human being.

"Billionaire Gordon Reese?"

"Yep."

More silence. I can feel through the phone the calculating going on as Duckey weighs any number of things, and I'm almost sure that trust is one of them. Duckey left the CIA long ago, and although he keeps former contacts in his back pocket, government-issue favors come with strings.

"What am I looking for?" he finally asks.

"Good question," I say. "Any recent change in his circumstances. Something big." I know I'm not giving him much to go on, and I feel some guilt for asking him to do this on his vacation. I don't really know why I'm asking, when there's a good chance I'll be backing out of this deal, except that it's one of those open questions I want answered—if only to satisfy my own curiosity. "Sorry, Ducks. I wish I could be more specific."

"I'll see what I can do," he says. "But you'd better have an explanation par excellence."

"Do you want me to make up something believable, or do you want the truth?"

"Surprise me."

"Thanks, Ducks. This means a lot."

He releases a sigh. "Are you in trouble?"

"Not yet."

When I end the call, it's with a smile, one that can only

be granted by finding something familiar in the midst of uncertainty. I glance at Espy.

"You all right?" I ask.

"Just fine." She adds a smirk, which is what I get for trying to get in touch with her feelings.

We drive in silence for a long time. I think the guy in the back—Marco—is sleeping, but it's dark and I can't see him very well in the rearview mirror. I feel myself drifting and I'm about to turn on the radio when Esperanza says, "Will you be catching a flight home tomorrow?"

Her question catches me without an immediate response, even though it's one that should occupy the bulk of my mind. I let the question hang there while the road passes beneath us.

"I honestly don't know," I finally answer. It's a hard thing to admit. This business, in the best of circumstances, is difficult. With all of the other things attached to this particular project, I have to face the possibility that I might not be able to keep up.

As the silence lingers, I realize that, yet again, I'm not on Espy's wavelength. I'm still considering her question in terms of the job. There are areas in which I am none too bright, and I'll be the first to admit that relationships fall within that province. Duckey will attest to that, as will Angie, and just about everyone else I've ever met. I think even my cactus is figuring that out. Here I am thinking that Espy's foul mood has something to do with the task at hand, when it has everything to do with us.

"I'm sorry." I let my eyes leave the road long enough to make sure she knows I'm not talking about Reese's project. It's difficult to see her in the darkness, but before I disengage I think I see surprise on her face. It's a sentiment I share. "I'm sorry for leaving the way I did. If I'd had any sense . . ."

I trail off, not knowing how to navigate this type of terrain and feeling more than a little weird.

I guess she finds there's little to say because she turns away. I'm out of my depth. My current closest relationship with a woman is with Angie, which consists of little more than our having coffee together, some innocent flirting, and a theft of miniature chocolates that by now probably approaches grand larceny. I've suppressed the knowledge that this week has to have been difficult for Espy. I've heard often enough that women need closure, but instead of that, I've given my former fiancée *open*-sure, or whatever you call it when you rip a scab off a wound that hasn't yet healed.

What's worse is that I may well still love this woman.

The SUV is bottoming out after a steep descent, where I bring it around a bend. I'm getting irritated because Antonio has his truck so close to mine that I can't see the headlights in the rearview, just a diffused glow that tells me he's there. I can see the lights of San Cristóbal not far off, and we'll be coming off the mountain in a matter of minutes, when it won't matter so much that he's tailgating.

"Listen," I say right before the windshield explodes all over me.

Esperanza screams as I slam on the brakes and try to keep the truck on the road. I yell for her to keep her head down, but before I can get a word out, Antonio rear-ends us. I bite down hard on my tongue and the pain is such that I'm blinded, and it's never a good idea to lose one's sight while navigating a mountain road with no guardrails. I force my eyes open just as our right front tire flirts with the drop-off. I overcorrect, angling for the rock wall to my left, when I hear a succession of popping sounds. More glass explodes, this time from the back of the truck. Marco shouts a curse in Spanish right as the SUV hits the wall. I have the sensation of flying, and then nothing.

It can't be much later that I awaken, because the wheels of the belly-up truck are spinning. I smell gas. As my senses right themselves, I hear the sound of tires screeching, receding. It's black outside, except for the beams from the headlights that cut at an odd angle into the darkness. Somehow the hazard lights were activated, and their steady blinking casts the landscape around the truck in a periodic yellow light. My side hurts and I run my hand over the spot, feel the ripped shirt, then something protruding from the flesh. There's a slickness that has to be blood. I shift position and pain shoots through my torso. I resist the urge to pull out whatever it is that's stuck in my side. For all I know, it's all that's keeping me from bleeding to death.

From what sounds like far away I hear another volley of gunshots. They propel me to my feet, despite the agony ripping through my body. Stumbling, working hard to keep my feet under me and my eyes focused, I make it to the truck, the smell of gas much stronger now. The tank is ruptured, the fuel dripping its last onto the ground. I try not to imagine my body doing the same thing, but my hand is soaked where it's pressed up against my side.

Right now, checking on Esperanza is more important than anything else. I can see the truck's passage down the road; we must have slid two hundred feet. It's amazing that we didn't slide off the mountain. It's the kind of accident that can kill instantly, and I feel more than a little panic as I sink to my knees and peer into the cab. Marco is the only one inside, in the back, his neck twisted at an odd angle. Even though it's pointless, I reach between the broken glass and feel for a pulse. Nothing.

I feel something catch in my throat but I quickly force it back down. I must find Espy.

I push myself upright and scan the road. As I take a step away from the truck, out into the darkness, there's a hollow sound of metal on metal, and I feel something whiz by my right ear. I lunge and my knees buckle, and as I hit the ground, the object in my side dislodges. I ignore the pain and scramble over the dirt, the ground behind me getting shot up in staccato clods. My path carries me into the darkness, toward the mountain wall. After I regain my footing, I stumble over something near the road. I drop to my knees and am about to feel for Espy's pulse when something hard strikes the back of my head and darkness claims me.

More than anything in the world, I need an aspirin. My head feels as if several very small men are on the inside of my skull, using equally small hammers to work over the gray matter. I open my eyes but can't see anything, and I feel a moment of panic that I've been blinded.

Everything comes back in a rush.

Where am I? What I know is that I can't see, my side hurts, my tongue hurts, I have a headache, and I can't move my hands. I try to bring my arms around to the front, but they're pinned behind me. It occurs to me then that I'm sitting up.

"Hello?"

There's no answer. I rock in the chair, testing the strength of whatever it is that binds me. It's thick, coarse rope that rubs against my skin the more I struggle, and I stop when the pain in my side approaches unbearable. I wonder how much blood I've lost. I try calling out again and there is an echo, which doesn't tell me a lot. I'm worried about Espy. I have no idea if she was alive when I stumbled over her, and the more I think about it, the sicker I feel.

I hear footsteps, then someone is touching my head and the hood is yanked off. The lights in the room are bright and I blink several times. I'm in an office, but one of those that's attached to a warehouse or factory. There's a large glass window that makes up one wall, with pallets of boxes as far as I can see. These observations are secondary, though, to the sight of the three men in the room with me. Two of them, the ones with guns, are strangers, while the third, the one sitting behind a desk, is not.

"Hello, Jack," he says with a smile.

Ernesto Ramirez is one of those men who perpetuates the caricature of a South American drug lord from the movies. The difference is that he isn't very successful at it. Contrary to prevailing belief, it's not an easy matter to send large quantities of drugs into the United States. It takes more connections, money, and intelligence than this man possesses. To supplement his income, he has a hand in just about everything that passes through San Cristóbal, illegal or otherwise. Few business deals get done here without Ramirez getting his cut. He's been successful in this venture because the logistics are nowhere near as complex as they are in drug smuggling. All he needs are hired muscle and meanness, and he has both of these in abundance.

"It's been a long time, Jack."

"It certainly has," I manage to say. "How have you been, Ernesto?" I wear a cheerful smile, ignoring the incongruity of not being able to move.

"I'm well, thank you."

"This is about the money, isn't it?"

"In a manner of speaking."

I'm terrible with money. I met Ernesto back when we were excavating Quetzl-Quezo, when Henry helped facilitate a deal with him to allow us to move some of the items out of the country through San Cristóbal. Ernesto never got his cut. I imagine he still holds a grudge that my word was not my bond.

"Where's Esperanza?" I ask, and there's a hardness in my voice that I can't remember having put there before.

"You mean the pretty young lady riding with you?" He waves the question away. "Don't worry about her. She's fine."

I have no confidence in his assurances. I pull against the ropes but it's no use, and Ernesto's goons have the firepower.

"How much do I owe you?" I ask.

"You have an outstanding bill of seventy-five hundred dollars, if my memory serves."

"I can cover that."

He gives me a pitying look and shakes his head. "You don't understand, Jack. I've received a better offer."

"Excuse me?"

"Apparently you've left a few more angry people in your wake. I've been paid the sum of fifty thousand to kill you and your associates."

"You've got to be kidding. Who would want to have me killed?" Even as I ask the question, I have the answer, and it sends a chill through my body. I feel light-headed and the room fades for a second. When I steady myself, I look down at my injured side. Bandages have been wound around my stomach, and a large section of the fabric is soaked through, but there is no blood dripping onto the floor.

He shrugs.

I'm in a panic now because, although I've had guns pointed at me before, this is the first time I can see myself actually being shot.

"Has he already paid you?" I ask.

"Half. I'll receive the other twenty-five thousand when I provide proof that you're dead."

He's fishing. Otherwise he would have just killed me and collected his fee.

"What if I can beat the offer? Cover the twenty-five, plus get you that much more?"

"We've already been down that road, Dr. Hawthorne. You weren't able to come up with the money, remember?"

"That was then," I say. "But you'll need to let me make a phone call."

His eyes narrow and bore into me. I don't know this man well, but I know his type. He has little compunction about killing, but he's also smart enough to know when a murder can unduly complicate his other business activities. I'm a foreigner, which would bring the government here were they to find my body in a ditch somewhere. And Esperanza's death would make the national news: University Professor Found Dead in San Cristóbal.

"That's fifty-seven thousand, five hundred," he says, lifting my cell phone from his desk. "Twenty-five to cover my losses, another twenty-five for the lives of you and your associate, and"—he smiles—"the seventy-five hundred you owe me."

"Will you accept an account transfer?"

He nods.

"But first, I need to see Esperanza."

Ernesto raises an eyebrow. "I don't see as you are in any position to make demands."

"If I'm buying her life, as well as my own, shouldn't I make sure she's all right?"

After brief consideration, Ernesto gestures to one of his men, who leaves the room. The other man adjusts his grip on his gun—a reminder. I'm made to wait a long time, and Ernesto watches me without saying a word, almost without blinking. It's more than a little unnerving. The first time I met him, his stare reminded me of the dispassionate gaze of a crocodile. I'm about to make idle chitchat, just to break the awkward silence, when Esperanza walks into the room, her arm held at the elbow. Relief greater than I have ever known washes over me and, after her escort unties me, I struggle to my feet and gather her into an embrace. I guess I'm not used to these extreme emotions because, while she seems to share my joy at the reunion, she is the first to push away, and I find it difficult to let go.

"That's beautiful," Ernesto says.

"Jack, what's going on?" Espy asks.

I mouth *later* and reach for my phone. I have a moment's hesitation as my thumb hovers over the speed-dial option for Duckey. I reconsider.

Reese answers on the second ring.

"Hello, Jack."

Before those two words finish their digital echo, my brow is furrowing, although it will take a little longer for me to figure out why.

"Gordon, I need a favor."

There is a few seconds' pause before he asks, "What sort of favor?"

And then it clicks; one of the things that has most impressed me about this man has been his accessibility. When we've talked, the atmosphere has been one of equals. Now I sense a patrician iciness, and I can't keep a sick feeling from swelling my stomach. Despite that, and what it might portend, I press on. "Mr. Reese, I need you to transfer fifty-seven thousand, five hundred dollars to the bank account of a man who is holding me at gunpoint."

I see Ernesto frown, but he does not move to end the call. Even he understands that the bold truth is sometimes the only way to go.

Reese doesn't answer right away, although I can hear him breathing so I know the signal hasn't cut out. It's an odd request, even of a man with his fortune, so I give him the time he needs. Meanwhile, I keep an eye on Ernesto, knowing that his magnanimous sensibilities won't last long. Finally he asks, "What will happen if I do not transfer this sum?"

The question chills me. "Then this man will kill me," I say.

I don't have to look to Ernesto for confirmation. He will kill me for the money, whatever the consequences. What I do see is the look on Esperanza's face—the realization that our situation is even more precarious than she may have thought. I give her a wink.

Gordon releases a sigh, and my heart begins to work its way up to my throat. I do my best to keep panic from surfacing on my face, but when Gordon gives me his answer, it's all I can do to keep from dropping the phone.

"I'm sorry, Jack," he says, and the line goes dead.

There's no telling how long I hold the phone in my hand. I can't focus on anything until I hear Ernesto clear his throat. With that, it hits me that Gordon Reese has just signed my death warrant. My mind is a vacuum, despite the half-formed thought that I've just been fired—which I will take a great deal more offense at if Espy and I survive. When I look up, it is not

Ernesto's eyes I search out, but Espy's, and it doesn't surprise me that there's nothing but calm in them, even though she has to know what has just happened.

"Am I to assume that you'll be unable to make good on your debt yet again?" While he sounds smug, there is also a hint of disappointment in Ernesto's question. He would have preferred to earn his money without the inconvenience of disposing bodies.

"Wait," I say as Ernesto gestures at one of his associates. When the man wraps an arm around Esperanza, gripping her throat in beefy fingers, I repeat, "Wait! Please!"

Before Ernesto can say anything, or make whatever gesture means *break the pretty girl's neck*, I stab at the buttons on the phone, praying I get the number right the first time and angered with myself for not putting it in speed dial. I hold my breath as the phone dials, and it's into the fourth ring before Romero answers.

"Romero! It's Jack. I don't have time to explain, but I need to ask for a very large favor."

"Jack?" It takes my friend a moment to orient himself, but when he does, he doesn't hesitate with his response. "What do you need?"

"I need you to transfer money to a bank account." I clear my throat and add, "I'm good for it, I promise."

"How much?"

"Fifty-seven thousand, five hundred . . ."

There is a sound that might be a muffled curse, but while I feel for my friend, I have no other choice. Romero is a high-end supplier of artwork and antiquities to the world's wealthiest people, and I know what his markups are. Out of all the people

I know, Romero is the likeliest to have this sort of available cash.

Ernesto is watching me with the expression of a man pondering which of the lobsters in the tank looks the tastiest.

Romero knows that his sister is with me, and it's probably that knowledge which prompts what he says next, even though I'd like to think it's the result of a trust built over a decade of friendship.

"What's the account number?" Romero asks.

I look to Ernesto, who provides me with a bank account number. When I relay the information to Romero, there's a pause as he writes it down.

"I have it. I'll call my bank as soon as we hang up." He then says in a quiet voice, "And if anything happens to my sister . . ."

"Understood," I say.

"Are you going to tell me what's going on?" Romero presses.

"I'll tell you when we get back. Thanks, Romero."

I hope he can hear the gratitude in my voice, but his acknowledgment is a mere grunt before disconnecting.

Several anxious minutes follow as we await confirmation that Ernesto's account—one I'm certain is a dummy, untraceable back to him—has taken the transfer, and Espy is silent throughout. But when Ernesto, with a phone call, verifies that his account has grown by a considerable amount, and he graces us with a satisfied smile, she says, "Are you going to tell me what's going on now?"

Ernesto offers a smile that is almost gracious. "Dr. Hawthorne and I simply had an old debt to settle."

When she hits me this time, I am wholly unprepared. And

since my midsection has suffered a grievous injury, the solid blow does more damage than she'd likely anticipated.

"You owe someone else money? What's the matter with you?" And then she starts in again with the cursing in Spanish.

"I still don't understand why someone would pay that much to have you killed," Ernesto says. "I'm not certain you're worth it."

"I've wanted to have him killed," Esperanza responds. "And I would have probably paid a lot to see it happen."

Ernesto laughs. "I like her."

"Now that we're settled up," I say to him, ignoring the budding camaraderie, "can you tell me anything about this guy?"

After my brief conversation with Reese, I'm convinced that, rather than the Australian who has entwined himself in my affairs, the man who made the deal with Ernesto was Gregory Hardy. The timeline fits; Ernesto's visitor made his offer two days ago, and Hardy showed up at the dig site the following day, yesterday. I don't believe in coincidence. It doesn't help me understand why Reese would want me dead, but at least it's a plausible theory.

"My curiosity got the better of me, too," Ernesto answers. "Which is why I had him tailed."

"You beautiful human being." I'm choosing to ignore the failure of that statement on so many levels.

"He's smart. Three vehicle changes. We almost lost him."

He's waiting for some sort of vocalized appreciation for keeping an elusive quarry in his sights, but he's not going to get it from me.

"Whoever he was," Ernesto continues, "he spoke with an accent that at first I thought was South African, but we determined it was likely Australian."

The chill that seems like a frequent visitor returns now. Ernesto's information would seem to indicate that my Reese theory is wrong. "How did you determine that?"

"Because he caught a charter flight to Caracas, where he boarded a plane bound for Sydney," Ernesto says with a wink.

Criminal distrust is a wonderful thing.

"Anything else you can tell me?"

"Regrettably, no."

"How were you supposed to prove that you killed me?"

"By emailing a picture of your carcass to him."

"Oh."

Ernesto has walked us to the door of the business, which is a legitimate industrial supply company where he rents office space. He's told me that the other SUV escaped and, while he had orders to eliminate anyone traveling with me, he thought that bringing the chase into the city would have been imprudent. I'm glad Antonio got away. I imagine the superstitious man thought he was being punished for desecrating holy ground. He probably drove all the way back to Caracas, crossing himself the entire way. I wish him Godspeed. Ernesto had no information about the car driven by Gregory Hardy. According to his men, there were only two vehicles in our party at the time they opened fire. At this point, I can't spare the resources necessary to care about him.

Ernesto leads us outside and, with no parting words, allows a metal door to close between us. Esperanza and I are alone on the sidewalk in the less-than-touristy part of San Cristóbal.

Warehouses rise up on either side of the street, and there is a smell in the air that more than hints at chemicals and burning rubber. The ground is wet, and there are brown puddles everywhere and hundreds of drowned worms around us.

I start walking, picking a direction that takes us away from an alley filled with people sitting amid refuse. There's an intersection ahead, where we may be able to catch a cab.

"What kind of life do you lead?" Espy calls after me. "People with guns, mysterious Aussies taking contracts out on you, a trail of bad debts all over the world?"

I can't help but laugh. It's funny because of the truth: that I am a boring college professor who seldom leaves my apartment. It's this place—this crazy country—that has made me into something else.

"Why are you laughing? I'm hungry, my leg hurts, and I want to be back in my apartment taking a long bubble bath."

Despite her irritation, I laugh harder, until there are tears pooling in my eyes. This whole thing is absurd. How did I get here? Evanston University seems like a world and a lifetime away. It's something I want to get back to, but I'm not sure how. There are things left unfinished—things I have to see through if I ever want to have even a modicum of peace teaching. The irony is that I was leaning toward giving up. I was going to let my fear of opening up something large—something quixotic—keep me from pursuing the matter. I would have stuck my head in a hole and kept out of the whole sordid business. I would have flown to Dallas, reported to Reese that I could find no evidence to support his theory, and that would have been that. If they'd left me alone, that would have been the end of it. Instead, someone tried to have me killed—either Reese or this mysterious Aussie who has inserted himself into my life. Maybe they're part and parcel of the same entity. Regardless, they've proven that I cannot return to my former existence—not without forever looking over my shoulder.

I get control of myself and put my arm around Esperanza's waist.

"I'm going to take you home. You can take your bubble bath, and I'll let Romero hit me a few times for putting you in danger. After that, I'm getting on a plane to Sydney."

It takes a long moment for the last part to sink in.

"You're what?"

"I'm going to Sydney."

"What on earth for?"

"To find out who's trying to kill me." I pause before adding, "And who killed Will."

The look on her face is one for the ages, and it almost sets me to laughing again, even through the fresh pain. Instead, I give her a reassuring squeeze.

"I'll explain everything. I promise."

We walk a ways in silence and I imagine she's wondering what connections she's missed, how I've linked this to Will. Too, she's probably going through a litany of arguments she can use to talk me out of it. But she knows me—knows that I am going to Sydney.

"Sydney's a big city. And you have no idea who you're looking for."

"That's why I'm glad I know your brother."

Chapter 11

Seldom does physical confrontation rear its head in educational circles, and for good reason: anyone who has ever witnessed two academics engaged in fisticuffs can testify to the wrongness of the activity. I suppose that's why I'm a bit jumpy. Within the last week, I've been hit—twice. By the same woman. I've also had guns pointed at me three times, with one of those instances resulting in the firing of actual bullets, as well as the violent crash of an expensive truck. So I think I can be forgiven my anxiousness as Romero's large hand comes toward me, offering a piece of paper.

"It was a light manifest," he says.

I take the paper, a Qantas moniker in the top right corner. Under a heading for Flight 2976 there's a list of perhaps fifty names. My friend has crossed through a number of them, the obvious female ones. That still leaves more than half, and I'm beginning to realize that this might be more difficult than I'd anticipated.

"Thanks."

My gratitude covers both the manifest and the fact that Romero has decided not to injure me. Even though I'm not directly responsible for his sister having been in danger, I understand that brothers don't always react in a reasonable manner. How could I have known there might really be a global conspiracy intent on keeping some ancient and dangerous secret? None of us thought the outing was anything other than an interesting academic exercise.

When we called Romero from San Cristóbal to fill him in and to let him know we were on our way back, I thought he might come through the phone. I'm not sure whom he would have fixed his anger on: the ones who forced us off the road, or me. I'm thankful for the hours that separated us from this meeting. And when we finally arrived at the Caracas airport, his eyes were hard and looked dangerous. They still do.

We are in Esperanza's apartment, and she has yet to sink into the solace of a bubble bath, even though she favors her right leg. She showed me the bruise during the flight. It's an ominous discoloration of flesh that covers much of the area above her knee. I showed off my own injury while still in San Cristóbal, removing the bandages, cleaning and rewrapping the wound. With any luck I'll avoid an infection. I'm amazed we walked away from the crash. There is a certain giddiness that comes from having survived something that would cause an actuary to soil himself. That might explain the grin I'm wearing.

"What will you do now?" Romero asks. He is standing near his sister as she rests on the couch, her injured leg spread across the cushions and covered with three ice packs.

The answer to that question became obvious during the flight back. I know who and where Reese is, whereas the Australian exists outside of any parameters I can place around him. Right now he commands most of my attention.

"That's simple. I have to match one of these names with a picture in my head, then find out who wants me dead."

"If that's the criteria, I may be on that manifest," Espy says with a smirk.

"And how will you do that?" her brother asks.

"Hopefully with a phone call." I don't have any delusions that it will be that simple, but I cling to optimism anyway.

Romero settles onto the arm of the couch with a grunt, careful to avoid bumping his sister's hurting leg. He fixes a hard gaze on me, much like one of the looks I've suffered from Duckey, as if I'm a specimen beneath a magnifying lens. The years of bearing up beneath the looks of my professor friend serve me well here as I maintain my smile under the Venezuelan's scrutiny.

"It's a fool's errand," he says. "You're rushing off to a big city half a world away, picking a fight with someone with enough resources to know where you were and what you were up to. You'll end up getting yourself killed."

When I do not answer, he says, "Think about it. An alarm bell went off somewhere, and it told them that you were messing around in something you shouldn't have been. And I think you were reasonably discreet. If you go off half-cocked to Sydney, do you think they will not know you're coming before your plane leaves the ground?"

"You forget. They think I'm dead."

"Not for long. When they do not get any pictures in their email, they will know they've been betrayed."

"By that time, I'll already be in Sydney."

"That's what I'm afraid of." He glances down at the floor, then back at me. "I'm going to hate myself for telling you this, but I found a reference."

"To what?"

"The little research project you assigned me." The words come grudgingly.

I feel a tingle along the back of my neck, that feeling I get at the moment of discovery which can make months of exhausting labor worth every pulled muscle and incidence of second-degree sunburn.

"A reference book at a library in Berkeley mentioned a family disinterment in 1629. They moved an ossuary from Samarc to Gatai."

"Did it say why?" I ask.

"No. As far as I can tell—and remember, we're talking about material almost four hundred years old and written by a French expatriate—a group with the Chevrier designation purchased an estate in Gatai in1628 and then sold it in 1641. And there's no mention that any dead relatives went with them back to Samarc."

My brain is working furiously now, trying to fit these small bits of data into a scheme that makes sense along the timeline. At the same time, I'm humbled that Romero took my request as seriously as he did. I hate to think how much research he had to do to find that one reference book.

"Is it too much to ask if it gave the name of the person they moved?"

"No name, but the text used the word *uncle*. And we both know how little that says."

He's right. In the genealogical parlance of the period, uncle could mean anything from the brother of one's parent to a respected cousin from five generations ago. Still, it wouldn't have been common to dig up and transport remains of someone beyond an immediate family member or a respected patriarch. There's some meat to chew on here. Before the idea can take hold of anything, I dislodge the information and stuff it into the cranial cavity designated to hold unsubstantiated musings, like who really killed Kennedy, or what comprises the Colonel's spices.

"I'm sorry, my friend. It's all I could find."

"Don't apologize. It's just what I needed."

"Except that all I've done is to encourage you, when I should be attempting to get you to abandon this nonsense."

I appreciate his sentiment. On the flight back from San Cristóbal, I went through all of this in my mind. Do I really want to add a globe-spanning pursuit to the list of things I've done over my vacation? Shouldn't I just be happy I'm alive and that I can leave this crazy place and go back to Evanston? It's possible that if I show obvious signs of giving up, they will leave me alone.

The only answer that makes any sense is that I don't believe I have a choice. I feel as if some veil has been lifted, and it has shown me the mechanism that controls my life, and the man with the errant balloon who operates the levers and pulleys. I feel as if events outside of my influence have wrapped me up and carted me hither and thither. Now that I'm aware of the manipulation, there is that indefinable something inside that may want to explore choosing the destination. And, despite the fact that everything in my life over the last five years demonstrates disengagement, I can't deny I have a need to see some light shed on what happened at KV65. It's a need strong enough to set my destination away from where I'd rather go. Ethiopia will have to wait. In my mind is a picture of the man who killed Will; I have no doubt of it. And unless I do something, I don't think going back to Evanston will provide me sufficient distance from myself.

As if on cue, my phone rings.

"He's dying," Duckey says.

"Hello, Ducks."

"Reese has liver cancer. His chart lists it as undifferentiated hepatocellular carcinoma. It's stage four."

I don't ask how Duckey got hold of Reese's medical records. Nor do I tell him that I already knew Reese is dying. It will give him a sense of accomplishment to think he uncovered that by himself. "Thanks. That's helpful," I say. "Did you find anything else?"

"The fact that he's dying isn't significant enough?"

"We're all dying, Ducks."

"Some of us not quickly enough," he grumbles. "Hold on, I have a few things jotted down here."

There's a span of several seconds, during which he drops the phone and I hear several choice phrases as he retrieves it.

"All right, here's my list, in no particular order. Reese Industries netted more than three hundred million last year. Their stock split. He named his son CEO in March. He's flown three times to San Diego, and once each to Vienna, Paris, and Addis Ababa—all in the last twelve months. He has four children and seven grandchildren, and one of the grandkids has terminal cancer." He pauses, then adds, "She's the one in San Diego."

As he finishes, I'm working through the information, seizing on the bit that I find most alarming.

"He's been to Ethiopia?" I try to keep the panic out of my voice.

"Got back yesterday. He spent two, maybe three days there."

I quickly go back over the timeline. If Duckey's right, then Reese left for Addis Ababa within a half day of my last conversation with him. I have no idea what to make of that. How could he have known of the Ethiopian connection before I'd connected the dots? It takes a moment's silence—during which

I can hear Duckey's children yelling in the background—before the obvious answer presents itself.

"He has another team."

"If you say so."

I'd forgotten that I have yet to reveal the particulars of my employment to Duckey. He has no idea why I'm interested in Reese, much less that I'm leading a research team for the man. Rather, I *was* leading a research team for him. Now it appears I was just one of Gordon's bets—one late to pay off. I find myself wondering, however briefly, who's leading the competition?

The unpredictability of this enterprise has just increased by a factor of ten, and some of that has to do with the revelation of the granddaughter's illness. I force myself to avoid thinking of her as a person at this point; as harsh as that might seem, obsessing over the impending death of a child I've never met does me no good. At the moment, she is a puzzle piece, only I'm not sure where she fits. Reese's uncharacteristic behavior is the sort of thing that might be driven by worry, but it doesn't explain why he would sabotage one of his chances at finding the bones. Unless he's already found them . . . My eyes widen as I consider that; it makes my stomach knot to think that someone else may have beaten me to a quarry that, within the last few days, has started to take on substance.

"Duckey, you have no idea how much you've just helped."

"Then why do I feel like I just gave you the go-ahead to do something stupid?"

I chuckle at that but do not answer, because he's right. I'm so enthralled with the information he's provided, I almost forget to ask for my second favor. "Ducks, I hate to overdraw from my account, but I need another favor."

"You do realize I'm on vacation, don't you?"

"If I send you a list of names, can you get your buddy at the State Department to run them through their system?"

It's the sort of request that can change the entire nature of a conversation. Indulging a friend by collecting information about a reclusive billionaire is one thing; leveraging the resources of two government agencies in one week is quite another.

"What's going on, Jack?"

I sigh, understanding the position in which I've put him. "It's important, Ducks. I can't go into it right now, but I wouldn't ask if I had any other options."

For the second time in as many days, I've asked him to weigh the level of trust that exists in our friendship. Fortunately, it appears I still have enough in the account to cover this one.

"Send me the names," he says. "But that explanation you owe me? It had better be the most eloquent thing I've ever heard, or else every one of your classes will be at eight A.M. next semester, got it?"

"Got it."

"What am I asking them to check for?"

I tell him and then, after ending the call, I turn to Romero.

"Do you know if there are any direct flights to Addis Ababa?"

Chapter 12

Addis Ababa sits in the foothills of the Entoto Mountains, and as we travel north along Menelik II, I can see their greens and browns through an unseasonable haze. It's been more than a decade since I've been here but there are some things that leave a lasting impression. And looking out over the Ethiopian capital from a mountain ridge is one of those things. My knee aches and I shift as much as the cramped space will allow until I'm rewarded by a relaxing of pressure.

I gaze out the window as the minibus slows to pass a donkey train that is navigating a boulevard shaded by a long line of eucalyptus trees. As the man next to me—the one virtually sitting on my lap—shouts again into his cell phone, the thought of conveyance by a smelly, cantankerous animal seems pleasant by comparison, and that's taking the flies into consideration. As if to validate that desire, the weyala leaning out the door of the vehicle calls to a group of pedestrians in Amharic, gesturing toward the oversized taxi. My command of the language is suspect, but it's a good bet he told them we're headed to Arat Kilo Square, and we've got plenty of room. There are no takers, and the blue and white bus speeds off.

Across the aisle, Espy is sandwiched between two young men who look like students. She wears a smile, and I can tell it's not manufactured. Even though twenty-two people are jammed into a vehicle built to seat twelve, and the air is filled with a dense mixture of unpleasant smells, and the weyala—in between collecting fares—is making off-color remarks about her, and one of her seatmates keeps smelling her hair, she seems to be having a great time. It's a full cultural immersion; more than that, it's an embrace of her circumstances. I have to smile, despite the fact that cell-phone guy has turned so he's shouting directly into my ear.

The fact that she's on the bus is a testament both to her stubbornness and my inability to hold the line against a hostile front. It encourages me to know that even her brother had been unable to keep her from coming along, and for as much as he maintains a fear of his sister, he can be an impassioned and convincing orator. In the end, after more than an hour spent arguing the matter, it boiled down to the bruise on her leg. She has a stake in this; her pain is her ante.

The fact that I'm on the bus is a testament to something else. I'm no longer on Reese's payroll, which means I'm working for free. But there is an understanding between Espy and me that we've invested too much to give up. Now I just want to find the bones, regardless of any power they possess. I want to spite Reese. Too, I want to see the things that Will may have died for.

The driver navigates the turns to get us onto King George Street without going anywhere near the brake, and we ride the wrong lane for the few harrowing moments it takes for us to slip back into the flow of traffic. Through my window I have a clear view as the Arat Kilo monument—a monolithic structure that sits in the center of the square—comes into view and the bus screeches to a halt. But our destination is beyond this; I can see a dome beckoning. The weyala shouts "Mercado!" several times into the crowd, announcing the destination for the return trip, and a few people climb aboard before the bus lurches and speeds off to its last stop before returning to the open-air market.

When Esperanza and I are, to my relief, deposited within a short walk of our objective, I take in a large draught of air and execute a sleepy stretch and then start down the narrow access road—almost a long driveway—that will take us to Trinity Cathedral. Espy is in step and, in contrast to my condition, she looks energized. Some people just travel well, and I'm a bit envious of that.

Most descriptions of the massive church ascribe European sensibilities to the structure. But to my eye, there's a visible, if minimal, classical North African element evident amid the Old World lines. In terms of most sacred buildings in Addis Ababa, Trinity is new—completed in 1941. But the builders stayed true to all that makes Orthodox construction unique. The details are beyond exquisite, showcasing a love of iconic imagery and ornate design.

As we enter the courtyard, its borders defined by a low stone gate with spaced pillars joined by chains, I notice Espy running appreciative eyes over the architecture. Our progress is slow through the courtyard; we almost dawdle as we pass the statues of the four writers of the Gospels.

Finally we reach the entrance, where there's a steady stream of people entering and exiting—tourists and the devout carrying cameras or prayer books. Espy and I slip into the tourist line and pay the fee.

It takes my eyes some time to adjust after entering, and I bump into someone I can't see enough to avoid. After turning down a tour guide who appears out of nowhere, we both remove our shoes and walk deeper into the cathedral. I'm taking in as many of the details as I can while still remaining mindful of the reason I'm here. After spending some time appreciating the cathedral's interior, we head toward one of the two doors on either side of the altar, my right hand running along the back of a wooden pew. Ignoring the few men and women praying in various parts of the sanctuary, I disappear through the door, Esperanza in tow, before someone tries to stop us.

Following the directions he gave when I called from the plane, I proceed to the end of the hall, make a right, and stop at the second doorway.

Alem'nesh Wuhib must have a sixth sense, because a tennis ball is in the air before I've cleared the threshold. I catch the ball a few inches from my face, somehow doing so without dropping my shoes.

"Hello, my friend," Alem'nesh says with a wide smile. He stands and comes out from behind a desk and gives me a warm embrace. I'm still clutching the tennis ball at eye level.

"Hello, Al."

As he steps back, I toss the ball into the air between us and he fields it and, as smoothly as a magician, slips it into a pocket of his sticharion.

Alem'nesh is Oromo, the largest ethnic group in Ethiopia. He has sharp features, highlighted by a strong nose—the nose of a pharaoh. And he has eyes that see everything.

"You look good," I say.

A close perusal—without the prospect of dodging various objects—reveals a touch of salt-and-pepper to his dark hair, and a pudgier face. But he looks largely as he did the last time I saw him, which is largely as he looked when we went to college together. It was then the projectile game took its form, at a time when a silly contest could compensate for the stress built into the lab-partner dynamic—an arrangement made more difficult by the language barrier between us. He has since become fluent in English, and I've learned just enough of his language to find a bathroom and count out cab fare. Alem'nesh left the study of archaeology for the ministry the next semester. I had harbored guilt for a while because I was certain it was our pairing that ruined the field for him.

His eyes stray to my right. "I do not believe I have had the pleasure," he says to Esperanza, extending a hand, which Espy takes in her own.

"Reverend Father," she says, bowing. "Bless, Father."

Alem'nesh beams at the proper usage of the honorific, and the customary request for a blessing, spoken in his native Amharic.

"Please, I'm Alem'nesh. Or if you are challenged by relatively simple, if foreign-sounding, names," he adds, looking at me, "Al will do."

"Esperanza Habilla. It's a pleasure, Alem'nesh."

He leans toward her with a conspirator's twinkle in his eye. "How does someone like Jack merit a traveling companion so obviously superior to him in every way?"

"Oh, you and I are going to be good friends, I can tell," she answers.

I can only shake my head and wonder if the fact that I'm always the butt of the joke when people I know meet each other says something unpleasant about me. I feign a pained expression that seems to please them both. What I keep to myself is my own appreciation for Espy's talents. I learned back on the bus, when I heard her conversing with her seatmates, that she has added Amharic to her language pantheon. And now to find her familiar with the customs of the Orthodox Church on the other side of the world . . . It's a reminder that even people you think you know can surprise you. I'm hoping—*praying* is not too strong a word—that Alem'nesh will surprise me.

As if sensing my unspoken request, Alem'nesh releases Espy's hand and gestures to a pair of chairs facing the desk.

"Come, sit," he says, taking each of us by an elbow and guiding us to the seats. Once we are situated and he has claimed his own spot behind the desk, he offers a knowing smile. "It's been a long time, Jack. I was very surprised to get your call."

"It's hard to believe it's been ten years," I say.

"What's ten years among good friends?"

There's a lot of history between us, and I feel a measure of guilt for popping up after so long because I need something. But I can't spare the time it would require to complete the cultural niceties. Fortunately my old school chum understands Western sensibilities; he's used to our brand of narcissism.

He is quiet, except I hear him making a clicking sound with his tongue that indicates he is thinking. It would always annoy me when he would do that.

"There is something wrong."

"I need a favor, Al." It's become my mantra, my own personal bumper sticker: *Itinerant archaeologist needs a favor*.

"You're not going to ask to see the Ark of the Covenant at St. Mary's, are you?" he asks with a chuckle.

"Tempting, but no. I'm here for something else."

"Then tell me. What has brought you to see me from so far away?"

Since I'm in a church, I reason that honesty is the best policy. "What can you tell me about the bones of the prophet Elisha?"

There's a reason that I wanted to be here when I asked the

question. I wanted to see his face, in that instant before lucid thought would provide a mask. I hate the knowledge that our past friendship does not engender sufficient trust so that I would accept his answer as gospel. The truth is that when one buys into a religion, protecting that belief system can become more important than anything else. Alem'nesh is a man I haven't seen in a decade; and he's not Romero.

The moment comes and goes, too quick, but what I catch, what I see fly past his eyes, is enough to incline me in one direction. Unless I'm clinging to something that's not there, and his expression was the simple result of an odd question.

The answer he gives is of the one-size-fits-all sort. "You came to see me so that I could tell you a Bible story?"

"I came to see you because you're my friend. And because you're the only Ethiopian Orthodox priest I know well enough that I can ask strange questions without feeling like a complete idiot."

Alem'nesh appears to digest this, and he starts that tongue-clicking thing again. I can't read his face. Finally he says, "You must help me understand your question. You do not wish a recounting of the biblical story, but what more could I give you?"

It's a valid point. Fortunately, Espy saves me from the duty of clarification.

"What we want to know, Reverend Father, is if the bones of the prophet Elisha are part of some international conspiracy spanning over twenty-five hundred years, several families, the ancient Egyptians, the Coptic church, and at least one South American trade organization." When she finishes, she offers a smile, yet it does nothing to fill the silence that settles on us. If

I'm grateful for nothing else, it's that Al has stopped making that infernal noise.

I'm not sure what I was expecting, but what I see on Al's face isn't it. There is something resembling incredulity, that's certain, only it seems the degree is off a bit. I imagine my expression looks more surprised than his—a result of hearing how outrageous my hypothesis sounds when stated so concisely. No, what I see in Alem'nesh is something else—not fear, but something like it. Worry, perhaps?

I don't know how much time passes, but it seems like a great deal. During the interval, the worry, if that's what it is, melts away, replaced by something I can't qualify. The eyes that see everything are also able to reveal nothing. I'm comfortable waiting for him to speak. I suppose that's a result of bearing up under so much of Duckey's scrutiny.

He's the one who breaks the silence. Al leans forward in his chair and steeples his fingers on the desk. I can't read his expression; I can only acknowledge that there are a number of things fighting for premier placement.

"I do not know how to respond to something like that, Ms. Habilla," he says. "Where did you come up with such an engaging story?"

"Al, I have the evidence," I say. "It's not enough to prove anything in court, and it wouldn't stand up under peer review. But I can follow clues as well as the next guy."

"Clues that say we are involved in the preservation of holy relics over a period of more than two millennia?"

"In a nutshell."

"Preposterous."

"Why? Your church makes no secret of the fact that you have

the Ark of the Covenant. Now, you never let anyone actually look at it, but you say you have it."

"Careful, my friend," he says after a few beats. "There is no cause for insults."

"That's not what I meant, Al."

"I know what you meant." He sighs. "I'm not certain what this is all about, why you are chasing phantoms, things with no substance, but I cannot help you in this."

There is finality to the statement, and in retrospect I'm not sure what I was expecting. He's a priest, one who will never become a bishop because he chose to marry. Why would he be privy to one of his faith's most well-kept secrets? I'd hoped that because of the church in which he was placed, and the fact that he has a talent for cultivating the right contacts, and because there are always rumors whispered in the dark, he would know something. Still, I have one more card to play.

"What's at Lalibela, Alem'nesh?"

He reacts with a start—one that no amount of preparation could have kept in check. He knows now that I'm not just fishing, that I have some of the pieces to the puzzle. I watch as his eyes darken in resolve.

"Again, I cannot help you, my friend."

"My brother died because of them," I say.

He looks as if I've pained him. I'm not even certain he knew my brother was dead. I go on to tell him about Egypt, about the man I saw there, and how I saw the same man in Rubio. I leave out most of the details, telling him just enough to get him to see the connection. I'm in the risky position of needing this man's help yet having to be wary of revealing too much to him. As I speak, the effect of my words is obvious; it's akin to the way things changed for Espy when she stood in front of the symbols in the temple, instead of flipping through pictures in a book. When I've finished, Al is quiet, but I can see that he's deep in thought.

"Alem'nesh," Espy begins in near-perfect Amharic, "people have died because of these things."

It elicits a sad smile from the priest. "People die for many things, Ms. Habilla."

I do not add anything. I've said all I can say, and Espy has provided support. It's now Alem'nesh's decision, and I will not fault him whatever choice he makes. For once, the eyes that see everything, show everything, and it's a fierce battle—a weighing of allegiances. It's a painful thing, this reconciliation of past loyalties and current responsibilities. The silence, broken only by the sound of a ringing telephone in another office, is so complete that I almost jump when he speaks.

"What did our Lord say, Jack, when the Pharisees told Him to instruct His disciples not to exalt His name? He said, 'If they keep quiet, the rocks and stones will cry out.' " Alem'nesh leans in, closing the distance between us as much as the desk will allow. "You've found the place where the stones cry out, Jack—where worship comes from the rock. Now let the dragon speak to you."

He will not say more. I don't understand the part about the dragon but I won't press him. I can guess what even this little bit has cost him. I am beyond grateful.

Chapter 13

The one good thing about flying into Lalibela, rather than attempting the drive, is that the twenty-three-kilometer road from the airport to the town is paved, unlike many of the roads we might have taken had we braved ground travel from Addis Ababa. Coming in from the air, it was at first hard to see the town. It sits in the mountains, where it rests amid the natural greens and reds of the surrounding land. When I did locate it, by spotting the hotels and other larger buildings sitting at the top of a very steep hill, I couldn't help but feel my heart kick out a few more beats per minute. The name of this place was carved on a floor on the other side of the world; this dusty town contains something of great importance.

Lalibela holds somewhere between ten and twenty thousand people, and much of it consists of modest stone dwellings with thatched roofs. One of the unique architectural identifiers is a preponderance of round two-story homes. The first story holds any animals owned by the family, and the people live above. I pulled up a few pictures on my laptop while on the plane and determined that the houses resemble small silos.

Right now I'm not researching anything beyond the flavor of the cigar I'm smoking. I've given the Cubans a rest and instead fired up a Clasico Robusto from San Cristóbal. I don't have to worry about bothering the driver, who is enjoying one along with me. Espy has expressed her displeasure by lowering the window but is allowing me to retreat to the familiar for the time being.

It's always when you're most comfortable that something demands your attention. In this case, it's my phone.

"Hey, Ducks," I say after battling to extricate the phone from my pants pocket.

"There are five possibles."

"That many?" I'm disappointed. I'd been hoping Duckey's friend in the State Department would cull a definite bad guy from the list. Maybe someone who specializes in international hits.

"And let me make sure I put the proper emphasis on *possible*. There's not a one of these guys with a criminal record that goes beyond minor traffic violations."

My mood suffers further deflation. "Then how did you pick these over the other twenty?"

"Money. These are the only ones with access to the kind of money you mentioned."

"That sounds reasonable, I guess."

There's a pause on the other end, and it occurs to me that I'm not exhibiting the level of appreciation Duckey probably expects.

"Jack, it's not like in the movies, where some computer spook pulls up a nice picture of a single suspect with the push of a button. Travis says if this was a domestic case they were working on, they would assign a few agents to it, watch these guys for a while, and see what gives."

"You're right, Ducks. Sorry."

"Not a problem. I'm just the messenger." He clears his throat. "Look, I'm not going to pretend to know what you're doing. But this just doesn't seem smart. What am I supposed to tell everyone when you wind up dead?"

"You'll have to tell them to cover my classes. And watch out for my second-year Asian Archaeology course. I've got a couple of sleepers in that one."

"Funny."

"I'll be careful, Ducks. And clear your conscience. You didn't force me to look for adventure over my break. It just sort of found me."

"You better be careful. I'm too old to break in someone new for breakfast."

"That's my own personal penance. Can you email those names to me?"

"Soon as I hang up."

Within sixty seconds of ending the call I have my laptop open and am booting up. True to Duckey's word, a new mail icon pops into place in the task bar once the screen clears. Espy leans close as I move the cursor over the message. I hesitate, feeling distaste like bile in the back of my throat. I'm fond of personal privacy, and so it bothers me that when I open this message, I'll see neatly compiled information about five men I've never met. It's likely that four of these people are innocent of any wrongdoing, yet I'll have a dossier on each. Their only collective crime is that they share some common physical characteristics: about six feet tall, brown hair, somewhere between one hundred eighty and two hundred twenty pounds. If I had been on the same plane with these men, it's likely I would have made the list according to those criteria. That is, until one accounted for my financial situation. Having only 132 dollars in the bank generally eliminates one from suspicion in a high-stakes murder scheme. Pushing aside my discomfort, I continue on, telling myself that one of these men may well have been responsible for the attempt on my life.

I open the message. It's a list of names, along with addresses, short bios, and pictures. "Thanks, Duckey," I say.

"He looks mean." Espy points at the first picture, one Bruce Burney. His face is thick and he has heavy jowls, with a monochrome tattoo on the loose flesh of his neck. His bio says he owns a chain of clothing stores. Espy's right; he does look mean. But he's not our mystery man.

"That's not him," I say. "Besides, even if I didn't already know what our guy looks like, this would be too obvious."

"Sometimes what you're looking for is right under your nose."

I'm afraid to, but I glance over to see if that statement has any hidden meaning. If it does, she's keeping it to herself. Her eyes never leave the screen.

There are three pictures visible in the window, yet none of them match the image in my head. I scroll down and, as the fourth suspect comes into view, I feel my body tense as anger rises to the surface. The Aussie's name is Victor Manheim. In an instant I am back in the Egyptian desert, looking up at him from the bottom of the RV's stairs. Minutes later, Will was dead.

Espy sees the change and says nothing, but she reads his bio along with me. Victor's a political attaché to the undersecretary of agriculture. His parents own a great deal of land in Australia's southwest region. He matriculated in the States—Harvard—where he received a law degree. As Esperanza said of poor Bruce, Victor looks mean, but it's an aristocratic meanness.

"Is that him?"

I nod and close the window. There's a sick feeling in my stomach, and I know that it's because I made the decision to come to Ethiopia first. My reasons seemed solid at the time, but now that I have something concrete to connect me with Will's killer, I feel as if I've made a horrible mistake—even though I know I haven't. I couldn't have known that Duckey's associate would provide me with anything useful. Without this information, I would be wandering around Australia with no direction. Ethiopia was the right choice, and Manheim will be there when I'm done with this business.

Espy puts a hand on my arm as if to confirm my self-therapy. Still, my mood is more sour than it was and I resolve to make an effort at improving it. We're in a new place, and the possibility exists that we will find something unique here—if Reese has not already found it.

I watch as the car tops a rise and the town spreads out before us. It's the kind of thing one might see in a postcard—one of those where it looks as if the photographer stumbled onto a spot where everything that's wrong with a place comes together to produce something marvelous, frozen in the instant the shutter clicked. The difference now is that the scene is in motion; a movement of people for whom this is much more than a backdrop. They live and breathe this place, this rural community that remains much as it was four hundred years ago.

As the car follows the only paved road through the town, climbing the steep hill that leads to the Seven Olives Hotel, I see many more people roaming the streets, slipping into and out of rustic shops and eateries, than I would have expected. It looks like a carnival midway. Children are everywhere, forming and reforming into groups that flit from one side of the street to the other and back.

"Why are there so many children?" Esperanza asks.

"They are following the pilgrims," the driver says in passable English.

I'm not sure what he means but I look more closely and I now see that the children are not just engaged in aimless flocking. There are nuclei to these undulations of small bodies. As I watch, a group of eight or so detach from two people who disappear into a tearoom, only to run ten yards up the road to encircle a trio of adults in western clothes.

"Of course," I say. I should have realized this would be the case. For most of the year I imagine that Lalibela is off the map, entertaining sporadic visitors with off-season vacation schedules. At this time of year, though, the place takes on special significance.

"Care to share?" Espy prompts.

"This is one of the holiest spots in the country. If you were a devout member of the Orthodox Church, where would you go for Christmas?"

"By the time Christmas comes, there will be fifty thousand pilgrims here," the driver adds.

Espy's eyes widen and she mouths a silent *oh*.

Something the driver has said gives me pause—something about Christmas. I glance at my watch, a Relic, to check the date, then shut my eyes, annoyed with myself. I reach into my jacket pocket, pull out one of Duckey's cigars, and offer it to Espy.

"Merry Christmas," I say.

It makes me feel better to see by her reaction that the day slipped past her, too. She takes the cigar and gives it an appreciative sniff. Much to my surprise, she removes the end with her teeth and spits it out the window. When she leans in for a light, I fumble to provide one, and seconds later she's puffing away.

"When in Rome," she says, sinking back into her seat. She

draws the smoke in and releases it through her nose. If it stings, she doesn't show it. "If it's Christmas," she says, looking out the window, "where are these fifty thousand pilgrims?"

"Good question."

"Christmas is still almost two weeks away," the driver says, looking back at us in the rearview mirror. "January seventh."

I nod as if I knew this, and I think that somewhere among the growing catalog of things I've forgotten is floating the knowledge that the Orthodox Church celebrates the holiday two weeks later than most of the rest of the world. I try to picture these streets with ten times this many people and it's hard to visualize. I'm hoping we will not be here by then. For now, though, I decide that the increase in foot traffic is not a bad thing if it can cover our arrival and our activities while we're here. I've been turning something over in my brain since leaving Addis Ababa: the chances of running into another team hunting for the same thing.

Our Peugeot is passing through the center of town, and several children run by the car, peeking in, some reaching hands through the half-open windows. The driver honks on the horn once and revs the engine, and the kids back off a few steps. The driver hits the gas a touch, sending the car up the steepest portion of the hill.

Once inside the gate of the Seven Olives, the driver pulls around to the front and stops. Clenching the last of the cigar in his teeth, he gets out and begins to remove our few belongings from the trunk. When he's finished, I tip him and, with another thanks for the cigar, he hops in the car and speeds off back the way we came.

"It's nice," Espy says, and I have to agree. The hotel is a bit rustic looking, but I'm betting that's half kitsch. Inside, it's probably as modern as anything you'd find in most small towns back in the States. And I doubt many of the hotels back home boast a garden like this one. Espy has long held an interest in botany, and the well-kept grounds surrounding the Seven Olives could keep her busy for days if we didn't have another pressing matter to attend to. Even my untrained eye spots a few flowers and bushes that merit attention, so I can only imagine what she sees as her eyes play over the foliage. Rather than compete for her notice, I pick up both our bags and my laptop and walk inside the hotel.

It's just as nice inside and I see that my initial assessment was incorrect; the bucolic look is organic. It's the other stuff—the technology—that has been added, built upon something that has been here for a long time. I cross to the front desk and navigate the process of reserving rooms. I'm hoping there are some left, what with the influx of people here for the celebration. I need not have worried. Espy and I each get a room, one right next to the other. As the desk clerk hands over the keys, he gives me the rundown on hotel services, their gift shop and wireless Internet access. The clerk also talks up the hotel's best feature—the terrace, from which one can sit and enjoy the view of Lalibela from above.

When our business is concluded, I look back and see that Esperanza has not yet entered the hotel. So with a shrug I determine to check out the vista from the touted terrace. I deposit our bags by the restaurant entrance, trusting that no one will walk off with them, but I keep hold of my laptop.

The place seems full for this time of day, and I chalk it up to the seasonal visitors. Seeing the exit to the terrace across from me, I work my way through the restaurant and past the small, unoccupied bar.

I cross the threshold and look out over Lalibela. The clerk was right; it's a spectacular view. But what makes it so is not so much that the town's laid bare before my eyes, but that it seems so insignificant when compared to the landscape that hedges it into the mountain. I would probably be humbled if I wasn't as tired as I am, but I do appreciate it. When I wake up tomorrow and come here for coffee and something unhealthy with which to start my day, I'll give it another try and see what feelings the view evokes.

I turn and walk back into the restaurant, glancing again at the bar. There are now people there—three of them, with drinks poured. It's obvious, even from the back, that they're foreigners. I'm almost past the bar when one of the men leaning against the rail half turns to talk to one of his companions.

I'm not sure I ever fully understood the flight-or-fight response until now. And the unusual thing is that it's not because of any perceived threat; rather, it's the degree to which I am shocked by seeing a familiar face in this setting. I almost stop walking, and I feel the handle of my computer bag slipping through my fingers before I can tighten my grip on both the handle and my thoughts.

I suspected Gordon Reese would have sent another team but I never even considered . . . He hasn't noticed me, and I keep walking. With any luck I'll be out the door and checked into another hotel before he's done with his first drink. What kills that plan is curiosity—the trait mentioned by Reese himself, and the one that has me casting another sidelong glance behind me. It's then that another person turns away from the bar, and her eyes, as if following a laser pointer, catch mine. I'm speechless for two reasons: the first is that I never expected her to still be in the field; the second is that she's even more attractive than she was five years ago. In that instant I'm certain that further subterfuge would be wasted and so I change direction. She watches my approach, a surprised and amused smile on her face, but doesn't alert her companions, for which I am grateful.

"I read your paper about Nordseta in the AJA," I say from behind Brown. "Very thorough."

When he turns to see who's speaking, there is a moment I will likely remember for the rest of my life. It's the instant when he goes from being puzzled to experiencing a near-debilitating shock. The look on his face almost makes my blown cover worthwhile.

"Hello, Brown," I say, allowing him to collect his faculties.

The first word out of his mouth is a garbled sound but, with a second effort, he manages a "Dr. Hawthorne?"

I haven't seen Brown—now Dr. Billings—since KV65. But occasionally I'll hear about a project he's leading, or read something he's written. He turned out to be as brilliant as I thought he was and, as I surmise by the fact that he's standing and all of his appendages appear to be intact, he's learned the art of caution. Not quite thirty, he's among a select group of archaeologists whose services are held in high esteem. Even so, there's something about running into a former teacher that can make someone, no matter how accomplished, revert to the student role. And while I never instructed Brown in a classroom, that's splitting hairs.

"I think we're beyond the 'Dr. Hawthorne' stuff. Call me Jack."

He looks mortified at the prospect, which is funny because I don't recall finding the transition from Dr. Winfield to Jim at all difficult.

"I can't believe it," he says. "What are you doing here, Dr. . . . Jack?" Aside from the surprise at seeing me, I gather that he's genuinely pleased, and that means two things: no one told him he'd be competing with anyone, and he never considered the possibility on his own.

"I imagine the same thing you're doing." I'm getting used to this showing-all-my-cards tactic. If nothing else, it puts the other person on the defensive. And I'd be kidding myself if I thought this would not get back to Reese before the day is through anyway. And then my former employer will realize that I'm not dead.

"Hello, Sarah," I say, allowing Brown some time to digest what I've just said.

"Hi, Jack."

The smile she gives me is one I remember well, and it still makes me want to look away first. In my periphery I see a troubled look on Brown's face, which makes me wonder what relationship dynamics I've walked into. Of course, he could also be reacting to the suggestion that we are here for the same purpose. As much as I'd enjoy continuing the flirtation with Sarah, Espy doesn't give me the chance.

"Jack?"

She has appeared at my elbow, carrying both of our bags.

"Esperanza, I'd like you to meet two of my former colleagues. Dr. Brown Billings and . . ." I pause, looking to Sarah to validate an advanced degree, but she shakes her head. "Sarah Ward. Brown, Sarah, this is Dr. Esperanza Habilla."

There are the requisite nods and pleasantries and I'm observant enough to see the brevity of the exchange between Espy and Sarah. I'm not sure what Espy picked up on but I know her well enough to see the frost. Seeing them together, though, puts Sarah's charms in perspective. Espy's in a different league.

The third member of Brown's party, who has been left out of the introductions, clears his throat. "My name is Fifth Wheel," he says with a good-natured smile. "And I'm going to go take a nap."

"That's Miles Lincoln," Brown says as the man walks away.

I know that name and, when I connect it to the man who is now disappearing out the door, I have to fight the urge to chase after him. "Miles Lincoln, the art specialist?"

Brown nods.

I shake my head, envious of Brown and his opportunity to work with someone like Lincoln. The man's presence, however, sets off a few alarm bells—which I'll have to attend to as soon as I can. Right now I file the fledgling thoughts away and focus on the task at hand. And since I've already taken a step down the path of direct inquiry, I see no harm in continuing.

"What brings you two—three—to Lalibela?"

I see a wall come up, but it's of the general kind. I think he actually missed my earlier reference to our having similar purposes. He thinks this is a random meeting. I see Sarah smirk—an indication that, unlike her companion, she heard my every word.

"We're doing a fluff piece for *Archaeology Quarterly* on the churches," he lies. "They wanted it for their December issue, to run before Christmas, but I wasn't available until now."

I offer an interested nod, but I almost feel badly that I haven't given him sufficient time to come up with a more believable prevarication. There isn't a periodical in the world that would send an archaeological team halfway around the world to conduct noninvasive research that could be accomplished with existing records. That's throwing money into a stiff wind.

"Sounds interesting," I say in what I hope is taken as patronization.

He looks embarrassed and, even worse, Sarah appears discomfited for him.

"Why are you here, Jack?" Brown redirects.

"Would you believe that I'm working for a billionaire, who's hired me to hunt for religious artifacts?" I grin and shake my head. "What a way to spend my winter break, huh?"

I don't know who is more incredulous: Brown, who has been blindsided, or Esperanza. I'm not looking forward to what words she will use on me later, once we're alone. Sarah, on the contrary, has a twinkle in her eye that tells me she put it together as soon as she saw me. I give her a wink, and the gesture is not lost on Espy.

The brilliant Dr. Brown Billings is speechless, and despite the fact that the man has never done me a disservice, I am tickled by the whole encounter. At some point, perhaps even today, he will find out that I'm no longer in Reese's employ, and yet we're far beyond even the billionaire's reach.

"Who do you think Reese is paying more?" I prod.

The comment earns a laugh from Sarah, one that pulls red to Brown's cheeks. I'm enjoying myself—until I catch Espy's eye. I have a feeling that I'm going to pay dearly for the last five minutes.

Chapter 14

The place where the rocks and stones cry out.

I know that the biblical allusion is poetic rather than literal, but as Esperanza and I stand on the edge of a forty-foot drop-off, looking down on the roof of a nine-hundred-year-old church carved from a single piece of granite, I would be hard-pressed to think of another place on the planet that better embodies that description.

The rock-hewn churches of Lalibela are among the architectural marvels of the world, and they're among the short list of things I've seen which assure me that, under the right circumstances, man can accomplish anything he sets his mind to. It's early morning, the breeze is blowing through the valley, and there are few sounds to interrupt us. Espy and I might as well be standing at the edge of the earth for the sense of almost alien beauty that rises from the granite cathedrals.

"It's unbelievable," Espy whispers.

I'm in perfect agreement, especially considering the tools the medieval Christians had to work with; but I'm also cognizant of time. I have no idea how many days Brown and his team have already put in. And I'm certain that Reese now knows we survived that unpleasantness in San Cristóbal.

"Ready?" I start down the narrow steps, themselves carved out of the rock, my hand trailing along its cold surface. It's like walking into a canyon, with sheer cliff faces rising up on either side. The ancient quarry workers began with trenches, pulling granite out to, in some places, a depth of forty feet. And like Rembrandt, only on a massive scale, they formed the lines of the churches, hollowed out the insides, and cut doorways and windows.

Espy and I are descending to Bete Medhane Alem, the largest of the churches. When we reach the base, it's easier to appreciate the scale of the structure. Several freestanding pillars support the roof, also framing an intricately latticed doorway. The ancient artisans formed perfectly round pillars, cutting out the rock behind them, maintaining precise dimensions from top to bottom.

Even though there are already a large number of visitors in town, I see only a handful of people awake and eager to see the sites. The resident monk is out front, his colorful robes a counterpoint to the muted rock. He holds a long prayer staff and appears ready to outlast the day in that one spot if need be.

He greets us with a broad smile. Another man then appears at our side, gesturing at our feet. I've been warned about the shoes, so I slip them off and hand them over, Espy following my lead. I give the man a small tip and head toward the entrance.

"What is he going to do with our shoes?" Espy says, glancing back over her shoulder as the man to whom she has entrusted her pricey togs disappears.

"They'll be waiting for us on the other side."

She looks less than convinced but follows me in.

The interior is modeled after a basilica, and as I walk deeper into it, I count five naves. I can't think of many churches this size with that number. There are more than thirty square pillars supporting a cornice, and Espy runs a hand along one of them. There are places that appear to be rubbed smooth—likely by the hands of countless visitors over the centuries. There's a lot to take in and I'm trying to oblige, but I can't move too quickly; I have to trust my gut to see something my eyes might pass over.

I'm drawn to the frescoes. Most of them are badly damaged, and it bothers me that they haven't been preserved. The parts I can see appear to be the recounting of biblical scenes. Yet several rock carvings have, by their nature, navigated the passage of time with more integrity. There's more than one theme to the carvings, but I fixate on the animals. I see representations of at least eight different animals, and I can't decipher any connecting thread between them. I have Alem'nesh's dragon in my mind, trying to tie it to something, but I feel handicapped by having no idea what I'm looking for.

There are eleven churches, each with its many details, carvings, and murals. And I'm presupposing that what I'm searching for is something that's visible to the naked eye. That could be a risky premise yet I have nothing else to go on, and I have to believe that as much as it pained Alem'nesh to confide in me, I don't think he would send me out here with no hope of finding something.

We spend perhaps a half hour inside, while other visitors come and go around us. When we leave, it's through a tunnel connecting to Bete Maryam—the first of the churches to find its liberation from the rock. It is much like Bete Medhane Alem, but with its own peculiarities such as the windows, which were carved in odd shapes, allowing the light to fall on the Holy of Holies and on the tabot that rests there.

Another half hour passes and neither Espy nor myself are struck by anything out of the ordinary. There's the very real possibility that we've walked right by whatever it is we are here to discover. I'm not sure what I was thinking, how I thought we could visit this place and find what we're looking for without the months—perhaps years—of exhaustive research that something like this necessitates. Esperanza must catch the souring of my mood because she leaves her perusal of a Maltese cross to link her arm in mine.

"Two down, nine to go. I'd call that progress."

Although I appreciate the gesture, I do not share her optimism. "You know as well as I do that we could have already missed it."

"You're right, we could have. But the way I see it, a few weeks ago I was home writing a grant proposal. Now I'm on the other side of the world, in a nine-hundred-year-old rock church, and I have no idea where my shoes are."

"I see your point," I say with a smile. Before I can say anything else, another person enters Bete Maryam and I turn, expecting to see a small group being led about by a private tour guide. Instead, I spot Sarah, who sees us at the same time. When she reaches us, she is almost out of breath.

"I knew you were in this section but I didn't know which church," she says.

"How did you know we weren't over on the eastern side?" Espy asks, her tone frosty.

"Because *we're* on the eastern side," Sarah answers. "Besides, I saw your shoes outside. Cole Haan Air Gabis? You were wearing them last night. Very nice."

Espy's eyebrows shoot up. "Thanks. You know, I almost didn't buy them. They just seemed too extravagant."

"I know, but they're comfortable, aren't they?"

"Excuse me, ladies . . ." It's fine if they want to chitchat about fashion, but Sarah has sought me out for a reason.

She gives Espy an apologetic shrug.

"I just wanted to tell you that a man named Gregory Hardy arrived thirty minutes ago. He works for Reese."

I nod. "We've met."

"Brown told him you were here and—" She stops, appearing unsure where to take this. "Look, Jack, I don't trust him. He's a lot more dangerous than he lets on."

I exchange looks with Espy, who gives me a grim smile.

I release a sigh, thankful that Sarah cared enough to warn me, yet irritated that we might have another obstacle to contend with before we're finished here.

"You're right. He is dangerous." I put my hand on her shoulder and lean in closer, locking eyes. "But he's not here for you. Or Brown. So go back and do your job and be careful. You'll be fine."

"I don't doubt that," she says. "It's you I'm worried about. When Hardy heard that you're here, he didn't seem happy about it. And he does carry a gun."

"Thanks for the warning, Sarah," I say. "I'll be careful, too."

She nods, and then a smile touches her eyes. "Just so you know, Brown is bothered enough about your being here that it might be him, and not Hardy, that you need to watch out for."

That prompts a laugh. I give her shoulder a squeeze and then, with as charming a smile as I can muster, ask, "Since we're being forthcoming, can you tell me why Miles is here?"

"Nice try, Dr. Hawthorne," she says with a chuckle. There's something in her expression that is new—that I would not have seen had this conversation taken place five years ago. It's open competition, a fierce desire, a need to win. It's unfortunate we're no longer working together, because I like this version a lot more.

"You can't blame me for trying."

"It'll be more fun if you earn it," she says. Suddenly she turns serious, looks down at her feet, then back up, and her eyes are glistening. "I never told you how sorry I was about Will."

She leans in and leaves a kiss on my cheek, and then she's gone.

I'm not sure how long I stand there, how many ticks pass before I can think a coherent thought. When I finally reengage, I find that Espy is watching me, and there is nothing there but muted grief, something we didn't get the chance to bear together.

Oddly enough, I don't feel like sprinting away; a brisk walk will do. I think that might be progress. It's as I'm searching for something to say that will extract me from the present moment that suddenly Esperanza slaps herself in the head.

"I'm an idiot," she says with a vehemence usually reserved for pointing out *my* failings.

At my questioning look she says, "Alem'nesh said to look for the dragon, right?"

"Right."

"I don't think we're looking for a dragon so much as we're looking for a saint." At my blank expression she continues, "See, that's why you should have been raised Catholic. At least then you'd know your saints."

"And I would have had real wine at church. I still don't follow."

"Alex, I'll take saints who are popular in Ethiopia and who have also killed a dragon, for two hundred dollars."

She's enjoying this and, once again, her amusement comes at my expense. I'll be the first to admit that my knowledge of saintly lore is thin. I shrug my shoulders in surrender.

"There's even a church named after him," she says. When she takes my hand to lead me out of the tunnel, I'm beyond exasperated. The glint I see in her eye tells me that she's well aware of this, even as it tells me there's not a thing I can do about it.

If it had been any more obvious, the flame from the dragon's mouth would have singed my hair. Espy and I are standing in the nave of Bete Giyorgis, the Church of St. George. It's the newest of the churches, and the most finely executed. Looking down on it from above, one can see the church was fashioned in the shape of a Greek cross. Its interior is less ornate than those of its older cousins, but the structure itself possesses a stateliness absent from the others.

Espy has filled me in on the particulars, and what she has told me does not jog anything in my memory. I'm reasonably certain that my knowledge of the lives and times of Christian saints is so sparse that I have never heard the story of how St. George killed the dragon. Espy, on the other hand, knows all the details, down to the name of the lance—Ascalon—that George used to slay the beast. She learned her catechism as a child and it has come back to serve us well.

There are more people around than were here when we began, but Espy and I still have a measure of privacy. Few visitors linger for more than a minute or two; there are so many churches to see before the flies become unbearable. The church stands as a testament to the saint, for his image is pervasive in the minimalist decoration.

We are still faced with the question of where to start but, buoyed by Espy's revelation, we have our investigative second wind. What adds to my enjoyment is that Brown, Sarah, and Miles are on the wrong side of the compound. What I try to avoid considering is the possibility that Esperanza is wrong and that the other team is working with hard evidence rather than conjecture. My thoughts go, again, to Miles Lincoln. How does his specialty fit here?

St. George's has its share of artwork—which is the province of Miles—including a lovely relief over the doorway, and some carvings. What I'm most drawn to, however, are the murals that bring color and character to the walls. There are several, of varying sizes and subject matters, though most of them feature St. George in one fashion or another. There is one, in a prominent spot on the wall, that stands out from the others; I noticed it when I walked in, and I stare at it for a full minute, trying to convince myself that it can't be as obvious as this. It's a representation of the saint slaying the dragon, jabbing his lance into the neck of a beast that does not seem as formidable as the dragons I remember from childhood stories. This animal is no larger than the horse on which George sits.

"Esperanza."

She follows my line of sight and gives a perfunctory nod once her eyes play over the mural. Both of us move closer to the painting, neither of us sure what we're looking for.

It's two minutes, perhaps three, before I come to realize that we're out of our depth. I could attempt an interpretation of the symbolism, but I don't have the background to make that worthwhile. There are things in the mural that could be representative of ideas or events. The man in the white robes in the bottom left corner, right next to the skull, could be a reference to the resurrection story in Second Kings. An image in one of the left panels appears to show someone secreting something. It's subjective, unless you know what you're looking at, and how the symbols were understood when painted. Processual symbolic analysis is not among my areas of expertise.

"I guess this is why Brown needs Miles," I say.

No response from Espy. When I look at her, it is to see that she's focused on the mural. Her eyes are not moving.

"What's that?" she asks after a time.

Without waiting for an answer, she closes the distance to the mural and sets a finger on what appears to me to be a squiggle or smudge over the shoulder of an angel. It looks like part of the background—a tree root, a bush. Espy traces a line that I can't see, her finger picking a path amid the painting's white noise. She mutters something to herself and takes a half step away from the wall, leaving her hand on whatever it is that's caught her attention. I watch as she studies this section of the picture with an intensity I've never seen her display, even when we were trying to translate the symbols in the temple. I remain still, fearful of breaking her concentration. Another few minutes pass before I see her lock on to something and, when she does, she breathes a triumphant sigh.

"It's Teutonic," she says. Her hand moves across the mural, two fingers coming to rest on another squiggle. She looks back, glowing. "These are Teutonic letters. Jack, they're hiding in plain sight."

I've always trusted Esperanza, and I have no reason to

doubt her now. On the contrary, I'm near giddy at her discovery. Except I wonder how it could be that of the hundreds of thousands of visitors who have passed through here over the centuries—noted scholars among them—not one has discovered this. I must look more skeptical than I imagine because Espy's glow turns to a frown.

"Whoever painted this made the letters part of the background; they're almost indistinguishable from the rest of the painting." She shakes her head. "We don't need Miles. They need a linguist."

I move to her side. While I'm familiar with several languages, each of them has gone part and parcel with my work. If I haven't worked a dig in some country, or if a particular language is not in common use in archaeological parlance, it's doubtful I could even offer a simple greeting in the tongue. Espy, though, devours languages with a voracious appetite. She's the expert here.

"All right," I say, "we have Teutonic letters. What now?"

Esperanza steps away from the wall and, hands on hips, takes in the whole of the painting. "They can't be randomly placed. There has to be a legend somewhere."

"But who's to say that a legend wouldn't exist separate from the mural?"

"Be quiet."

"Excuse me?"

"I can't think with you talking."

I know when I'm licked, so I do what will move us forward: I remain silent.

Espy studies the mural for a long while, walking around to change perspective. I'm doing my own analysis, looking for something to help us locate and organize Espy's Teutonic letters, when she steps in front of me. We're both at the part of the picture where St. George is delivering the deathblow to the dragon, driving Ascalon through its neck. I lean over Espy's shoulder, drawn by the lance itself. To me it looks more like a staff, a walking stick, because of the irregular notches.

It seems the thought comes to both of us at the same time.

"I need a straightedge," Espy says, and I think it takes every fiber of her being to keep from shouting.

I understand and start hunting through the church for something that will work, but everything I see is nailed down or bolted to something. Then I remember the monk.

"I'll be right back," I call as I run out the door. Outside, it takes some convincing before the monk decides it's all right for me to borrow his prayer staff. When I get back inside, there's a tour group studying the murals, and so we have to wait until they leave before we can test our theory.

I find the first of the Teutonic letters and guesstimate the corresponding notch on the lance. When I line up the prayer staff and it runs through the letter, a rush of exultation threatens to take my knees out from under me. I have to make certain, so I perform the experiment with the second letter, with an identical result.

Success breeds urgency. We've done what should have been impossible within our narrow time frame, and it would anger me to have the other team walk in while we're transposing letters. I stand ready with the staff as Esperanza pulls a notepad and pen from her jacket pocket.

I start at the top, careful to line the staff true with each notch. We spot a few letters right away; others take more time and often we're forced to stop the work as people file through. I grow more uneasy the longer it takes, but Espy works with calm efficiency. The process takes less than half an hour. When finished, we have a series of twenty-five or so letters written down on the notepad.

There is mutual agreement between us to get out of here and go somewhere halfway private before we begin the work of decoding. We're both breathing heavy as we leave, and it has little to do with exertion. I return the prayer staff to its rightful owner as Espy finds our shoes.

We're now sitting in a small café in the busiest part of Lalibela, our bags near our feet. I've chosen a table in the shadows, which allows me to keep an eye on the traffic passing by the open door. Prudence dictated a discreet checkout from the hotel, followed by the rush to find a place where we could give the painting's Teutonic letters a serious look.

Espy has her pencil in hand, ready to form the characters into different groupings and orders—a lengthy, medieval anagram. Except that the pencil hovers over the page as a frown creases her forehead. She looks up to make sure I'm watching and then, with careful deliberation, draws a vertical line between two characters, then a second line farther to the right. That done, she slides the notepad across the table.

"Couldn't you at least make it look difficult?" I ask.

"Do you remember the first patronymic in Reese's research?"

"Chevrier."

"And we wondered how Reese got the bones from the cemetery to there?"

"You wondered. I just nodded and hoped you wouldn't hit me again."

She taps the notepad, indicating the group of characters on the left. "Chevrier."

"What about the others?"

"This one on the right," she says, pointing on the page. "It doesn't translate as well but it's also a name. Vuk Stefanovíc."

"Son of Stephen." I shake my head. It can get tricky trying to trace names earlier than the thirteenth century.

"This is going backward, Jack. Vuk Stefanovíc transferred the bones to Chevrier. That's where Reese's record picks up. And if we keep following it backward, it will become nearly impossible to track them. Relying on patronymics makes it sketchy enough as it is."

I can feel the frustration building up inside me, yet I refuse to believe the clue we fought so hard to attain is simply a name to add to the list—and one going in the wrong direction. Then I see Espy's smile, which makes me realize she's not experiencing the same irritation as me. When I follow her eyes down, her finger has moved to rest on the group of characters connecting the two she's rendered.

"The best translation is *broker*," she says.

"Broker? As in *to trade*?" It makes sense, and it's further evidence that a transfer of something valuable took place between these two families. Still, I'm not sure how helpful it is to have the action defined for us.

"It's a noun."

Those three words are the aural equivalent of a lightning strike. I hear them, and understand their individual meanings, but don't discern their thunder until seconds later. When I tear my eyes away from the page and back to Espy, she wears an expression that's unadulterated satisfaction.

"Here's your organization," she says, leaning in. "Arranging the transfer."

Her body language is all earnestness but, while I'm near dizzy at the possibility, I need time to think. It's as I'm fumbling for the right words to express both excitement and caution that I see Brown walk past the café door.

"Put it away," I say to Espy. After a brief, puzzled hesitation, she flips the notepad closed and hides it in her jacket pocket, then fights the urge to turn around to see what has my attention. I continue watching the entrance but do not see my former protégé backtrack. Still, if he's looking for us, it means Hardy can't be far away. I motion for Espy to grab her bag just as Brown comes into view. I see him glance into the café, but the only light in the place comes from the open doorway and a single window. From his spot in the afternoon sun, I wonder if he can see anything at all in here. As if to validate that thought, he looks away, seeming ready to start off again, when, perhaps in some act of submission to his subconscious, he changes direction and takes a single step through the doorway. When he sees us, I lock eyes with him for several seconds until, with an expression I can't read, he disappears back onto the street.

"Let's go," I say. Without waiting for Espy's reply, I toss money on the table to cover our untouched coffee, then head for the door. After what Sarah told us, I have no doubt that Brown has gone to find Hardy, and although the odds are slim that he would try anything in front of so many witnesses, there's nothing to be gained by us sitting in the open.

We join the flow of people beneath the blinding sun, and I pause to get my bearings. There's a taxi depot down the hill about four blocks away. With any luck, we will avoid any more run-ins with Brown and company and be on a plane within the hour.

I tell Espy our destination and she starts off first. As I follow her, my knee testifies to the steepness of the hill. I promise myself that if I ever make it back to Evanston, I will snatch up the first unit available on the ground level of my apartment building.

We've covered two blocks and the slope begins leveling out. I can see the taxi sign ahead and am gratified to see a car parked in front. The crowd is thicker here and I come near to losing Espy in the crush of pilgrims. Once, I feel a hand slide along the shoulder strap of my laptop but send the pickpocket—a child of nine or ten—scurrying with a look. I quickly move my wallet from my back pocket to the front. Meanwhile, Espy is getting farther ahead as the crowd grows even denser. Someone bumps into me and I feel my knee give; it's all I can do to keep from falling. By the time I regain my balance, Espy is out of sight. A mild oath finds its way past my lips, and I pick up speed, hoping to catch sight of her through all the people.

A narrow alley opens up to my left and, as I hurry by, a flash of movement catches my attention. There's a moment of disconnect between my brain and my body, with the latter stopping before the former can commit to action. I stumble and catch myself on the shoulder of a gentleman carrying two large boxes of onions, both of which tumble from his arms and send their contents cascading down the sloped concourse. Ignoring the man's protest, I retrace my steps back to the alley, and anger sucker-punches me in the same part of my midsection that Espy worked over in Caracas. I push my way through the crowd and step between the buildings, because I know that's what the man with the gun expects of me.

Esperanza's eyes are large but free of panic, even though Hardy has the muzzle of a sleek pistol pressed just below her ear. I can see Brown standing behind him, but I can't spare him more than a passing thought except to wonder at the strangeness of a world that can chart such a path for a man with his potential: an esteemed archaeologist serving as patsy and betrayer. More important is the man who stands between Espy and me—a local who is pointing the business end of a WWII-era machine gun in my direction. Behind me the street rings loud and bright, and no one pays any attention to what's happening in this alley mere feet away.

"Hello, Dr. Hawthorne," Hardy says.

"Why?" It's the only question that means anything.

He shrugs, and I flinch as the gun moves over Espy's skin.

"Because he doesn't need you anymore."

"And a pink slip wasn't sufficient?" The weak attempt at levity sounds out of place even to me as the anger still pulses in my ears.

"Mr. Reese ties up loose ends."

I have to believe it, because Reese's puppet is here, and my continued existence is very much in question. Yet it's difficult to jell my present knowledge of Gordon Reese with the genteel man I met in Dallas.

"Why doesn't he need me anymore?" It's a play at buying time. There's only one reason why Reese would no longer need my services.

"He knows where they are, Dr. Hawthorne. That makes you a liability."

I half process Brown's reaction to that pronouncement.

"Then why not fire me and let me get back to teaching? How could I possibly be a threat to Mr. Reese?"

At this, Hardy laughs, and I am again watching the gun move.

"I'm sure you've realized by now that there are forces at work larger than one man—even if that man happens to be Mr. Reese."

The man with the machine gun glances toward the street, then at his boss, and I can read the question in his eyes. He wants to know why this is taking so long.

So someone else is directing Gordon's paces? But Hardy will not be baited, and I'm getting the impression that he's on the verge of giving the nod to his hired hand. My mind frantically searches for something that will prolong this vignette, and it seizes on the first thing that promises to throw an unknown into the mix.

"How many teams does Reese have working on this?" I ask. "And are you supposed to kill all of them, too?"

This time I'm watching for Brown's reaction and am rewarded with something resembling realization. Hardy can feel it, even with Brown behind him; his eyes become slivers. But Brown's response is more muted than I'd hoped, meaning my gambit has crossed the line meant to assure self-preservation without a satisfactory payoff. I'm left scrambling for something that can halt what seems inevitable, and hoping it will be painless, when all eyes shift to a point over my left shoulder.

"You didn't answer the question, Mr. Hardy," Sarah says, walking into the alley a few steps past where I stand. "Once you're done with Jack and Dr. Habilla, are you going to kill us, too?"

She stops near the man with the machine gun, and I almost

feel pity for him as he wonders what he should do in response to this woman who is standing close enough to reach out and put her hand on the weapon.

Hardy forces a laugh, perhaps realizing he's allowed things to go off the rails. It's never wise to foster suspicion in your allies when one of said allies is standing behind you. I see that Brown has taken a step forward with Sarah's arrival, and that his nearness makes Hardy uncomfortable.

"You'll get the standard pink slip, Ms. Ward," Hardy answers, but his tone is unconvincing.

"That doesn't reassure me as much as you might think," Sarah says.

From my angle, I can't see her face when she looks over at machine-gun guy, but his response is a sheepish smile—and the lowering of the gun by the smallest of increments.

It takes me by surprise when she lunges for him, wrapping both hands around the gun barrel and forcing it to the side. But she gives up a hundred pounds to the Ethiopian mercenary, and the man yanks the gun toward his body, bringing Sarah with it. He quickly releases a hand to wrap his arm around her shoulders, then brings his forehead down on her nose and there's the sick sound of popping cartilage.

I will my own feet to move and join the one-sided fight, forcing the gun aside now that he has only one hand on it, and popping him in the face as hard as I can with my free hand. In my peripheral vision I see Espy struggling in Hardy's grip. With a snarl, the Ethiopian releases Sarah and she falls to the dirt. The man then shoves me away. He outweighs me too, and it doesn't take him long to clear enough space to get his hands back on the gun. I use all of my strength to keep him from bringing the weapon back around.

From deeper in the alley I hear a gun discharge, the sound deafening in the confined space, and I feel white-hot fear. I throw my shoulder into my opponent's sternum and I feel his grip loosen on the machine gun. As he doubles over, I swipe at his temple with an elbow, connecting with a loud thud. He drops to his knees and, as he slides from view, I see what's playing out beyond. Brown is lying facedown, blood pooling around his head. I watch as Hardy turns back toward Esperanza, and is met with a solid kick to the crotch, which sends him to the ground.

The man I'm dancing with, although dazed, is still holding the gun. With one final pull I wrench it away from him and toss it toward the far wall. He hasn't yet caught his breath so I leave him and run to Espy, grabbing her hand.

"Let's go!" I yell. I help Sarah to her feet, grab her elbow, and lead both women out of the alley.

"That was stupid," I say to Sarah.

She offers a tired smile. "It worked, didn't it?"

I give her arm a squeeze at the same instant I hear a loud peal of thunder. It happens in slow motion. A spray of red erupts from Sarah's temple, and before I know what's happening, she is falling. I know she's gone even before I lose my grip on her arm. The sound of the gunshot echoes in my ears as Sarah comes to rest on the ground, her hair covering her face.

As I stand there, numbly looking down on Sarah's lifeless body, Espy pulls on my arm, shouting in my ear, "Jack! C'mon, we have to go!"

She doesn't wait for a reply but digs her nails in and keeps pulling until I follow. Before we hurry out onto the street, I look over my shoulder and see Hardy struggling to his feet, trying to steady himself so he can squeeze off another shot. The Ethiopian has reclaimed his gun, and he meets my eyes just before Espy gives a final tug that jerks me around the wall.

The street is near to empty now. The smattering of people I see—the ones watching the alley from which Espy and I emerge—look like Europeans. The locals have all fled, gone somewhere to hide, probably waiting it out until the violence is over. I'm still only half there, even with the urgency caused by knowing what's behind us. I see the taxi station ahead, a straight shot.

I have the presence of mind to start running with Espy toward the first car I see, a beat-up Peugeot. It's downhill, and every step threatens to upend me, but I keep the pedal down as I hear a volley of gunfire behind us and see puffs of dirt explode far too close to our feet. As Espy and I narrow the distance to the car, it occurs to me that there's no driver in sight. I'm just about to turn to Espy and tell her we need a new plan when I see a man in long shorts and a knee-length shirt exit the taxi station and rush toward the Peugeot. He enters through the passenger-side door and scrambles behind the wheel, beckoning with frantic hand gestures. Espy is there first and she yanks on the door and dives across the seat, and I perform the same maneuver, albeit with less grace. Before I can reach to shut the door, the driver puts the car in gear and pulls everything he can from the engine. Racing away, I hear a rapid series of impacts as bullets pepper the car, and then I'm wearing the shattered remains of a window.

As the car fishtails around a corner, taking us out of Lalibela, our savior looks up into the rearview mirror, flashing brilliant white teeth.

"I save your life. You pay double the fare now, yes?"

It's been just three days but it feels as if I'm returning to Addis Ababa in a different season than when I left. Winter has replaced summer, even if the change is reflected in nothing beyond my mood. I've been quiet for the last few hours, since we boarded the plane in Lalibela, and Espy has allowed me this. I know I'm doing her a disservice by retreating, but she's strong enough to get by while I try to figure out everything that's happened—not just recently but since this whole business began back in Dallas. And it's not just Sarah's death, even though that's something I'm grappling with; she signed on to this thing on her own, and my gut tells me that Hardy would have killed her team regardless of my involvement. But what I'm trying to figure out is how this job has come to define my life. This quest has dragged me from retirement and forced me to engage elements of my personal history that I was quite happy ignoring. It has unearthed people, events, and connections I once kept in separate compartments. Now I'm coming to realize that these things are all linked, and it's a bit more than I'm prepared to process.

We are near Trinity Cathedral, in a coffee shop off Arat Kilo Square. From where I'm sitting, I can see the front entrance of Trinity. I reach for my new cell phone. We bought it in the airport terminal, working under the assumption that the people involved in this drama possess the resources necessary to monitor my old phone. I have no delusions that we will remain untracked for long, which is why I'll try my Reese Industries card one last time for a hefty cash advance. The advance will tell Reese that we made it here, but if Espy and I are careful we may escape Addis Ababa before anyone can lock on.

I'd used a pay phone at the airport to facilitate this meeting. Alem'nesh picks up on the first ring.

"We're here," I say.

He hangs up without saying anything. I put the phone down and reach for my coffee cup.

"Do you know how bad he probably feels right now?" Espy says after I've taken a sip.

"I have an idea."

In our earlier call, I gave Al the highlights of our trip and I could almost smell the incredulity coming through the phone. As Espy said, there also has to be guilt there—from two fronts. On one hand, he provided information and furthered something that almost got us killed; on the other, he violated an oath to his religion by divulging their secrets.

"I don't think he has them," I say.

Espy gives me a questioning look.

"The bones. I don't think Reese has them. If he did, he would just stop paying us."

Espy frowns, and I see her parsing my logic.

"He'd cut the money, not answer my calls. Basically he'd wait for me to give up and go back to my real job." I shake my head. "No, the reason he's trying to execute his teams is because he knows where they are—"

"And he doesn't want anyone else to get to them first," Espy finishes. I see her working through that revelation until a thought hits her. "He meant to kill you all along. Even if everything went according to his original plan, and you found the bones for him . . ."

I look out the window, watching the sun drop behind Trinity, the church casting a lengthening shadow that will soon encompass Espy and me.

I've been trying to make sense of all the players. There's Reese, whose role and motivations seem obvious. And Victor Manheim has stepped from the shadows, but he's a cipher. I have no idea how he fits into this, beyond the knowledge of his involvement at KV65. What I feel confident about is my belief that Manheim and Reese are not on the same team—even if they employ similar methods. I've considered the possibility that Manheim is tied to someone like Reese, who wants the bones found, but every time I give that more than a passing thought I go back to the Valley of the Kings. Manheim didn't have the air of someone searching for something; he acted like a man trying to keep others from finding it.

What keeps me from rushing off to Egypt, though, is the irrationality of thinking the bones are in that tomb. Even if they'd been there when we were excavating—unlikely, considering that KV65 was sealed when the research has the bones passing to Fraternidad de la Tierra—they would have been removed after the accident.

What hovers just out of range of these considerations is the hypothetical secret organization for which we seem to have found evidence. As much as Reese and Manheim must occupy my attention, I wish I had the time and resources needed to research this third entity, this group that might precede the birth of the Christian church. I take another sip of coffee and chuckle to myself. I still haven't attached Victor Manheim to any vested party; for all I know, he's a representative of this ancient society.

I have to push those thoughts away. What's important now is our destination. There are two men who have tried to kill me, both in different parts of the world. Heading for Dallas will move me only toward vengeance, while going to Australia might lead me closer to the bones. If I want this to end, I have to do what Reese doesn't want me to do: I have to find the bones before he can get to them. And with Victor Manheim as my only connection to the bones, vengeance might make a showing after all.

Watching out the window, I catch sight of Al crossing the Trinity courtyard. I've wondered what role Alem'nesh's church has in this whole thing. It would seem to be a significant one, even if their recent historical origin, relatively speaking, precludes them from being the original organization. I don't think he will tell me anything more, not after the events his last intel spawned. But I have to try, so that I can be as prepared as possible for what might await Espy and me when we touch down in Sydney.

Al recommended this coffee shop. He said he stops here every day on his way to the church. He reaches the street, and I see him looking this way, maybe searching for us through the shop's dirty window. Al steps from the curb between two parked cars and starts to cross. I offer a small wave, and he sees it. He waves back.

Then the world outside the window disintegrates in a mix of light and deafening sound. Before Espy and I can react, the window ruptures, spraying us with glass. Instinct kicks in and I turn my head to avoid the worst of the shower as I throw myself to the floor. Espy does the same, coming down hard a few feet away from me. I'm at her side almost before the last bits of glass land.

"I'm fine," she says, rising on one arm.

I ignore her words and do a battlefield check, but she's right; I can't see that she has been injured. I spare a few seconds to determine that I have fared almost as well, save a single, albeit large, piece of glass stuck in my left shoulder. I pull the glass from my skin and toss it to the floor. The shopkeeper chooses that moment to rise from behind the counter, his eyes wide. He looks at Espy and me, and I give him a wave to assure him we're all right. His eyes move to take in the scene outside.

With the same idea, I pull myself up, using the table for support, then to steady myself as I take in what has happened. It looks like one of those war zones one sees when watching CNN. Smoke fills the air, with debris scattered about in the street. People are running to and fro, and there's a car—one of the cars that Al was walking by—that's in flames. Only a crater remains of the other vehicle. I don't understand why, but the sounds break through only after the images have made their mark. The first noise that cuts through is that of distant sirens. I hear people crying, screaming; the crackle of flames.

I don't see a body but I have no doubt that Al is dead.

Smoke is drifting into the coffee shop and I begin to cough. Tears start to form, and I can blame these on the smoke, too. I take Espy's hand, and together we head outside.

On the street, an atmosphere of chaos reigns. I watch as a young man, dazed, wanders toward the flame-engulfed car. I run to him and guide him in the other direction and get him to sit down on the other side of the street.

Then I force myself to stop. There's a hollow feeling in my stomach, as well as a larger portion of guilt than Alem'nesh carried. Even this close to the event, I have no doubt that Al was targeted, for the detonation was too well timed, too precise, to have been anything but a hit. Which means that whoever detonated the bomb might be watching me right now, and that means Espy and I must leave immediately.

Chapter 15

The smells of salt and fish ride the wind that spills through the cab's open window. The wind passes over the harbor to collect the sea, to deposit it in odor and moisture on a city of almost four million, as reminders of the industry by which it was built. Tourism has long usurped fishing as Sydney's chief domestic product, but to me the place's chief identity is that of a sea town. A very large sea town. At almost sixteen hundred square kilometers, Sydney's sprawl matches that of London, covering twice as much territory as New York City.

"I'm cold." Esperanza shivers and pulls her sweater tighter around her shoulders.

Actually, the weather's perfect. When we got off the plane, the display at the airport said 23° Celsius, which translates to around 73° Fahrenheit. It's the sort of temperature that would have one walking into any public place and spotting people wearing light sweaters, right next to others in shorts and T-shirts.

I put the window up.

"Thanks."

I watch out the window as the driver navigates Cumberland Street, heading toward the Cahill Expressway and the Sydney Opera House. Traffic is thick and our slow progress gives me a chance to absorb the people and the atmosphere. A man on a unicycle passes us, going the opposite direction down a sidewalk that slopes several scary degrees in a direction I would not think someone on a single-wheeled conveyance would attempt.

"That's something you don't see every day," Espy says.

"Then you're not looking in the right places."

She doesn't respond. Under the circumstances, casual conversation seems forced. Both of us are still reeling over Al's death, made more difficult by it happening so soon after the murders in Lalibela—although Espy was a godsend during the first few hours after it happened. She kept me from disengaging, kept me in the here and now. She kept me from placing the blame for Al's death on my own shoulders. Now her own emotional reserves lowered, she needs time to think these things through and in her own way.

"Where are we meeting your friend?" Espy asks.

"The beach."

Our destination is Station Beach, northeast of Sydney. I'd wanted to meet at her hotel—the Observatory, a five star in the Rocks District—but Angie was insistent that, if I was going to crash her vacation, I would have to work around her schedule. When she got my call from Ethiopia, she wouldn't believe me when I told her I was paying her a visit. I had to put Espy on the phone to prove to her it wasn't a joke meant to ruin the tail end of her vacation. When I got my phone back, all Angie wanted to talk about was the woman traveling with me.

Seeking out Angie penciled its own way into our plans when I discovered that my Reese Industries credit card had been canceled. The ATM in the airport swallowed it and wouldn't let go. I could deal with that. What really threw a wrench in the works was when the nice young man at the airline ticket counter gave me an apologetic smile and proceeded to cut my personal credit card in half. Had Espy not had a card of her own, and sufficient available credit, I don't know what we would have done.

Espy accused me of another bad debt, and my track record has not left me in a good spot from which to defend myself. But although it's true I have occasionally allowed a debt to remain unpaid, I have never played anything but nice with Visa. This has to be Reese's doing. Or Manheim's. I know Reese has the connections to turn off a poor archaeologist's credit spigot. I have to assume Manheim does, too.

So I'm hitting Angie up for money. She doesn't know that yet. I left the reason for our visit a mystery so that she wouldn't go into hiding.

But I'm irritated that I had to revert to my old phone to reach her. I called half a dozen times with the new phone and couldn't get through, and her voice mailbox was full. The only thing I could think to do was to call with my old phone and hope she recognized the number, which she did. Now if anyone has been eavesdropping on my calls, they know my short-term itinerary.

As our driver takes the taxi up the 14, I see signs for Palm Beach and the city's congestion gives way to green and sand and the bluest water in the world. According to the driver, Station Beach is on the opposite side of Barrenjoey Head from Palm Beach. It's quiet and the water of Pittswater Bay is calm enough to keep surfers and their like away. It's warmer in the car now, so I lower the window. Espy doesn't complain. Like me, I think she's coming out of her mild funk. It's too pretty here to hold on to anything negative. We ride in silence the rest of the way until the driver pulls into a small parking area, beyond which I can make out the pristine white sand and lapping surf. I give some thought to asking the driver to stay to take us back, but then change my mind. There's only one other car in the lot and I'll bet it belongs to Angie. I'm hoping to talk my way into a ride to a car-rental agency.

I'd been wondering how easy it would be to locate Angie once we arrived and now I see I needn't have worried. As we step out onto the sand, I can see only one person from my vantage point. She's stretched out on a towel and turns her head to watch us approach. As we get closer, I see her sit up and raise her sunglasses.

"What in the world happened to you?" she asks.

"It's a long story."

I know how I look. While I'm wearing new clothes, and most of my injuries are not visible, I imagine that my overall weariness has become obvious. That, and I haven't shaved in several days.

Espy leans toward me and says, "She's pretty." She doesn't sound pleased about it.

Angie rises to greet us. She looks many shades darker than when I saw her last, and she wears relaxation like a second skin.

"Hi, Jack."

"Hi, Angie." I glance around at the empty beach. "I wouldn't have pictured you here. Isn't Bondi more your style?"

"Let's just say I'm spending the last few days of my vacation recovering from my vacation," she says with a wink. "What about you? This is a far cry from being holed up in your apartment."

"Aren't you the one who told me I need to get out more?"

She chuckles and turns to Espy. "Hello, I'm Angie."

"Nice to meet you, Angie. I'm Esperanza."

"So what brings the two of you here?"

Angie is still taking in my condition, and there is genuine concern in her question, alongside the curiosity about my traveling companion.

"Angie, I need a favor." I offer my most charming smile, but Angie knows me too well.

She looks back and forth between Espy and me and I see her fixate on my shoulder.

"You're bleeding," she says. "Jack, what's going on?"

Blood from the wound in my shoulder has seeped though the bandage and is staining my new shirt. I sigh. It's just another minor complication in a growing list, and it's not one I'm going to worry about right now.

"Let's take a walk," I say.

The three of us walk up the beach, angling for the thick tree line and rising ground of Barrenjoey Head. I tell Angie about the last few weeks, giving her the highlights only. The more I share, the more her eyes widen. I remind myself that of all the friends I have called on since this job began, Angie knows less about my past than any of them. To her, I'm just a typical archaeology professor with no social life. Picturing me in the field, much less engaging in something this dangerous, must be difficult for her. What's more, many of the details I leave unsaid are ones that would likely send her to the unbelieving camp. What I give her is enough for her to see that we're in trouble without making it sound like some James Bond adventure. When I've finished and we turn to head back toward the parking area, leaving the rough terrain and treacherous cliffs behind, Angie is silent. She is walking next to me, her eyes on the sand.

"So what do you need?" she asks when we have neared the parking area.

I half register that Angie's car is not the only one there. I don't see anyone else on the beach, but it's just a short walk to the other shoreline, where the ocean meets Palm Beach.

"We need money, Angie. Otherwise, we won't be able to finish this."

She nods, giving my words consideration before saying, "And would that be such a bad thing? Not being able to finish? Teaching archaeology seldom causes blood loss."

I think that even as she asks the question, she knows the answer. In the short time we've talked, my guess is that she's picked up on the fact that I'm not the same person who walked out of her apartment two weeks ago.

"How much do you need?" she asks with a resigned sigh.

"You're my girl, Angie. I'll make good, I promise."

With a laugh, Angie wraps her arm around mine and leans in close.

"You'd better. And I think you have yourself a new girl now." She delivers this last in a stage whisper, meant to be heard by Espy.

As Angie gathers up her belongings, she makes certain I know how irritated she is that I'm taking her away from the beach. What redirects her is when Espy asks about her hair, and the two of them enjoy a conversation about current styles as we walk to Angie's car.

The other car is still there, parked two spaces away from Angie's. It's a new Lexus—beautiful lines. The windows are tinted so that an observer can see nothing of the interior. It's a car I can appreciate even if it's something I'd never buy for myself.

It's as Angie is popping the trunk of the rental to stow her belongings that the driver's door of the Lexus opens and my heart is shocked nearly to stopping to see Hardy step out. Even through my disbelief I start to move before Hardy is all the way out of the car. But he raises a gun before I can gain more than two feet. He's wearing the ever-present dark suit, only this time it's accessorized with sunglasses.

"Hello, Dr. Hawthorne," he says.

I have never wanted to punch someone in the teeth more than I do at this moment.

He gestures with the gun. "To the beach," he says, no doubt realizing that anyone would come up from the busier Palm Beach side and see what's happening here. When we do not comply, he makes a move toward Angie.

"To the beach, or I will kill Ms. Bernard right here. The trunk is open; it would be quite a while before someone finds the body."

Espy and I start back for the beach, and it's only when we have almost reached the white sand that I realize Hardy used Angie's last name. It's proof that my phone is indeed bugged, and that Hardy can access avenues of information as easily as I can with Duckey.

Hardy marches us toward the Barrenjoey Head. I know that if he succeeds in herding us there, we're all dead. If he hides the bodies in just the right spot, it could be a year before someone finds us.

I stop and turn to face the man.

"There's no reason for you to involve anyone but me," I say. "Let them go and you can do whatever you have to do."

Hardy has his gun pressed into Angie's side and, while she's doing an admirable job of maintaining her composure, she looks only a handbreadth away from giving in to her fear.

"It can't be that way, Dr. Hawthorne. Dr. Habilla knows too much." He grins and jabs Angie in the side with the gun and I see a single tear roll down her cheek. "And it's your fault that Ms. Bernard is caught up in this now."

"Like Alem'nesh was caught up in it?" I accuse.

A flash of what appears to be genuine puzzlement appears on Hardy's face.

"Who?"

"The priest you killed in Addis Ababa."

"I can assure you that I wasn't involved in any operation that called for the killing of a priest."

I don't know why, but I believe him. Something in his manner tells me he wouldn't dance around the subject. If he'd killed Alem'nesh, he would have no qualms about admitting it.

"If you're going to kill us no matter what," I say, "then I'm not walking anymore. If you want to kill me, you'll have to do it right here."

Hardy seems to give this serious thought and, as he does, I realize I've made a mistake. In a situation like this, isn't it a cardinal rule that you prolong the inevitable for as long as you can; that the longer you stay alive, the more the chance increases that something unexpected might happen? Now I've given him an ultimatum that can only end one way.

"Very well, then," he says, pointing the gun at me. It happens in slow motion that I see his finger tighten on the trigger and for the second time in just a few days I find myself hoping that it won't hurt. I don't have time to steel myself, or to offer even a quick apology to these two women who will die with me.

I hear a crack, and Angie screams, and my eyes snap shut. A few ticks pass before I realize I'm not dead. I open my eyes and see Hardy still standing, the gun still pointed. A trickle of red runs down his nose and, when I reach over and grab Angie by the arm, pulling her away from him, he tumbles forward into the sand.

The bullet took most of his skull when it exited, and I feel Angie growing faint as she sees the gory sight.

"We have to go!" I say.

I don't know who fired the shot, only that it came from behind me, hitting Hardy with a single shot from an impressive distance, if my recollection of sound versus projectile speed is even half accurate. It means we're sitting ducks.

I start to run back the way we came, guiding Angie. Espy is nearby, and I see that she has scooped up Hardy's gun. When we've traveled a good distance away from Hardy's dead body, I glance over at Angie. It seems she's allowing determination to replace the fear. She gives me a look that is both wonder and accusation.

"Welcome to my world," I say.

Australia's capital city has much to recommend it as one of the most unique capitals in the world, not the least of which is that it didn't exist prior to being named such. Before the government hired a Chicago architect to build them a ready-made city from which to govern, there was nothing here but a juxtaposition of swampland, savanna, eucalyptus forest, and a few adventurous souls staking their claim to the country's riches.

What I like most about the city, though, is its lake. The Molonglo River winds through Canberra, and previous generations dammed it to create a scenic body of water in the City Center. It can make traveling through the area a bear, especially at the height of the tourist season, but I can remember canoeing down the Molonglo with Jim, and how the city looked from the water.

Esperanza appears wide awake as we navigate Forest Avenue, the loop around downtown that passes the National Gallery, then the Parliament House. We came in through Kings Park, crossing Lake Burley Griffin, because I wanted her to see the city at night, with the lights on the tall, silent edifices of government. We have to go back across the water on Commonwealth to find someplace to stay. But from what I see in Espy's eyes, the extra miles are worth it.

The Mustang makes a noise somewhere between a purr and a grumble, as if torn between appreciating the rest, and anxiety about returning to do what it does best: ripping up the road at over a hundred miles an hour. When we rented the car, I was surprised to find out we could get the Mustang for only a few dollars more a day than it would cost to rent an economy car. And after all that's happened over the last few weeks, I decided to indulge the juvenile urge of feeling the powerful engine coursing through my body.

I ease the car off the roundabout and head north toward the National University. I remember there being a selection of hotels somewhere near the university. At this point I'd settle for anything, no matter how cheap, just as long as it has a clean bed. We have to be judicious with the money Angie provided. She floated me five thousand, the max that she could coax from her credit card company.

The events in Sydney shook Angie—to the point that I'm amazed she went along with lending me the money. Someone shot a man standing behind her, the bullet passing just inches from her head. It's enough to frighten anyone half to death. What sort of relationship we'll have should I return to Evanston in one piece is up in the air. I wouldn't blame her if she greets me with profanity and violence. Hardy was right about one thing: I'm to blame for dragging her into danger.

My mind shifts to the identity of Hardy's killer; the question has followed me over the miles separating Sydney from Canberra. Whoever pulled the trigger was an expert marksman. The shooter had caught Hardy with his head sticking out from behind Angie, the timing and placement of the bullet perfect. I still believe the shot came from a considerable distance. A sniper, a one-shot kill. But why were we spared?

This is one of the reasons we stayed on course. While Hardy has been a thorn in my flesh of late, I can't forget that Manheim and I have a personal history. It's possible he's the one who killed Hardy and Al. All I know is that I have to stay on task. And now that Hardy is dead, there's some cushion built into any dealings I may need to have with his boss.

The university scrolls by on the left and I see that, as much as she'd like to, Espy is now too tired to appreciate anything beyond the promise of a place to sleep. We're almost to Braddon before I spot the yellow sign of the Days Inn. I pull the car into a parking spot but do not hear the light snoring until I cut the engine. I pop the trunk, get out and remove our luggage, then walk around to the passenger side and wake her enough so that she can follow me to the lobby.

The lobby is dark, with dim lights running along its perimeter. A petite young woman sits behind the front desk, her blond hair pulled back into a severe-looking bun. She's wearing red lipstick, too bright for her waxen face. But her smile seems genuine, and I'm glad to see another human being who looks happy to see me, even if the expression is nothing more than theater.

"Hi there," she says, and her voice is as chipper as her smile.

"Hi back. Do you have any rooms available?"

"We do," she says without consulting her computer. "Smoking or non?"

"Smoking."

She makes a face at that and then swivels on her stool and taps at the computer's keyboard. After a moment's study, she says, "We have two rooms available in the smoking wing. One has a queen-size bed, the other a king." Tabitha—I've only now noticed the name tag—gives me an expectant look.

"Great. We'll take both." I would ask Esperanza if she'd prefer something in the clean-air section, but given the way she's leaning against the desk, I get the feeling she wouldn't care if I led her to one of the couches in the lobby and left her there.

"Both?"

"I snore."

A few minutes later, the elevator deposits us on the third floor. I have the room keys in my pocket—128 and 133—as I set off down the hallway, lugging both of our bags. We reach 133 first, where I set one bag down so I can fish the key from my pocket. Two key cards and I have no idea which one is for this door. The first swipe has no effect on the lock's red light. The second card produces a welcoming green color and the sound of the lock disengaging.

I push open the door, step inside and drop Espy's bag on the floor, then turn on one of the lights. The room is of decent size and with no foul odors. It looks like she's getting the king-size bed.

"I'll come and get you in the morning," I say.

"Not too early," she says, but the last part is lost in a yawn.

I give her a smile and, stifling my own yawn, start to leave. I'm just passing by her in the narrow entryway when I catch the scent of her shampoo. It's the same one she used when we were together; it's another one of those old memories that people attach more meaning to than the thing deserves. But now the subtle floral smell catches me sleep-deprived. I reach my hand around her waist and pull her in for a kiss. It's funny how something can be immediately familiar and startlingly new at the same time. They're the same lips, but we're different people. I wonder, in that brief moment that passes before we disengage, if that's a good thing.

I can't read the answer in Esperanza's eyes, yet she doesn't push me away. We're close enough that I can hear her breathing.

I'm the one who pulls back. "I'm going to get some sleep."

Without waiting for a reply, I make for the hallway, pulling the door closed behind me. Right before it clicks shut, I hear Espy say something about flossing. I stand in the dimly lit corridor for a time before resettling my bag on my shoulder and heading off to find my own bed.

Chapter 16

The seat of the Australian government is a mammoth building forever fated to be reminded of its humbler beginnings. Parliament House occupies the ideological center of South Canberra, forming the southern point of the Parliamentary Triangle that claims a large section of the Lake Burley Griffin shoreline. Looking north from its main entry, though, one cannot help but notice the smaller but elegant Old Parliament House that oversaw the birth of a self-determining nation.

Espy and I ascend the fifteen or so steps to the entrance, where two guards are posted, facing straight ahead with matching staunch postures. We join the stream of people entering the building, most of them tourists hoping to visit the nonessential rooms set aside for the curious. Among these are a smattering of professionals in suits and skirts—government officials, aides, lobbyists, grifters of all shapes and sizes. I can probably include Espy and myself in the latter designation.

Inside, we stand in a massive foyer with wide white pillars reaching up to the vaulted ceiling and then slender brown wood columns supporting a second story. We follow the foyer until it empties into the Great Hall, where my shoes echo across the immaculate hardwood as I step into the open chamber. At the far end of the hall hangs an earth-toned tapestry that covers most of the wall.

I reach for Espy's elbow. "Ready?"

I'm sensitive to the speed with which she pulls away from my grasp and walks back the way we came. As if we didn't have enough baggage between us, now I've gone and ruined the whole thing with a single kiss. It's a reminder that, once this sordid business is concluded, there's something of greater importance which needs tending. Yet there's little I can do about it right now. If she wants to sulk, I'll just have to let her sulk.

At the end of the foyer is a stairway leading to the visitor gallery overlooking the main Committee Room, where one can see a portion of the legislative process in motion. It's the most popular tourist destination, and I see at least fifty people ascending and descending the steep steps, which seem to open up toward nothing, reminding me of the proverbial Jacob's ladder. I'm glad we don't have to set foot on them, because my knee is complaining again. I haven't walked this much in years, and my subpar leg is telling me it has no loyalties to anything beyond its own well-being.

I pull out my cell phone and dial the international number that came with the file from Duckey.

Someone answers on the first ring with an irritated "Yeah?" This tells me that the man I'm here to see is reticent about giving out this number—that there are a select few who would ring it.

"Hello, Mr. Manheim."

A cruel part of me enjoys the brief pause that follows my greeting. As he struggles to place my voice and come to grips with the fact that he's been caught off guard, I can almost smell the consternation via satellite.

"Who is this?"

As I think of how to respond—after days of travel, dead

ends, and dead bodies—I harbor a desire for something direct, something akin to ripping off a bandage in one quick pull.

"This is Jack Hawthorne."

What follows is a sound that might be an intake of breath, but I can't be sure. What I do register is the look of surprise on Esperanza's face. She doubtless assumed that we would engage in some sort of ruse for as long as we were able.

"I don't believe I know a Jack Hawthorne," the other man says, recovering.

"Did you enjoy your trip to Venezuela?" I ask. "I hear San Cristóbal is lovely this time of year."

Esperanza is mouthing something but I ignore her. I can almost see Manheim clenching his teeth and drumming nervous fingers on his desk. Probably what he's weighing now are the merits of maintaining obtuseness.

"What do you want?"

I can respect a man who, seeing the world crumbling around him, makes a desperate lunge toward salvaging the situation. Manheim did a rapid calculation of the particulars, for he understands that I've nailed him. And his response is unadulterated survival.

"There are a lot of things I want. A nicer car, a lighter class load." I pause, then say, "And to find out why you want me dead."

For a moment I think I've lost him. Finally he says, "I don't know what you're talking about." There's a hoarseness in Manheim's voice that I can only attribute to anger.

I don't feel like playing games. I could stay on the line and string him along, maybe drop Ernesto's name, the dollar figure, the email address. I have enough of the pertinent information to, if not prove in court that he set up the hit, then at least unnerve him enough to force his hand. Instead, I'm feeling a sudden sympathy with Esperanza, and with all of female-kind: I want closure.

"If you're interested in talking, I'm in the lobby."

Before he can answer I end the call and, for good measure, cut the power. It wouldn't do to have Mr. Reese try to call when I'm in the middle of holding my own against a man like Victor Manheim.

I barely have the phone back in my pocket before Espy grabs my arm. "What are you doing?"

I give her a wink. "I don't have any idea."

I'm trying to ignore the small fountain twenty feet beyond Manheim's chair, but it's difficult to avoid looking at it. An exquisite black onyx representation of the Egyptian god Anubis is sending a stream of water arcing from its muzzle, and I'm positioned at just the right spot for the water to appear to enter Manheim's left ear and exit out his right. It's all I can do to keep from laughing because, no matter who this man is, the illusion makes him seem anything but threatening. It's equivalent to a public speaker imagining the audience in their underwear. I shift in my chair to change perspective and focus on the man who wants me dead.

By the time Manheim arrived, less than five minutes after our phone call, he had reclaimed the trappings of the consummate politician. He greeted me with a gracious smile and a handshake, as if we're two old school chums reconnecting after several years, but I refuse to exchange pleasantries with Will's, and possibly Al's, killer.

We are semisequestered in a small oasis of comfortable chairs in a lounge area somewhere behind the Members Hall, only accessible by traversing a corridor barred to the general public.

A distinct odor of cigars lingers in the air, and this, coupled with the fact that it's hidden in plain sight, gives the room a Masonic feel. I imagine this is one of the areas where the more senior representatives gather to unwind, to share in a camaraderie that transcends their respective political affiliations. With a start, it occurs to me that this is what I'd been expecting when Reese's butler led me to the old man's drawing room.

It bothers me that Espy and I are alone with this man, that we have been whisked away from the more public areas. Still, if I concentrate, I can hear the muffled sounds of people talking and milling about on the other side of the wall, which teases me with an unwarranted sense of safety. If Manheim has a gun equipped with a silencer, it is no help that we're close to the main transit area. He could pop us both, and the gawking tourists would never know. And yet my impression is that, whatever his other work, the business that involves me is separated from his political service. He will not bring it to this place.

Manheim's hands rest on the knee of his pressed slacks, and his expression is one of patrician warmth. Esperanza occupies a seat to my right, but beyond a perfunctory greeting back in the lobby, the Aussie has all but ignored her. This isn't about anyone but Manheim and me.

"Can I ask what brings you to Canberra, Mr. Hawthorne?"

"You can ask, but I think it's a waste of time. You already know why I'm here."

At first he offers a smile and a head shake, but then his lips compress and the smile disappears. He leans forward and his eyes flick over me with undisguised distaste. "I'm going to have to ask you to remove your coat."

"Excuse me?"

"Your coat, Dr. Hawthorne. I need you to take it off."

I'm sure the look on my face conveys my puzzlement, yet Manheim seems unmoved.

"If you wish this conversation to continue, you will do as I ask."

His body language leaves no doubt that if I do not comply he will end this meeting. And I've come too far to allow something unexpected, something seemingly harmless, to derail this train. I stand and slip out of my coat and then hand it to the Aussie when he reaches for it. He gives the thing a thorough pat-down, even turning the pockets inside out like a jail guard searching for contraband. The effort yields a few receipts and a half-empty pack of chewing gum, and he replaces these and then returns my coat. He looks at Esperanza.

"And you?"

Espy's first response is to glower at him, but then she, too, seems to sense the tenuousness of the situation. Without a word, she slips out of her jacket and hands it to Manheim. He repeats the pat-down procedure, then returns the garment.

"Satisfied?" she asks.

"Hardly."

He reaches a hand into his own jacket and I tense, waiting for the gun, even as I hold to my earlier assessment of Manheim's willingness to act here. Too, for all its secluded feel, surely other people use this room. I am relieved when the item Manheim pulls from inside his coat resembles a small wand more than it does a firearm. Before I can get a good look at it, he leans close and runs it down my body, holding it about three inches from me. This lasts less than twenty seconds, after which he repeats the procedure on Esperanza. My guess is that he's looking for some type of recording or eavesdropping equipment, and I'm more than willing to put up with the indignity, because Manheim's careful approach indicates he has something to hide.

He returns the wand to his pocket and settles back in his chair. There is silence in the room for a while, broken only by the muffled sounds of activity filtering to us from other areas of the building. It takes me some time before I recognize the distasteful atmosphere as something familiar. In my younger days I hated having to prostrate myself before one grant board or another, dumbing down my research enough so that dour, unqualified people would loose the purse strings and give me enough money to dig in peace for a year. I feel the same condescension now coming from Manheim. And the problem is that, unlike those sessions before the financial gatekeepers, this time I might not be the smartest one in the room. At least I don't have the same level of information that Manheim possesses. It puts me in the weaker position, a place where my footing isn't as solid. It irritates me.

"Now that we're done with the cloak-and-dagger routine, would you mind telling me why you tried to have me killed?" Directness is my only party favor at this bash.

Manheim waits a few beats before answering. As I watch his face, I'm pleased to see the same irritation I myself am feeling. He's wondering how I found him out, how I tracked him here.

"Out of more than thirty million people in Australia, why would you pick me as this so-called assassin?"

"Out of the fifty million people in Venezuela, why would you pick me to do in?"

Manheim leans forward in his chair and crosses his arms over his knees—the posture of a confidant. "Maybe you were the only one digging somewhere you didn't belong."

I ignore the widening of Esperanza's eyes, half seen in my peripheral vision. My heart, though, picks up its pace. I'm not sure what I was expecting, but thinly veiled admissions were not on the list.

I, too, lean forward. "What wasn't I meant to find?"

He snorts and settles back in the chair. "How much is your employer paying you?"

"Who says I have an employer?"

"You're using a Reese Industries corporate card. You might as well hand out business cards."

He's got me there, although it pleases me to learn he doesn't know I'm no longer in Reese's employ.

"I'm a consultant."

"A treasure hunter."

"Semantics."

"Indeed," Manheim says.

He pauses and seems to be considering something, then gives a half smile.

"You're obviously resourceful, Dr. Hawthorne. I'll grant you that. Tell me—is it that quality, or pigheadedness, which makes a man stumble blindly through a dangerous neighborhood after nightfall?"

"Interesting analogy, Victor. Am I the blind man? Or is that you? I have trouble with metaphors." I was wrong: directness is not my only party favor. I also have false bravado. It's like an insincere charm. And inflating beneath it all is a latent anger that I want to nurse until it is large enough to force me to kill this man with my bare hands. And I want him to know it's for my brother that he dies.

"Don't think I've come unprepared for this meeting, Dr. Hawthorne. I know a great deal about you. I know that you were born in Athens, Maine. That you graduated from Cambridge with a 3.7 GPA. You then spent three years working with Dr. Wherle in Peru, and another three with Dr. Winstead in several locations." He pauses then, and I see what might be the hint of a smile. "Your brother died while you were excavating a site in the Valley of the Kings in 2003, and ever since then you've been teaching at a charming little institution in North Carolina."

It's like being forcibly undressed—my life recited in a pithy paragraph. The fact that I'm astute enough to understand what he's doing is of only marginal help. I affect an unimpressed smirk, even though he's picked at the wound that is my brother's death.

"All public record," I say. "A few minutes with a search engine."

"Your parents are John and Madeline. Your father is dead and your mother lives alone in your family home on Denton Street. She spends her time volunteering at Athens Presbyterian and sitting on the board of the Fitzgerald Art Museum." He stops, fixes me with a look of pure malevolence, then says, "On Tuesdays and Thursdays she leaves her home at precisely 3:30 in the afternoon, arriving at the museum between 3:50 and 3:55, depending on traffic at Broadmore."

Even with my knowing the reaction he wants to elicit from me—even this doesn't insulate me against what's been revealed. Without putting a voice to it, he's just levied a threat against both me and my family. As I try to formulate a response, the chief thought in my head is that Manheim is something more than a second-rate political hopeful. And he's just demonstrated resources enough to make good on his threat. That in itself should be enough to force me to gather up my toys and go home—to promise to never again stick my nose where it doesn't belong, and return to teaching uninspired youth. The urge is magnified when Esperanza places a cautioning hand on my arm, a gesture that barely cuts through the red haze starting to cloud my vision.

Manheim nods. "I see you understand."

I understand that I want to beat this man until his face is an unrecognizable pulp beneath my fists. But that would accomplish only the assuagement of a personal need. If this man is more than bluff—and his past actions force me to believe he is—then there's more at stake than my own satisfaction.

With the stakes raised, and made personal, the need to know is accentuated. It's like a slow burn in my blood—a lingering of hot sauce on the tongue hours after the meal. "What was in KV65?" I ask.

I think the man sitting across from me understands my need, because the question causes a slight break in his façade. For a brief instant I see something—not quite empathy but maybe an acknowledgment from one who can understand this desire to fill in the gaps. But the look is gone before it can solidify, and it does nothing to make me hate him any less.

The silence in the room grows heavy, absolute. If I were sweating, I would hear each drop strike the floor. When Manheim leans forward, a strange energy passes between us. I can feel it crisscross my skin, run beneath Esperanza's hand that still rests on my arm. And when he speaks, I can almost hear the words before they leave his lips.

"Dr. Hawthorne, there are some things that were never meant to be discovered."

Chapter 17

I sense more than see Espy beside me. I sense her through the worried anger that threatens to upset the rhythm of my feet, the sun full in my eyes as I hit the white stone steps, dodging a pair of elderly women in matching sweaters, embroidered Scottish terriers wearing green hats. Because of urgency, I've reverted back to my old phone. I come close to a snarl as I will Duckey to answer, as I imagine him in the throes of some holiday ritual while his phone emits an impotent ringtone in an empty room. It's never felt less like Christmas than it does right now. I'm detached from all the familiar things I associate with the holiday season. I'm on the outside of it, and I find that I'm resentful—of Duckey, of his family, of whatever it is that's keeping him from answering his phone.

By the time I reach the bottom step, the phone is on its eighth ring and I'm about to jam my thumb onto the disconnect button when I hear a click and then my friend's voice.

"Jack?"

"Do you still have a friend in the Bangor police department?"

There's no hesitation in his voice, as if he can hear something in my own that registers the need for a quick response, for a setting aside of the usual playful banter. "Yeah. Carrie Preston. She's a detective in the fifteenth precinct."

I let go of a sigh that's been building inside my lungs, just waiting for an opportunity to escape, to mark the fact that something, however small, has gone right.

"I need a favor, Ducks."

"Name it."

"I need someone to get my mom away from the house. They have to take her somewhere safe."

What Duckey says next is a testament to our deep friendship, to a trust not easily granted. And it denotes another item on the ledger for which I'll be paying for the better part of the foreseeable future.

"Quickly or quietly?"

"Quickly." The word is out of my mouth before I've really considered the question, but I know it's the right answer. Manheim has shown too much of his hand; I know now what his people are capable of. I'm certain that my mother is under at least one set of watchful eyes at this very moment, so the odds of an operative secreting her from the family home are slim. In this case, then, bigger is better. "Black and whites, flashing lights, whatever it takes. I need her out of there and tucked someplace where even Santa couldn't find her."

"Denton Street, right?"

"Right."

"I'll make the call."

I know what those words mean for him. Duckey will have to call someone a thousand miles away and convince that person to utilize the resources of a big-city police department to collect and hold a woman on nothing but his say-so. I'm not deluding myself that things will be that easy, but I'm grateful for Duckey's willingness to try.

"Thanks, Ducks."

His answering grunt is cut off as he breaks the connection. I try my mom's house again but get the same busy signal I got before I called Duckey.

As I pull the phone away from my ear, I see that I've walked in a straight line away from Parliament House, following a path toward the lake, and the older building that stands all but forgotten except to tour groups and those susceptible to nostalgia.

Espy is still at my side. I slow and then stop as it hits me that we've nowhere to go at the moment. I know where my car is parked, and I know the location of the hotel, and yet neither morsel of knowledge helps direct me. I am, again, at the mercy of a force outside of myself, and even though a friend with proven loyalties is exercising this force, it nonetheless leaves me stripped of immediate purpose. I look around and my eyes settle on Espy.

Then her hand takes mine and she leads me to a weathered wooden bench near the path, where she makes me sit, forcing me down with her stern but gentle eyes. And despite myself, I'm grateful. The bench is comforting, and I sit and consider the idea that I feel adrift because the Australian to whom I've just spoken has shown an ability to affect peoples and events on the other side of the world, whereas I can't even get someone to water my cactus.

Esperanza squeezes my hand, as if to remind me that regardless of Manheim's vast resources, I've shown that I'm equally resourceful.

"What now?" she asks, and immediately I feel like I've let her down. Up to now, I've been somewhat in control. But after hearing Manheim's threat, everything's changed. There's a strange combination of emotions that comes from baring oneself, and I don't think I like it.

"I don't know," I say.

"Should we go back to Sydney?"

"I don't know."

It's quiet here, like a still pool of water carved from a fast-moving river. I know that under different circumstances I'd appreciate the quiet, were I not fighting the dual sensations of worry and weariness as I am right now. If the last week has reinforced anything, it's been an understanding that I work best when alone, when all I have to worry about is me, when a misstep means that I'm the only one in harm's way. Death as an abstract. But it's a completely different story when people I care about are drawn into my affairs. Al is dead because of me. Sarah is dead because of me. My mother is in danger because of me. It's hard to swallow all of this with my customary aplomb. And it's made all the more poignant because of the loss I've already suffered—the brother who, as it turns out, died because of this thing that has now ensnared me.

Death as something with power, with consequence. I think what I'm feeling is the idea that I'm no longer in my twenties. The great lie of that age group is work and reward—a universe with a munificent scale, where fear can be checked at the cloakroom. It's a lie because an absence of fear can only mean that we do not dread loss, and that we value nothing so strongly that it would injure us to see it snatched away. It's a world full of discovery and accomplishment and ego, absent honesty and loyalty. It's also something I understood, at least in an intangible way, when I took the job at Evanston.

Esperanza's thumb is making small circles on the back of my

hand, and the touch draws me back until I can smell the grass and the air and the fresh mulch laid on the flower beds along the path. Her hand feels good in my own, and there's a different quality to it that comes from age, from experience. I give it a squeeze and meet her eyes and, despite myself, I have to smile, because it's exactly what I need. A rebuttal to the presumed superiority of unfettered youth.

Together we sit in silence. As the sun makes its incremental way across the sky, we wait for a call that will tell me if my mother is safe. What goes unsaid is our destination, and for more than the obvious reason. For even if I'm compelled to continue—and that's something I'm not quite ready to wrestle with—I have no direction, no point that leaps out from a map, which would beckon the Mustang onward. So I'm at something of a dead end, and the only way I can rationalize anything beyond a return to the airport is to cultivate spite.

The thought brings a small smile. At least spite is something I'm good at.

The thing about waiting is that it can segue into a number of other things, depending on factors like the weather, one's personality, or even biology. In this case, the latter—principally hunger—causes Espy and me to forsake our serene outpost for the manufactured comfort of a nearby restaurant. With several eateries within walking distance of Parliament House, we leave the car parked and try our luck winding our way on foot through the crowds until we find something that looks good.

Less than an hour later, Esperanza is picking at the Trout Amandine, leaving the sides of broccoli and wild rice untouched.

A full glass of white wine sits on the table near her plate. It all tells me that she's in a contemplative mood. If memory serves, she rarely eats when considering a weighty matter, a response that's in direct opposition to her gastronomic tendencies when she's angry. I remember her eating a great deal toward the end of our relationship.

"What's wrong?" I ask.

Her eyes remain on the trout. She uses a single tine of her fork to flake away a tiny piece of fish, which she does not eat. There's a long pause before she answers, "I'm worried about you."

"Don't be."

She looks up from the plate with mild accusation in her eyes, but there's also warmth there that I would not have seen back in Caracas, or even Rubio. I'm not certain she'd have even been able to manufacture it.

"Always quick with an answer, aren't you? *I'm worried about you* because I don't think you understand why you're here."

"We both know why we're here."

She shakes her head. "I know why I'm here, and that's been enough for me up to this point. I've carried it for the both of us."

"All right, why are you here?"

"You're changing the subject."

"And you're avoiding it."

"Semantics," Espy says, parodying my earlier comment.

"Etymology." I smirk. "See. I can use big words, too."

I feel silly, especially seeing as I'm verbally jousting with someone who has crossed the globe for me. Someone who only last month would have ritually spat on my picture.

"Jerk," she says. "See, I can use appropriate ones."

That forces a smile and I reach for her hand across the table. I'm not used to this kind of dynamic with someone when, for the last five years, most of my relationships have consisted of surface banter and ego gratification. Espy is like a female Duckey, although I've never tried to hold his hand. The thought gives me a shudder.

"What do you want from me? I was hired to do a job, and that job has brought me—has brought *us* here."

"This isn't archaeology. You were hired to find some bones, not traipse around the world angering government officials. Not to hunt down someone you think killed your brother."

Or put my other loved ones in the crosshairs. I wonder, briefly, if Espy falls under that umbrella, but I quickly bury the thought. I don't have time to consider something like that. It wasn't on the agenda when this whole thing started, and I hate penciling things in. I let go of her hand.

"You've taken this far beyond where you should have," she continues. "It's become your personal crusade now."

"Even if it is, what of it?" I retort.

"For one thing, I'm still not convinced your primary target is Victor Manheim. Or Gordon Reese. I think you're angry enough at God to follow the bones anywhere they take you."

"There you go with God again. What's gotten into you?"

She shakes her head, as if in disbelief at my ignorance. "You're looking for bones that have the power to raise the dead, and you want to keep God out of it?"

"Yes, I do."

"Well, I can't."

Silence falls over us and I notice that everyone in the café is looking in our direction. Lowering her voice, Espy says, "You and I haven't talked about this. Way too much baggage. But

God means a lot more to me now than He used to. And before you go much farther, you should evaluate where you stand."

What saves me from having to respond is the ringing of my phone. I fumble in my pocket until I feel the phone.

"Ducks?"

"She's safe, Jack." He coughs. "But she wasn't happy about it."

That elicits my first genuine smile of the day. "I can imagine."

"Carrie called me and I talked to your mom and convinced her to go."

"I'm surprised she listened. I didn't think she liked you."

"It would have helped if you'd told her they were coming."

"The line was busy. I think she's still on dial-up. Where did they take her?"

"Carrie wouldn't tell me. Only that they couldn't use a real safe house because it's not official police business. But Carrie's good people, Jack. I'm sure your mom's safe."

"Jim Duckett, you're a beautiful human being."

"You're right, I am. But I'm also someone who needs a few good answers right now. Carrie said I better have something solid for her soon or she'd hurt me. And she's a cop, so she knows how to inflict pain."

Duckey is trying to keep it light but there's tenseness beneath the words—a suggestion that there have been too many unexplained favors. I know I owe him an explanation—several explanations—and so I give him what he needs. I tell him everything. By the time I've finished, I can almost see my friend processing the story. Were we back in the student union considering the same matter over dinner, now would be the time when he would lean back in his chair and run a hand over his breast pocket, feeling for his cigar case.

When he answers, his words are not entirely unexpected. "Isn't it time you got yourself back here?"

"Denver?"

"You know what I mean."

Of course I do. And yet, at a time when the most logical response would be a yes, preceded by some off-color exclamation, I find that I'm ill-equipped to make that call. It takes a moment for me to realize that my inability to answer the question in the manner Duckey wants is that I no longer understand where I belong. I have a brief and painful fear that I will never see Duckey again, but I shrug and the thought is gone.

"I can't come back yet, Ducks."

"When's a good time? Before or after you wind up dead?"

"I'm aiming for before."

"But the target's small and you've had way too much caffeine."

I have no reply but to smile, which doesn't translate well via satellite.

"What time is it there?" I think to ask.

"Dark."

The waiter comes by and clears my plate but I don't hear the few words he exchanges with Espy. I'm thinking about my friend, whose vacation I've crashed in all but body, sitting in his in-laws' kitchen in his bathrobe. "You have no idea how much I appreciate everything, Ducks."

The waiter has been by twice, yet it's not until Esperanza slides the bill in front of me that I understand. I reach for my wallet and extract some of Angie's cash.

After I hang up, I feel lighter. Walking through the whole

thing with Duckey—forcing myself to lay it out in linear form—was cathartic. It's helped me to get a handle on what we've done, and to begin to formulate what we need to accomplish still. As I try to answer that last question, I find that even if I don't have a good long-term plan, I think I have a place to start.

Chapter 18

Two hours have passed since I've seen another car, and I'm beginning to believe I'm the last man on earth. Like most people my age, I liked the Mad Max movies from the eighties, and I can understand how this setting spawned the post-apocalyptic feel of the films. There's a primordial rawness here—the sense that the place exists as some vast and important thing regardless of the dearth of humans crossing it. It is all desert and sky, mile after mile of two-lane road scorched by the sun and covered over by windblown sand, and nature battling nothing but itself. And it's an experience and a vista rendered impotent as long as the Mustang's radio can pick up even one signal.

In this case, it's an FM jazz station, originating from Leonora. I have off-tempo bass guitars and horns acting as fellow journeyers, and I'm grateful for the connection to the outside world, especially because Esperanza checked out over an hour ago. The music is a link to something beyond these environs—a reassurance that even this manifestation of nature is comparatively small as long as I have something else with which to occupy myself.

As the darkness gradually recedes, a coat of red dirt is revealed on the once-shiny body of the Mustang. With Sydney far behind us now, the road in front of me ascends and the Mustang's tires knuckle down on the dust-covered surface. A line of low hills—red dirt with sparse green cover—is the only thing to differentiate this land from the desert I see through the windshield.

Regardless of the circumstances, I'm looking forward to seeing Jim, even if I have to steel myself for the barbs he will surely throw at me about my becoming a professor. My hands tap a quiet rhythm on the steering wheel, an anticipation of sorts. The last time we spoke face-to-face was at Will's funeral and, while he fared better than I, even working for a few years after the tragedy, I don't think he completely lost the haunted feeling when in the field. I hope retirement has been better for him. When I called and told him I was in the country, his pleasure couldn't have been more genuine. Espy and I could stay with him and the lovely Meredith for a month and not be made to feel as if we were intruding.

The Mustang crests the top of the hill, and Laverton opens up before us, the whole of the town bordered by gradual rises that highlight the vastness of the surrounding desert, as well as offer a buffer.

Espy stirs. She does a half stretch, which one must do in a cramped car, then opens her eyes. It takes her a little while to absorb the scene outside the car. I can tell the second she's fully awake, because I see her grimace. Not that I blame her. A vista of sand, sky, barren hills, and a city so exposed to the elements must appear strange to someone used to jungle and urban areas, even if Espy is more traveled than most.

"Have we died and gone to hell?" she asks.

"Once you taste Meredith's cooking, you'll think we're in heaven."

It's the wrong thing to say; my stomach has been growling for the last two hours. I press down on the gas pedal, moving the dirty red car onward and hoping that Meredith has made her coffee cake.

While the house is old, an original of its period, the large pond it overlooks is all Jim's doing. My friend has always loved water, and although an affinity for the town and its people caused him to make his home here in the dry plains, he brought the water with him. I don't know how much it cost him to dig out seven acres of dirt and rock to a depth of ten feet, then fill the area with water, but it must have been an astronomical sum. His father was a steel baron in Britain, and Jim netted a grand inheritance when the man passed. Still, what he's accomplished here seems beyond the means of someone who has never appeared to have a lot of money.

What impresses me more, though, is that he built the wraparound porch by himself, along with the chairs on which we're seated.

The cigar in my hand has burned down an inch and a half, and its smoke, combined with the sweeter scent of Jim's pipe, is a simple pleasure enhanced by the setting.

My eyes are on the small motorboat tied off at the dock, gentle waves giving the vessel a light bobbing against the taut line. It's the same boat we took out to the center of the pond the last time I was here, when I'd failed to catch anything, even though the water was seeded with trout, which have bred to copious amounts within their liquid enclosure.

"I could get used to this."

Jim chuckles and says, "I don't think so."

I look over at him, and his eyes are focused on some spot far beyond the pond. "Why?"

He taps his pipe in the palm of his hand. "While you've always had a bit of the hermit in you, this sort of solitude would drive you crazy."

Jim has aged well, if such a thing can be said about the violating process of adding years at the expense of robustness. He is still slim but he's also softer, which, I suppose, comes from the fact that he has a house, and a wife, and nothing left to prove in his field. And the solidness of his work, his research, means that he doesn't have much left to defend.

"Maybe. But right now I can't think of anywhere I'd rather be."

"I would guess you said the same thing about Brazil, and Ecuador, and Burkina Faso, and Nizhniy Novgorod." He leaves out Egypt. "It's about the work, my boy. The setting is incidental."

I don't give him an answer because I'm not sure what to think of his assertion. The last five years would certainly seem to belie it but, considered through the filter of recent events, it sounds like a plausible hypothesis. I'm supposed to be back at Evanston soon, and I can't remember a time when a place seemed like such a distant idea. Except, of course, for my cactus, which I can see in my mind's eye withering on the windowsill beneath the winter sun.

Through the screen door I can hear Meredith and Esperanza moving about the kitchen. But except for a muffled word or two, their conversation remains their own. I'm not at all surprised they are getting on well. They're cut from different parts of the same cloth.

"She's a lovely woman," Jim says.

The old professor remains sharp, his intuitive skill bordering on the eerie.

"I know," I say.

He turns silent for a few seconds and then gives a small *harrumph* before taking a puff from his pipe. From somewhere out over the pond I hear a single bird call.

"You should have married her," he says.

I have no answer, except to suspect that he's probably right. He must sense that I'm not going to be baited, as if I were a grad student again and arguing some finer point of archaeological theory. He removes the pipe from his mouth and fixes warm and wise eyes on me.

"Are you going to tell me what you want?" When I don't respond right away, he adds, "I know you didn't come to the other side of the world just to sit on my porch."

"Technically, I was already on the other side of the world. So it was only a matter of a few hundred miles."

He shakes his head. "You were always saying something smart like that, as I recall. All right, have it your way. What is it that brings you a few hundred miles to here, Australia's premier vacationland?"

There's something inside me that doesn't care to broach the subject. I'm more at peace right now than I can remember feeling for quite some time, and forcing the conversation to the events of the last couple of weeks can only serve to dampen the mood. I let go a sigh that's louder than I intended, but Jim says nothing. He knows I'll tell him when I'm ready.

And I do. It's like some Jack Kerouac stream of consciousness that has me divulging everything that's happened since I took this job: the exhilarating finds, the mounting bodies, the flights from one continent to another. Through it all, Jim listens, and I'm not looking at him to gauge his reaction, even though the portion connecting my present circumstances with the events at KV65 must have hit him hard. My eyes stay on the calm water. I'm not sure how long I speak, or if my story makes any sense. Yet it doesn't really matter because it's another much-needed catharsis. If the trip out here proves to be nothing more than a visit to a comfortable confessional, it will have been worth it, even accepting the fact that I'm not Catholic.

After I've finished, when I've reached empty, Jim is quiet. I look over at him and see him mulling over everything I've said. The afternoon is beginning to cross into early evening, not noticeable so much by any change in the light as by a certain feel in the air.

"Do you believe the bones are real?"

"I don't know."

"It's an important detail. Whether you're a skeptic or a believer speaks volumes about where you go from here."

"You mean whether to continue the search or go home?"

"In a nutshell." He takes a long, thoughtful draw on his pipe. A moment later he pulls it away from his mouth and releases a cloud of gray smoke, then points the pipe at me. "If you don't believe the bones exist, then you're putting your own life—not to mention the lives of your loved ones—in jeopardy for no reason. If, on the other hand, you firmly believe they exist, and that they possess the power that Reese and the biblical record claim, then you're making a conscious decision to value this magnificent artifact above your own well-being."

I'm bothered by my friend's nutshell, because I'm not sure the Occam's razor principle works here. It's not an either/or, a belief or a rejection of belief. There's room for something else. Manheim's actions—and Reese's to a lesser extent—have woven me into the fabric of the unfinished narrative. I'm still here to dig into what was behind Will's death, and I want to see Manheim pay for what he did. For now, I can tell myself that the bones are incidental.

"What about Will?" I ask.

A cloud drops over Jim, and it's not something I'm happy about. I don't know what Jim has carried with him over the last five years, or what he's feeling now that I've told him what I know. He is quiet for a long time, until I'm not sure he's going to answer. But then his face gives way to a sad smile and he says, "I'm sorry I didn't do more to find out what happened to Will."

I start to protest but he waves me silent.

"I knew that what happened was no accident. Everyone knew it."

I'm gathered up in that sentence. I've always known, yet I ran away.

"I should have pressed for an investigation," Jim says. "Instead, I packed up and went home. And I let you do the same."

There's nothing I can say in response to this candid admission, except to be grateful that he's made the gesture. Sitting in silence with him is my forgiveness.

I ponder his words while whatever passes for the Australian equivalent of an erne makes a dive toward the still water. There is the barest hint of a splash before the bird beats its wings furiously to rise back up into the air. I think its talons are empty, although I can't be sure.

"Dinner's ready," Meredith calls from the doorway.

I grind my cigar in the ashtray balanced on the arm of the chair until the glowing tip dies and then I slip it into my breast pocket. As Jim gets up and starts for the door, I gesture that I'll follow in a minute. Once the door swings shut behind him, I pull out my phone and, after a brief hesitation, dial the one number I haven't wanted to call.

"Jack."

"Hello, Mr. Reese."

Neither of us speaks for a time and I imagine it's because we both know how much water has passed under the bridge.

He's the first to break the silence.

"Do you believe in them, Jack?"

I sigh, my eyes searching the sky. Finally I say, "Hardy's dead, Gordon."

"I know that."

"I didn't kill him."

Any answer he might give is forestalled by a coughing fit. It's a bad episode; I can hear the man gasping for breath. I am unmoved. We're all dying. A full minute, maybe two, goes by before he can talk. When he does, he says the only thing that can shake me.

"She's nine, you know. My granddaughter. Her name's Sophie."

I say nothing.

"She'll be dead soon. Unless—"

"I would have given them to you, Gordon. But then you tried to have me killed."

I end the call there, not moving for a long time. At some point I hear someone come to the screen door, but whoever it is leaves without saying anything.

———

Jim leans back in his seat, his hand resting on his belly as if he would undo his belt.

"I don't eat that well unless there's company," he says.

"Then I'm glad I could help."

"Don't believe him, Jack," Meredith laughs. "A waistline like Jim's doesn't happen based on the few people who come to visit us."

Meredith Winfield is a woman with whom I will always be partially in love, and I don't feel at all guilty about it. Even now, when gray has claimed most of her hair color, when wrinkles have found purchase beneath her eyes and along her forehead, she is one of the most striking women I've ever met. She has the type of beauty that's independent of age—a conglomeration of perfect attributes. She holds doctorates in both philosophy and political science, has a razor-sharp wit, infinite patience, and a pair of eyes that tunnel into infinity. Like Homer's Helen, Meredith's eyes could launch a fleet of vessels helmed by desperate men.

Jim scowls at his wife, who smiles back at him as she begins removing the dirty plates from the table. Espy rises to help. Reaching for his pipe with a mottled hand, Jim locates the matches in his shirt pocket with the other and relights its contents. I think about doing the same with my half-spent cigar but let the inclination pass.

"What are you going to do?" Jim asks.

"I'm not sure." I shrug. "Allow entropy to run its course?"

He doesn't reply but instead puffs away at the pipe until a haze forms above him and spreads through the dining room. There's no eye contact. His are focused on some point between here and God, and mine are on the grease spots that stain the tan tablecloth. Without a word, he rights his chair and stands and, with the look of the professor—the look that used to send his students scurrying—he beckons me to follow.

Cutting through the living room, we enter Jim's office, or rather library, where he heads for his computer. He takes hold of the mouse, moves and clicks, and a search engine pops up. He steps back and gestures toward the machine.

"Know your enemy," he says.

It takes a while before I realize what he's talking about, but when understanding strikes, it all makes perfect sense. Jim knows I'm going to keep pursuing this, that there will be another meeting with Victor Manheim. So it makes sense that I learn all I can about the man.

Grinning, I take a seat and get to work. I begin by searching through a large volume of query results using a wide array of keywords. Before I know it, an hour has passed. At some point Espy joins me. Together we go from site to site, document to document, looking for anything that would explain Manheim's involvement. Birth and death records, newspaper articles, press releases, business acquisitions—his is an impressive, influential family. What I'm not finding, though, is anything I can use against him.

When my eyes start to hurt, I take a break, and Esperanza slides into the driver's seat. It's as I start to walk away to peruse Jim's library, to relax a little, that Espy switches to an image search rather than the standard text. The first page that pops up features a bevy of people I've seen when digging through other sites. Victor has many entries; his mug has far too much presence in the cyber world. But he's in politics, so that is no surprise. Espy clicks to the next page. The images generate, hang there for seconds, and Espy is about to move on when something clicks in my brain and I tell her to stop.

I'm not sure how long I stare at it before the thing comes into focus, but it's like a shot to my nerves when I realize the meaning. My throat tightens until all I can utter are strangled noises.

It's there, right in front of me. A symbol I've carried with me for years, rubbed and photographed from the Quetzl-Quezo wall half a world away—the last in a line of strange glyphs that have defied translation. It's the Manheim family crest.

———

My eyes hurt. I blink several times in an attempt to lubricate them but can't seem to produce any moisture. I think this is nature's way of forcing sleep on someone too self-absorbed to understand what the body requires. Ever obstinate, I use both hands to massage my eyeballs, probably harder than I need to, and I convince myself they feel fresher, more alert as a result.

Esperanza is still in charge of the mouse, clicking on images, pausing for only a second or two, then flashing through several more without so much as a blink. After the shock of discovering the first symbol, an idea formed, and Espy and I have spent much of the evening following up on that idea. I feel guilty for involving myself in something like this when I've only just arrived, but our hosts seem to understand our need to see things through. Meredith has been in once with coffee.

"Can you slow down a bit?" I say.

"Even at this speed, it will take us two days to get through all these hits. Suck it up and deal with it."

Search engines are remarkable tools, but they have one main flaw: there's no way a user can know the exact combination and sequence of words that will produce the desired result. Usually the search terms are too narrow, so one is forced to generalize the criteria in successive attempts until, suddenly, there are a million hits through which to sift. There's no happy middle ground, no matter how smart they make the application.

We're at the million-possibilities stage, which means that even if my fledgling theory proves correct, it's like looking for digital needles in an information haystack. I'm about to tell Esperanza to keep at it while I go stretch my legs when an image flashes on the screen, then disappears, and although I didn't see it clearly . . .

"Wait, go back."

She stops, shifts the mouse, and clicks.

It's a color photo of a wall-mounted shield. On it is a picture of a thin-faced brown bear sitting on its haunches, holding a scale in one paw. Beneath it are three short lines, almost like a stunted paw swipe. The first thing to strike me is the fact that I'm seeing it in color. I don't have to guess what was in the mind of the artist who carved it into a limestone wall in the jungles of Venezuela. It's the most beautiful, oddly shaped bear I've ever seen.

Below the photo is a short description: *DiPastina Coat of Arms, Verona, circa* A.D. *1876.*

Espy takes her eyes off the screen, turns, and looks at me. She doesn't have to ask; she can see it on my face.

"All of them are crests, aren't they?"

"I'd bet everything I own on it."

Before Espy and I call a halt to our online search, and after we research the DiPastina clan back to the third century, we have another visit with good fortune when we're able to match a third Quetzl-Quezo carving to a line of Frank nobility from the seventh century. It's with the discovery of this third one that the appearance of an identical icon in each of the crests—the oblong disc with the *S* squiggle—earns avid interest. On the walls of Quetzl-Quezo, the symbol was an oddity. Incorporated into more than a dozen family crests stretching back more than a thousand years, the symbol is worth a great deal more study.

Espy studies the screen. She sees it, too.

"How big is this thing?" she finally asks.

"Much bigger than us."

Chapter 19

My eyelids fly open, and the first thing I realize is that apprehension fills my stomach like a solid ball of undigested cheese. It's always a bit unnerving to wake in a strange place, even for an experienced traveler. There's that moment between sleep and wakefulness—when one's unconscious mind is feeding stimuli rapid-fire to the part of you fighting off cobwebs, when everything takes on added poignancy. Usually it's that the bed is different and the mattress doesn't cooperate in the way one is used to, or there's an odd smell coming from somewhere in the room, or someone else's cat is watching from the foot of the bed. It's one of the brain's remarkable defense mechanisms.

Right now the absolute darkness of a rural night without moon or stars greets me, along with the feeling that something is amiss. Much of my professional life has seen me catching short, unsatisfying naps in foreign and uncomfortable places: in a Bedouin tent, or sharing a campfire with Cree tribesmen, or wedged between two large men in a Chevy El Camino while a surprise snowstorm blankets the Chechen Mountains. So it's possible that my senses are a bit more focused than those of people used to the same bed in a familiar room. I lie still for a while but don't hear anything beyond the noise of the wind running alongside the house. The clock on the nightstand shows 1:29 A.M. in large red numbers. I take a few deep breaths in an effort to slow my heart rate, which is engaged in a befuddled fight-or-flight response.

I consider trying to fall back to sleep, yet I know myself well enough to realize that, warranted or not, I've been startled from a dreamless slumber and will end up tossing and turning for some time. When insomnia strikes me back home, I spend an hour or two with a drink and a book until I feel my bed calling me back. I guess it's fortunate, then, that Jim has both a well-stocked liquor cabinet and a library.

Jim's library is larger than mine but small compared to those of many academics. It takes an exceptional book to wind up in his collection. His tastes mirror mine, and as I peruse the book titles, I find myself becoming jealous. My fingers pass over the leather bindings of valuable first editions from renowned poets and essayists, storytellers and historians.

His liquor cabinet is stocked with equal care, holding a mix of imported and domestic spirits. I select an aged bourbon with a Melbourne imprint. Filling a tumbler with the dark liquid, I take a sip and allow the burn to coast down my throat.

Another bookcase stands to the right of the liquor cabinet and I give the nestled tomes a once-over, looking to find something that will both earn my interest and propel me back to drowsiness. As I scan the shelves, I almost miss it. With a smile I pull the book from its shelf and turn it to see the front cover. *Story as a Conveyance of Culture in Mezzo-America.* I almost laugh, because I'm torn between competing thoughts. The first is that I'm honored that my favorite professor has included my work in his collection. The second is to recall that the book isn't very good, nor does it deserve a place here among such prestigious company.

I flip the book over to see the back cover and the head shot.

It's not a flattering photo. I shake my head and slide it back into its slot on the shelf. Next, I select a book about the Industrial Revolution and then settle into a comfortable chair by the inactive fireplace. I'm three sips and two pages into the book when I hear a sound—a single thud, muffled by distance and the closed library door. I lower the book and listen; the house has settled again into silence. Had I not woken up edgy, I might let the mystery pass by without rising from my chair, but the feeling I had earlier has now returned.

I set the book and the drink down on the carpet, stand up and cross to the door. I'm about to open it when I decide to flip off the light, plunging the library into darkness. I crack the door enough so I can see out, through the living room and into the hall beyond. It takes a moment for my eyes to adjust, but it's not long before I can make out shapes, indistinct and gray. Beyond that, all I register is silence.

Then, before I can take another step, I hear sounds that seem to come from somewhere near the kitchen—a rapid succession of muffled pops. At some point I hear another thud, then the pops taper off, and then nothing.

I start forward, toward the sounds. I don't know why except that to head into something—even unprepared as I am—is better than waiting and letting that thing come to me when I'm in my nightclothes. I quickly tiptoe through the living room and peek around a corner, just in time to see a man emerging from the master bedroom—only he's moving with the stealth and strength of someone much younger than Jim. I fight the impulse to jerk my head back, knowing the darkness is my friend but that I have a better chance of remaining unobserved if I hold still.

A sick feeling washes over me as I watch this person pause

and, apparently, get his bearings. I can only imagine what he's left in the room behind him. I hope that I'm wrong.

The intruder turns and I see his silhouette in profile, the gun in his hand. It's not until he starts for the stairs, toward Esperanza, that I feel a white-hot anger building inside me.

Then it hits me: I don't have a weapon. All I have is the element of surprise.

So I launch myself from around the corner, intent on tackling this person and wresting away the gun, but I haven't counted on the combination of hardwood floor and bare feet. My right foot slides forward on the floor and I feel my knee give, bending in a way for which it was never designed. Sensations of heat and tearing race through my leg, and for a terrifying second I can't see anything. But the immediacy of the pain recedes and I recover just as the man turns toward me. Mustering the remains of my balance and my anger, I lunge at him, reaching for his gun hand.

He gets off a single shot, muffled by a silencer, before I'm on him. I start beating his face with my closed fist while my other hand fights to keep the gun pointed away. I'm not sure how it happens but I'm suddenly on my back and he has my forearm in a solid grip. He brings the gun around as my free arm flails to grab hold of it. I still can't see his face—just a dark spot hanging a foot away. It's like fighting Death, with his obscuring robe and terrible sickle.

I bring my knee up into his midsection, causing him to break his grip. I pull back and aim a punch that connects with a jaw that feels like iron. The gun's muzzle emits a flash and I smell sulfur, and it takes me a moment to realize that the fact that I'm registering the smell means the bullet missed its mark. I lash out again and twist away, and I hear the sound of something hard striking the floor.

I'm looking for the gun before I've stopped rolling, and it can only be providence that has me land on top of it. I push myself to my knees and scoop it up. I have half a second to find the trigger and pull it before his shoulder hits me in the chest. There's a flash of energy and of unrestrained power, forcing my arm back so that my elbow strikes the floor.

And then I'm beneath two hundred pounds of dead weight.

I don't fully process that he's dead until I have the chance to breathe again. As I lie there, drawing large draughts of air, I realize that life has left him and that what's ended up on top of me is a husk. A very heavy husk. I struggle to push him aside, pressing the handle of the gun into his armpit and placing my other hand on his sternum to shift him enough so I can squirm free. I push myself up to a sitting position. As my eyes cross up and down the length of the body, I feel a numbness come over me. I've never killed anyone before, and my mind, while still in an agitated state, is grappling with the finality of what I've just done.

I stand and it's only then that I notice the large wet spot on my shirt, soaked through to my skin. Even without being able to see it, I know it's his blood on me and not my own. I have to fight the urge to vomit. Forcing myself to stay calm, I start toward the dead man, setting the gun down and rolling him over. In the darkness I can see little of his face, except to determine that he was young. I lean in closer—close enough that when he opens his eyes it's like a scene from a horror movie. I jerk back, a strangled yelp escaping my throat, and it is this distance I've put between us that allows him to reach his hand into his jacket pocket. Before I can stop him, he pulls out something the size and shape of a cell phone, and is pushing a button before I can grab his wrist. It's over almost before it begins, as his arm goes limp and the phone drops to the floor. My eyes dart to his face, and I see a thin line of blood trickling from his mouth, but I don't release the hand until I feel his neck for a pulse and find none.

After catching my breath, I scoop up the phone. I'm worried that he was trying to signal someone, because my guess is that this was no random event. It was too professional. The thing in my hand, though, isn't a phone but looks more like a pager. Yet if it has a display, it's too dark for me to see it. All that's evident is a single button on one end, which glows green. With a shrug, I set the thing on the floor and then start running my hands over the dead man's clothes. There's nothing on him that yields a clue as to his identity. This tells me he's neither a petty thief nor someone with a grudge. The professional theory looks stronger.

It's that last thought that forces me to move. If this is an operative, he might not be alone. I quickly retrieve the gun and stand on two shaky legs.

I almost resist the necessity of turning on the light in the master bedroom, but my eyes still cannot make out anything beyond a few feet. I shift the gun to my other hand and feel along the wall.

There are moments one wishes he could have back, and touching the light switch will forever be one of mine. After the light's brilliance forces my irises to snap shut and then reopen, I see Meredith caught in a grotesque pose between the bed and floor. Her nightgown is riddled with small, red-rimmed holes, and lines of blood have traced their way to the floor. And I see Jim lying in the bathroom doorway. His body has come to rest facing the opposite direction so that my eyes focus on his thinning white hair. A line of holes has splintered the wood along the wall and punctured the doorjamb.

I think time becomes something else in situations like this. It can either speed up, with everything seeming to occur in rapid-fire, or it can slow down to something approximating the dripping of a faucet. It's the latter that I find myself trudging through as I cross the room and go to Jim's side, where I kneel and put my hand on his shoulder. I turn him around and settle his head gently on the floor.

In the single moment I spare myself, I ponder a list of things with which I could regale an audience at his funeral, and yet it's enough for me that he was a mentor and a friend. I smooth a piece of his hair and then push myself to my feet, and go to move Meredith's body so it's fully on the bed. With the gun clenched in my hand, I exit the room as if the hallway can offer some salvation from what I've witnessed, except that there's another body out here. A flash of anger makes me want to kick the dead man for what he's done, but I resist the impulse.

My only thought is Espy, and I'm about to head up the stairs when, from my peripheral vision, I see a red luminance coming from the direction of the front door. It's like the blinking of an alarm clock after a power outage, only I remember no clock in that part of the house. The curious side of me wages war with the part that wants to rush upstairs, wake up Espy and get her to the Mustang, but the blinking light wins out.

I pad down the hallway, giving the dead man as wide a berth as I can, and pass the living room before flattening myself against the wall and peering around the doorjamb. On the ceramic tile, near the shoes that form a neat row against the wall, is an object the size of a toaster—the large sort that can handle eight slices of bread. I see most of it in shadow, except for the rectangular display that's flashing a series of numbers in a lazy pattern, which alternately casts an eerie glow in the small space and then snatches the meager light away. I step closer to the thing until I can see the display more clearly. It flashes 1:39 . . . 1:38 . . . 1:37 . . .

I can't remember moving but I'm suddenly at the foot of the stairs, my free hand on the rail propelling me upward. I now understand the purpose of the device thumbed by the dead assassin. Frantic, I fumble with the doorknob to Espy's room, then strike the door with my shoulder and it gives way with a loud crack. I'm at her side as she bolts upright.

"Get up!" I order, pulling hard enough on her arm so that she obeys, even before she sees it's me who is pleading. In my mind I can see the display of the malevolent toaster, and I know it's counting down with a single-mindedness, one that's immune to indecision. I grab her jacket off the chair by the closet as I consider our escape. The front door's no good—not only because we might not make it in time, but also because it might be wired to the bomb. Or it could be that the dead assassin has friends waiting out front. I consider for a second the back porch, but I'm not willing to play chicken with the countdown.

"What's going—"

I halt the question by tossing her the jacket. I hurry to the window and have to set the gun down so I can undo the latch. When I get the window open, the cold air rushes in. The ground is maybe fifteen feet below, and I see there are no handholds, no drainpipes, nothing but a free fall to the ground below.

I take hold of Espy's arm and pull her toward the window. Maybe it's the fact that she's still sleepy, or because I'm sending out a definite life-or-death vibe, but she lets herself be walked forward. Until she reaches the window. As her part becomes clear, she pulls back.

"Jack! What's happening?" she demands.

"You have to trust me! Please, I don't have time to explain."

The urgency in my voice causes her to reply with a grim nod. She moves to the window, tosses her jacket to the ground below, and places both legs over the ledge until she's sitting on the sill. She then flips over onto her stomach and shimmies down until her hands are all I can see. There's the briefest of hesitations before she lets go and drops out of sight.

The cold bites into me as I follow, the thin fabric of my borrowed pajamas no match for the elements. Like Espy but with less grace, I shift into a similar position on my stomach and then lower myself so I'm supported solely by my hands on the windowsill. Because I'm holding the gun in my hand, the maneuver is a bit more precarious. In my mind I can see the bomb's timer approaching the critical moment, and it is this, plus the fact that the fingers of my right hand are being crushed between the sill and the gun, that lets me release my grip.

I come down hard on a shrub, and my injured knee screams in pain. Ignoring it, I quickly look around in the dark until I see Espy standing a few feet away, shivering as she slips into her jacket. I stumble out of the landscaping. At this point, the darkness is both friend and foe, and I hold the gun in front of me with the certainty that I'll use it if I have to, that what I've seen this night has ripped civility from me like an old bandage.

I grab Espy's hand and, heedless of direction, start to run. My bare feet kick up the wetness of the grass, but by now I hardly feel the sensation. In fact, I don't feel much of anything on a physical level. Adrenaline has done its work, creating an insulating capsule of survival.

It seems as if we've traveled only a few yards before a concussive blast of sound and light lifts me from the ground and sends me hurtling into the darkness. And I find that I have only one thought during my flight, and it's that I can no longer feel Esperanza's hand in my own.

Chapter 20

I was sitting in the stands at Fenway Park, Section 86, right field, when suddenly the ball hit me in the temple. I was taking a bite from my chili dog, distracted, when I heard the crack of the bat like a gunshot. By the time I looked up, the ball was close enough that I could see each individual stitch. Now I'm facedown on the concrete, and people step over me as they head for the bathroom, or a concession stand, or back to their seats laden with nachos, dogs, and beer. A few of the careless ones slosh their cups as they step over my prone form, and beer drips down on my face. I hear the crowd roar as the batter crosses home plate. The Sox win . . .

I force my eyes open, blinking until I can see past the bright lights that dance over my retinas, the scent of ballpark hot dogs lingering. A sharp pain runs the length of my skull as I lift my head. I run a searching hand over the focal point of the pain and my fingers come away wet. With a groan, I roll onto my side and force myself up to something resembling a sitting position. A light rain has started, and it falls like a cold mist between the tree line and me. Somewhere on the tip of one of my brain's lobes—the one responsible for handling the fulfillment of immediate needs—is a sense that I should be concerned, that I'm in a situation where urgency is required, and this doesn't look at all like Fenway.

From behind, I hear a soft moan. And when I turn and find Esperanza lying next to me like a discarded rag doll, the cobwebs vanish. Instantly I remember where I am, and I see the leveled structure in my periphery as I rush to help Espy. The residual smell of hot dogs gives way to that of charred wood as flames engulf the ruins.

I put my hand on Espy's shoulder and give her as thorough an exam as one can give in the light provided by a structural fire, and in the rain, and when the other person's lying facedown and wearing a jacket. There are no obvious broken bones, but I have no way of knowing about internal injuries.

"Esperanza, you have to get up." I give her shoulder a little shake and feel her stir.

After another groan, she pushes herself off the ground on unsteady arms. I slip next to her and let her lean on me, brushing the dark hair from her face. Her eyes are clear, if rimmed by pain, and I can't see anything to indicate a concussion.

"Can you move?"

"If I have to."

"You have to."

While steadying her, I remember the gun. When she can stand upright without my help, I go back to where the blast threw me and start to feel in the grass, making an expanding circle from that spot until I find it nearly ten meters away. I hesitate for only a second before picking it up and, in a crouching run, returning to Espy. Our escape took us out a window on the side of the house away from the front entrance, and though it would seem we're alone here, I can't assume anything. While the explosion gutted the house, it remains an obstacle that's keeping me from seeing the driveway. Another thing I can't gauge is how long we were unconscious. My gut tells me I was out for less than a minute, but I have no way to know for certain.

I take Esperanza's hand and, in a move that catches my companion by surprise, start toward the fire. She tugs at me, but I strengthen my grip and pull her along. I take us as close to the burning house as I can, stopping just before the heat causes pain.

"What are you doing?" Espy asks.

With the hand holding the gun, I motion to the empty expanse surrounding us. "Look. We're in the middle of nowhere. The nearest neighbor is four miles away, and Laverton is almost ten. Neither of us have shoes. I don't have a coat. We'll either freeze to death or one of us will get bit by a snake before we can get help."

That seems to satisfy her. I begin walking toward the right because the fire seems less intense there. When I reach the corner—or what would have been a corner if the bomb hadn't done its job—I peek around.

"What—"

I cut Espy off with a quick squeeze of her hand. Three vehicles are parked in the driveway. Jim's Dakota lies under a coat of rubble, broken two-by-fours and roof shingles, and the windshield has a long crack on the driver's side. It's probably drivable. Which is more than I can say about the Mustang. Being nearer to the house, the car took more of the brunt of the explosion. The windows are gone and the interior is ablaze. But it's the third vehicle that grabs my attention. It's a high-end SUV, although I can't determine the make and model from where I am. The passenger door is open and a solitary figure in dark clothing stands next to it. He's watching the house and, if I can make some sense out of the expression on his face, I'd say he looks worried, indecisive. And no wonder; his buddy was supposed to be out of the house before it went up.

Despite the heat from the fire, I'm shivering in my wet pajamas, and my feet are hurting. Too, my knee throbs with some urgency, a warning that it will not put up with much more. I'm trying to think through my options, and the ugly truth seems to be that I have no enviable choices, only a slew of mystery doors to open, and the knowledge that behind each lurks something dangerous. The trick is in figuring out which risk is the most manageable.

"Stay here," I say, then release Espy's hand and take a step before she tries to stop me.

"What are you going to do?"

Rather than give her an answer, I gesture for her to remain where she is and walk out into plain view of the man by the SUV, the gun held tight in my hand. I move fast, closing half the distance before he realizes I'm there. When I see him begin to reach for something, I point the gun upward and fire a shot.

"Don't do it!" I shout, still striding toward him. The rain's coming down harder now, plastering my hair to my head and stinging the raw spot on my temple. The man hesitates, possibly because I must look like something out of a horror film. When his hand makes a sudden move, I shout again and pull the trigger.

His hand comes up just as he's hit. The force of the impact staggers him. For a moment that might seem comical were it not for the terrified look on his face as he glances down at the small hole in his chest. He reaches up and touches the place with his finger. He raises his eyes, looking at me. Bile rises up in my throat before the man falls to the ground. I'm retching before I can even be sure he's dead. It sickens me how easy it is to kill someone.

Once my stomach is empty, I call for Esperanza and head for the SUV where, for the second time in ten minutes, I go through the pockets of a dead man. Like the other, this one is carrying nothing of any value. But as I do a quick search of the SUV, I see one shiny piece of good fortune in the ignition.

Just seconds later, Espy joins me. Her expression as she takes in the scene is hard to watch, especially when her eyes come to rest on the gun that I hold with an ease born of necessity, and of years of hunting with larger guns with my father.

"Let's go," I say, sliding behind the wheel of the SUV. I fire the engine as she, after one final look at the dead man, climbs in and shuts her door. She's silent while I turn us around and start down the driveway, headlights kept off, our way guided only by the dim yellow of the running lights.

It's a Lexus. The odometer reads 234 kilometers. It's 220 from here to Melbourne, which means it's a rental, probably paid for with a pilfered credit card. Nestled in the dash is a satellite navigation system. On it are a few thin road markers and a single large dot in the center of the screen, the word *destination* along the bottom edge, and an address. Jim's house. The sick feeling returns as I become fully aware of the terrible fact that Jim and Meredith are dead because of me—because I showed up on their doorstep.

I guide the truck along the narrow driveway until we reach the main road. There I hesitate as I consider our options. Laverton is to the east, and there's a whole lot of nothing for a considerable distance to the west. I glance at the gas gauge and am relieved to see that it's nearly full. The engine sounds loud as we idle, but that has to be normal, considering the precision engineering that went into the vehicle.

I look over at Espy. She's watching out the passenger window, and she's much quieter than I'm comfortable with. I'm not sure what to make of it, and I find myself wishing for the more combative Espy to resurface. Her silence speaks volumes about the gravity of our circumstances. She must sense that I'm watching her, or maybe she just wonders why we're not moving, because she turns from the window and meets my gaze.

"You're bleeding," she says.

"I *was* bleeding. Now I think I'm clotting."

That earns a small, tired smile. She leans closer to examine my head, frowns, and raises a hand toward me but then draws back.

"You have a small stone in your head," she says.

"What?"

"There's a stone in your head. About the size of a marble."

She casts her eyes around the truck, taking in the dash and console and the seat behind us. She pops open the glove box and, atop a slim plastic folder that probably holds information from the rental agency, she spies a box of tissue.

"Hold still," she says as she pulls several tissues from the box. In the dim light she studies my head and begins moving the hair away from the wound. I exercise every adult muscle in my body to hold still, to keep from pulling away and screaming like a three-year-old.

There is a sensation of digging, and soon the ordeal is over and she's holding up something for my viewing pleasure. A jagged stone, covered in my blood. I feel a fresh line of blood running down my face, but quickly Espy applies a tissue to the reopened gash.

"Can you drive and hold this at the same time?"

"I think so," I say, then slip my hand over hers and she pulls away.

I give the Lexus some gas and use my free hand to crank the wheel, sending us toward Laverton. We'd accomplish nothing by heading in the other direction, other than provide distance from the horror of what just happened, and that would be a temporary salve. Jim and Meredith deserve to have the circumstances of their deaths made known.

Espy lapses into silence again. I pick up speed, and a small white sign indicating that Laverton is ahead comes into view.

"What now?" she asks.

"We have to tell someone what happened."

She nods, still focused on the passing terrain out the passenger window.

"Then what?"

"I don't know."

"I'm getting tired of hearing you say that."

"Do you want me to lie?"

"I want you to decide how far you're going to take this." She turns away from the window and I catch enough of the look in her eyes to understand that what she's saying is not coming from some emotional well. There's a calmness to her features that gives added weight to the words. "Six people are dead." She pauses. "Make that seven, with the one you killed. Jack, you're carrying a gun."

"Eight."

"What?"

"I've killed two people tonight, so that makes it eight. Just so you know."

"Eight. And for what? You're not even sure you believe in this thing we're chasing."

"That stopped being the point days ago."

"So what is the point?" Her eyes flash with the spark that's been missing for a while, and I mentally kick myself for wishing its return.

I'm not sure how to respond because it bothers me to think that the only honest answer is that there is no point. Beyond stubbornness, or spite, or the simple fact that I've become wrapped up in something that's carrying me along despite myself. I can't tell her those things. I'm saved from having to say anything when an insistent crackling cuts through the silence, followed by a voice.

"Status check."

Esperanza and I exchange glances and then she's bent over and rooting around the floorboard. When she straightens, she holds a radio. It's a short- to moderate-range model, with a green indicator light signaling its readiness.

"Status check two."

I'm not sure how to respond so, in this case, inaction seems to be the best option. We wait for the person on the other end to say something else but the seconds stretch into a minute.

"Now they know that something's wrong," Espy says.

"Which means they'll either disappear or go to the house to see what's happened."

"Unless they have a Plan B."

I have a feeling that there is, indeed, a Plan B. And we can't wait around to find out what it is. I press down on the accelerator and send the Lexus flying down the road until I see the outskirts of the town. The dashboard clock reads 2:13 A.M. The streets, like the people who would travel them, are asleep. I have no way of knowing how many of them there are, but it seems logical they would have some sort of presence here—a place to regroup. It means we have to be quick.

Years have passed since I was last here and everything is new to me. Once we get closer to the center of town, I start to look for something open—a restaurant, a store, a gas station. But every establishment looks buttoned down. For a town with a reputation of having been the Tombstone of Australia—the quintessential Wild West town—it seems oddly tame. And the ominously silent radio serves notice that at any moment any number of identical vehicles could converge on us. I wonder if they would be able to track us with the GPS?

Running low on choices, I pull up next to a building that looks promising.

"Stay here."

She puts her hand on the door handle. "I'm getting tired of hearing you say that, too." Then she's out the door, standing barefoot on the cold sidewalk.

I get out and walk to the back of the truck and find a tire iron under the rear seat. Then I join Espy on the sidewalk, where she shifts her weight from one foot to the other. Without waiting for her to say anything that might give me pause, I walk up to the large glass window of the storefront and, after peeking in to make sure it has everything I need, smash in the glass. No alarm sounds, and I whisper quiet thanks for small favors. Of course there might be a silent alarm that's been activated at a remote monitoring site. I use the tire iron to clear away the jagged edges, ignoring the fact that I can now officially call myself a burglar. Desperate times.

"Are you coming?" I ask as I stick my leg into the opening. When inside, I sprint to the men's clothing section, where I grab a pair of pants and a shirt that looks to be my general size. Next, I snatch up two packs of socks. Out of the corner of my eye I see movement across the store and spot Esperanza in the women's department. The last thing I take before heading down the shoe aisle is a coat—a thick, heavy one that can withstand an extended stay in the elements. I can barely hold everything now and have to set it all down in order to find some boots. That done, I gather up my bounty and double-time it toward the exit.

Espy's beaten me to the truck and, as I open the door and toss the clothing in, she's already changing into jeans and a sweater. Before I get in, I look up and down the street but don't see anything moving, nor do I hear the telltale sound of sirens converging on us. I shut the door and run back inside the store, and it takes me a minute to find the food section. There's only so much I can carry so I settle for a case of bottled water, a loaf of bread, six cans of soup, and a can opener.

I return to the SUV, load these into the back, and take off, all but burning rubber on the cold asphalt. The gas pedal hurts my bare foot, and I've sliced the leg of my pajamas on the window glass. Espy, on the other hand, looks like a new person in her stolen outfit. She even managed to ensure that everything matches.

"How much do you think all this stuff is worth?" I ask.

"I don't know but these boots were on sale. Marked down to two hundred."

"What a bargain."

"Why do you ask?"

"I guess I'd just like to get an idea of what degree of larceny they'll charge us with when they catch us."

Chapter 21

Calmly, without opening my eyes, I lift my hand from my knee and reach for whatever creature is burrowing between the seat and me, playing the odds that it's not one of the poisonous variety. The problem is that, in Australia, the odds are against me. As my fingers close around the creature and wrest it from its comfy spot, I feel cool, dry skin, and I think *lizard* as a best-case scenario. Which is silly because some species of lizards here are almost as lethal as their legless cousins.

I bring my hand back up in front of me. It's still dark in the truck and my eyelids, heavy with weariness, struggle to open. Two bulbous eyes, much more alert than I imagine mine appear, regard me with unblinking calm from only a few inches away. The yellow lizard's back legs are engaged in a slow-motion flail but find only air. Its tongue flicks out in a test of the environment, gauging its situation, and then it licks its own eyeball. If I needed any help beyond the lizard's coloring, the spiny pouch beneath its jaw tells me it's a Bearded Dragon lizard. Harmless. And it's not a spider. I'll take a venomous reptile over a tarantula any day.

"Looking for a warm spot?"

Even though I know that it's impossible for a lizard to manufacture a plaintive expression, the slight curl of the animal's mouth produces a close facsimile.

The windows of the truck are all shut, and there's no way the creature could have gained entrance via the ventilation system, so it's either the Harry Houdini of lizard-kind, or it gained entry earlier when the doors were opened. With the latter being the most likely case, this boy is a long way from home.

I look past my captive to take in the vista beyond the curved window of the Ford. When we dumped the Lexus in favor of a more nondescript vehicle—F-250, with a busted taillight and a bumper sticker that reads, *Maybe a dingo ate your baby*—we removed any doubt about the sort of larceny that would appear on our rap sheets. It gives me some small pleasure to imagine the moods of the men who will find—or have already found—the luxury SUV.

A hint of red is only now drawing a crayon line in the distance, but it's lightened enough so that I can see the entire desert spreading out in front of me. During the dark early morning hours, when I was driving through it, it was easy to give this place no more thought than I would the plains of Kansas. But the dawn reveals an entirely different animal.

Two hours' sleep doesn't come close to preparing me for the day. I yawn and open the door, and air with a respectable bite rushes into the truck. To my right, Espy stirs. I force my sore legs onto the uneven surface outside and stand—an exercise complicated by the fact that my right leg is numb from where it was pressed up against the console, and that I'm still holding my bunk buddy. I shut the door and then crouch and release the animal. As soon as its feet hit the ground it's gone, scrabbling across the rocky landscape and darting behind a group of large rocks.

My muscles protest as I stand. I slip my hands into my jacket pockets and breathe in a long draught of air laden with microscopic icicles. As it tickles my nose, I consider that the comparison to Kansas was inaccurate. I'm now getting a definite Montana feel. It's certainly remote enough to qualify as Montana, and since my cell phone and wallet are gone I might as well be on a desert island. The logistics of what I need to do—what I concluded as we drove through the darkness like exiles—are daunting under the best of circumstances, let alone cut off from my resources.

I decide to test my knee on the rugged terrain by walking slowly up the slope behind the Ford. The knee feels stiff and I take measured, careful steps. I grimace against the pain, knowing that if I don't work it out now, it'll only get worse, especially as we spend a good portion of our time driving.

By my estimate, it will take most of the day to reach our destination, and that's taking into account having to make our own road in some places. I almost wish we'd kept the Lexus, only because the GPS would plot for us a passable route. Now I'm forced to rely on a paper map and whatever survival skills I've collected during my time in the field, and most of those pale in comparison to those that come naturally to the average Boy Scout. On a positive note, the Ford has two full gas tanks and a good set of tires, and the bed holds plenty of firewood, a tarp, a fishing pole, and a toolbox. With a little luck, we should have enough to keep us healthy and moving forward while we're out here.

Out here is the Great Victoria Desert, via the Gunbarrel Highway. It's one of the most inhospitable places in all of Australia, and a place where only a fool would travel without extensive preparation. It's also something of a tourist draw for those people into bungee jumping over a waterfall, or free-climbing a cliff face, or any other extreme activity that involves taunting death. There's a slim chance we might run into somebody out here, but this part of the country is only now emerging from its dormant period, and the adventurous set won't descend en masse for another few weeks. And few of them will take the path Espy and I need to follow. Most will head north, directly into the MacDonnell Range, past Ayers Rock and through aboriginal lands. It's more than twenty-five hundred miles in which trekkers can test their self-sufficiency. Espy and I will take a circuitous route, crossing over just south of the mountains before heading southeast toward Adelaide, then on to Ballarat. And I doubt that anyone will look for us out there.

I reach the top of the hill where the vantage point affords me a view of the wide-open space between us and the distant mountain range, plateaus giving the red landscape texture. It's beautiful, and my mind starts to traipse down an old, well-trod path. I imagine all the artifacts these mountains might hold. Nothing can compare to the exhilaration I feel when unearthing something that has avoided detection for thousands of years. I have to admit that, regardless of what's happened over the last two weeks—the horrible things I've witnessed, as well as those I've done myself—the rush of discovery is what has kept me on course. More than anything, I want to find these bones—to hold them in my hands, to see if they're worth the price I and others have paid. There might also be something akin to a fledgling belief, although giving that any serious thought makes me uncomfortable and forces me down a path I refuse to travel at this point in my life. Religion, God, the metaphysical—I haven't had much use for these things for a long time, not since KV65. What was it Reese said? *"The power of God does not fade over time."* I grunt. That may be true, but I can still ignore it. And isn't ignored power the same as impotence?

I sigh and turn back toward the truck, my knee feeling somewhat better as I descend. The case of bottled water is in the truck bed, and I cut the plastic holding the bottles together with a pocketknife and then pull one free. I think about the soup but my stomach seems to rebel against the idea. I wish I'd thought to steal something more suitable for breakfast.

The passenger door opens and Espy joins me in the great outdoors. This time she does a full-body stretch and yawn, and I'm amazed at how good she looks after jumping out a window, enduring an explosion, robbing a store, and only getting a few hours of sleep. I must look like death; I certainly feel like it. Hands on hips, she takes in the forbidding view.

"Nice place."

"God's playground."

She walks to the back of the truck, lowers the tailgate and sits, reaching back to grab a bottle of water.

"Care to tell me where we're going? And I'm warning you, if you tell me you don't know, I'll hurt you more than I did back in Caracas."

I wince in remembered pain. Fortunately, I'm not without an answer to her question. The problem is that I'm not sure my response won't bring about the same beating that indecision would.

"We're going to the Manheim estate."

"Excuse me?" Esperanza's eyes darken.

"It's the last place they'd expect us to show up."

"Because they wouldn't think even you would be that idiotic."

"They'd certainly be wrong about that." I understand her feelings because it took a while to convince myself that going to face the beast is the most logical course of action. "We're off the grid right now, and I intend to use it to our advantage. Up to this point, we've been operating under a microscope, and I think it's time for us to do something unexpected."

"Getting ourselves killed would qualify." She almost spits the words. She's on the verge of slipping into Spanish, a good indicator of the level of her anger.

"I don't think so," I say with more confidence than I feel. "If I were Manheim, I would be watching the airports. I'd track all calls to anyone on my cell phone log. He thinks I'm going to try to leave the country. It's the only logical decision he thinks I can make."

"So you're going to act illogically."

"At least it's something I'm good at." The trouble with trying to charm someone who knows you well is that they become immune to it. Espy looks unmoved. "What else is there to do? We can't go to the police. With Manheim's influence, it wouldn't surprise me if you're on Wanted posters all over Australia."

That catches her off guard.

"That's not funny. No one knew we were staying there . . ." The words trail off as she remembers the rental car. "All right, why just me? The car is in your name."

"It'll take them some time because of the fire, but a forensics team will find three bodies. For a while, at least, they'll think that one of them is me. That just leaves the beautiful dark-haired woman who will likely turn up on surveillance cameras at the rental agency, and then they'll get your name from the Qantas manifest."

The curses that fly from her mouth, regardless of her newly touted religious faith, are in her native language, and by the time she's done I'm sweating. She hops down from the tailgate and stalks off, kicking a rock in her path. It careens over the uneven ground, striking the pile of rocks behind which the lizard disappeared.

It's going to be a long drive.

Two hours' worth of ground that can only be called a road by someone with a generous disposition has passed beneath us, with the sun beating down at us through the windshield. And Espy's stewing during the trip has made the truck's cab more confining than I'd like. I've tried the radio a number of times, but we're so far from civilization at this point that every station produces nothing but static.

We've reached a ridgeline—successive plateaus that act as buffers between the desert and the mountains. Foliage dots the rugged landscape, yet the barrenness of the place is only made more evident with the presence of a few scattered bushes and hardy plants. The only wildlife I've seen has been carrion birds, circling high on the dry desert winds. It looks as if they're following us, tracking our progress through an area where things die with regularity. I consider it a bad omen. I look down at the gas gauge. It's just over half full, and it's my only real concern right now, even though there's a second tank waiting in reserve.

"I'd guess it's about three more hours before we cut east below MacDonnell, and it looks like there's a road that runs along the base. And there's a town right before we turn south toward Adelaide, where we can get gas and some supplies."

"With what money?"

"I thought we could trade your boots. They're worth two hundred, right?" The punch that connects with my arm tells me that was the wrong thing to say, and I don't know if it is karma doing its business, or if the birds have jinxed me, but a red light appears on the control panel and I feel the truck lurch with some slip in the engine.

"No, you don't," I mutter as I ease up on the gas. But the Check Engine light stays on, and I smell something sickly sweet. Now I'm the one who's cursing. We cover less than a hundred yards before the truck loses power and I give the steering wheel a single brutal punch. When we stop rolling, the silence is deafening. I refuse to look in Esperanza's direction.

Above us, through the tint on the upper portion of the windshield, I see three birds making lazy circles.

I wake to the sound of Esperanza snoring. It's still dark and the desert air has cooled to the point where I'm uncomfortable. Overhead, the tarp blocks my view of the stars, and I like to think it also discourages the carrion scavengers from making any advances. The fire has burned down so that only a faint glow remains. We used two of the pieces of wood we brought with us, which leaves two more for tonight's fire, provided we need one. And provided we last that long. It was difficult to leave so much wood back at the truck, but there was no way we could carry any more with us, along with the water, the food, the tarp, and a dirty, stained blanket that Espy discovered beneath the passenger seat. She's got most of the blanket wrapped around her, and I make do with the corner she's left me. I'm glad for the coat I picked up during our nighttime shopping spree.

My body is tired but I know that falling back to sleep won't be easy.

There's no way to tell how far we walked after finally giving up on the Ford. I'm guessing that we covered a good fifteen miles, and I'm thankful there was an unusual layer of clouds that persisted for most of the day. And the ground is harder than I'd anticipated; I'll take that over wading through sand any day.

I shift position and Espy stops snoring until I'm still, and then the soft sound starts up again. I'm angry with myself for carrying Esperanza this far into things. If I thought her brother was going to hurt me when we returned from San Cristóbal, I'm doubly concerned about what he might do when we get back this time. I have to cling to that last bit; I refuse to entertain the possibility that we're going to die out here, even though hardier and better-prepared men and women have met just that fate in this wilderness. God's playground. I wonder if that makes me God's plaything? Like an action figure.

As much as I've tried to minimize the obvious connection, this business is like a bully, forcing me to think about things that I'd rather not consider. The problem is that you can't have bones with divine power and withhold the divine element. There's a part of me that hopes Elisha's bones, if they do exist, turn out to be nothing more than dusty relics. It would make things a lot easier; it would allow me to avoid dealing with the list of items I've ignored for a very long time. At least when Duckey pushes my buttons, he placates me with cigars.

I chose to continue on toward the Manheim estate. Going back the way we'd come would have been just as long, and we know what waits for us back there. No, if fate is forcing us to face a grueling march through this hostile place, we might as well try to accomplish something.

The fire pops and there's a momentary flare of light, enough so that I can make out the tarp overhead where we secured it to a nearby boulder. Staring at the glowing embers, I allow myself to drift off.

There's a scene in an old Western—I think it's a Clint Eastwood film—where a man comes crawling out of the desert, drags himself into the nearest saloon, and asks the bartender for whiskey. Women cross to the other side of the road to avoid him, shielding the eyes of their children, and men look upon the pathetic creature with contempt and no small amount of wonder that he's somehow managed to triumph over the elements. I imagine this is close to the response that Espy and I generate as we enter town on the single road that bisects it.

The sign we passed a half mile back when we reconnected with the road—coming down through rocks larger than the truck we abandoned five days ago—read, Kent Station, population 435. From what I can see, through a haze of weariness, we're approaching the town center: several one-story buildings built in straight lines on either side of the sun-bleached road. It really is like something from a movie; I almost expect to find that the structures are façades—that I could walk around them and see the angled beams that prop up the fronts.

Every step I take sends pain shooting up and down my leg and into my hip. But I've been dealing with the pain for the better part of three days, and it's become something I'm able to ignore. Like the blisters on both feet, and the sunburn on my face and neck. None of them carry an urgency rivaling constant thirst. My throat and mouth have had every bit of moisture sucked from them; I can hardly produce saliva anymore.

I stop and swing the gathered blanket from my shoulder

and set it on the ground. From it I pull our last nearly empty bottle of water. I hold it out to Esperanza, who accepts it with a weak eagerness. She takes three measured sips before handing the bottle back, and I down the rest.

Spotting a gas station on the corner, I return the blanket to my shoulder, then reach for Espy's hand, and together we head toward the station. Two cars are parked at the pumps, and a middle-aged man stands near one of them, attending to the tank. He slips his hand under his cap and scratches his head.

"You all right?" he asks.

I try to speak but can't utter anything beyond a croak. Instead, I nod and then push through the store entrance. There are two people inside: a young woman at the cash register, and an older woman buying cigarettes. The conversation between them comes to an immediate stop when they see us. Neither of them says a word as I pull Esperanza through the store, toward the cooler along the far wall. A blast of icy air hits me in the face when I swing open the cooler door. I grab two bottles of apple juice, noticing how weathered my hands have become, and give one to Espy. It's the most wonderful thing I've ever tasted. Deprivation enhances the senses; I had no idea that the flavor of something as basic as apple juice could be so satisfying. By the time I've drained the bottle, I feel immeasurably better, enough to notice the stares directed our way from the vicinity of the cash register.

"What on earth happened to you?" the clerk asks.

My initial response consists of a raspy chuckle—a sound which means to convey that condensing what's happened over the last two weeks so it fits in the span of a short answer is near to impossible. How can I describe even the last five days of walking through much of the night and early morning, huddling beneath the tarp, following the hint of road and hoping for a car in the hazy distance, taking the risk to leave the road and cut a half-day's travel from the journey, watching my companion fall three times in the space of an hour and trying to force warm water past her lips? Even fresh from the ordeal, much of it is a blur.

"Good morning," is about all I can muster, my voice carrying the timbre of a heavy smoker. "Can you spare a few sandwiches?"

Chapter 22

The estate is enormous. Seen from where I've been studying it over the last four days—from a hilltop half a mile away—it's a colossus of windows and gardens and well-manicured labyrinths, all surrounded by an imposing yet tasteful wrought-iron gate. It is as if some force gathered all the old buildings back at Evanston to form one complementary structure of aged stone and tiled roofs with Italian influences.

Using binoculars I scan every inch of the place, as I have numerous times in committing it to memory. Once again I count seven security cameras, but there's likely several more than that, just not that I can see from here. Either way, it's clear that there is little chance of anyone entering the grounds of the estate without attracting notice.

I lower the binoculars and return to the van. Esperanza is leaning against the fender, adjusting the ill-fitting legs of her borrowed pants. The rightful owner of the white uniform is taller, forcing Espy to roll up the pant legs to keep from stepping on them.

"Are you ready?" I ask.

She nods. The time for arguing logistics is over, finished sometime during our six-day convalescence. We spent a day in Kent Station, the only occupants of a run-down motel, licking our wounds and doing our best to avoid others' curiosity. There was also the problem of money. Everything Espy and I owned went up in flames with Jim's house, including the money we borrowed from Angie. And I couldn't think of a safe way to get a message to Duckey, not with the likelihood that, having lost track of us, the ones pursuing us would turn to bugging our friends and family. It was Espy's chance now. Through her network a message found its way to Romero, and soon we were five thousand dollars richer. Thus fortified, we bought a ride to Adelaide, then caught a bus to Ballarat, where we disappeared, allowing the city to swallow us up.

The Manheim estate begins ten miles south of the city limits and stretches for miles beyond that. From what I've been able to learn, most of the land is undeveloped, designated as a private wildlife refuge—a status with tax benefits, also exempting the owner from undergoing an inspection of the area by a local or government agency. The Manheims probably earn a tax write-off of a few hundred thousand dollars solely by leaving the land alone.

Espy and I have spent much of the last four days doing nothing but watching the grounds. We've noted and cataloged the comings and goings of every vehicle, the movements of the staff—who seem few in number, considering the size of the estate—even the pattern of light usage through visible windows. We're as prepared as we're going to be. There comes a point when one must take some decisive action to move things forward. I can't stay in this place forever, living under Manheim's nose. Nor can I return to Evanston while this thing remains unfinished. Each time I leave my apartment, I would be looking over my shoulder.

The landscaping van was Espy's idea. We watched them drive in on our second day here, and they spent almost six hours working among the multitude of hedge mazes, flower beds, and the lawn on the east side. By the time they knocked off for the day, we had our plan sketched in. I walked into the shop at Green Gardens Landscape Service expecting suspicious questions as I pried for information about the crew responsible for the Manheim grounds. Instead, I was met with an indifference that marked the employees as average working stiffs who didn't care about anything beyond their next paychecks. Soon I had the names of the two operators of van number three, even the location of their favorite after-work hangout—a dive located less than a mile from Green Gardens. Three rounds of beer and two hundred dollars are all it took to convince my new friends, Joel and Napalm—I never got a definitive answer about whether that is the man's given name—to take a paid sick day, misplace their uniforms, and lose their keys. According to Napalm, Green Gardens would cancel the next maintenance trip with a promise to double up the following week. That way, Espy and I wouldn't run into a replacement crew when we assume our new identities.

Behind the steering wheel of the van, Espy shifts gears as we turn onto the road that leads to the estate's entrance. It's almost anticlimactic when, less than three minutes later, we pull into the long and stately driveway. I barely have time to get my hat on before we're climbing a gentle slope of stone pavers, approaching the security gate. I glance at the shrubbery on both sides of the concourse—beautifully shaped, and the spacing is spot-on. I agree with Napalm: no one would know that the third bush on the left is new, a replacement for one that succumbed to a fungus. It matches the others in every way.

"Those guys do great work," I say.

I slouch down in my seat as Espy slows the van and stops

next to the security station. She leans out the window and presses a button, and I hear a faint buzzing sound coming from the call mechanism. I keep my head low, the hat all but covering my eyes, while trying to make it appear as if I'm not hiding. A moment later the gate swings open, and Espy drives through without any change in her expression. As we watched the crew do earlier, we park in the front roundabout, near the cherub fountain on the east side.

We exit the van and go straight for the back of the vehicle, where I open the door and pull out a gas-powered edger. Espy reaches for a wheelbarrow. It's upside down, resting on a cushion of pine mulch ten bags strong. She gives it a yank and then guides it into a twist while in the air so that it comes down on its wheel. It bounces once and she steadies it at an angle so she can reach the bags of mulch and pull them across and into the wheelbarrow.

"Nice," I say.

"I grew up on a farm, remember?"

"Just don't wear yourself out. We're not here to plant daisies."

"Daisies would never survive in this climate. The soil is mostly clay and there's too much sun."

"I'll remember that. Thanks."

I start the edger and work my way toward the front door, keeping my eyes to the ground. I pass three of the security cameras that I noticed during our reconnaissance, and two that are hidden in trees along the walkway. Whoever owns this place—be it Victor or his father or some other relative who exists solely for cooking the books—they exhibit an elevated class of paranoia.

While I've been edging, Esperanza has brought the

wheelbarrow to the bed of perennials nearest the front door. She sits a mulch bag on its end and slits it across the top with a pocketknife, then puts an arm along the side and hoist-dumps it along the curved line of the bed. I'm aware that she's faking it, yet she almost convinces me that this is her day job, so I imagine it's good enough to fool anyone zooming in with a camera.

I reach the break in the roundabout's curve and ease up on the gas, letting the edger idle. Espy turns in my direction and starts working her way toward the flower bed closest to the front door. She uses a hoe to push the new mulch between the flowers.

I cut the power to the edger, set it down, and walk up the front steps—immaculate white stone set in graceful curves that lead to a large open area of smaller blocks and hanging plants. It looks like the kind of setting in which a president or a captain of industry would stage a photo op with dignitaries. My work boots clump along the stones as I aim for the double oak doors, my head tilted down, hat pulled low. I'm a man asking to use the restroom.

An ornate brass knocker sticks out from each of the doors, and it strikes me as curious that the houses where one often finds a knocker are also those large enough for the sound to go unheard. I opt for the doorbell.

In less than twenty seconds one of the doors swings open and an austere gentlemen of perhaps seventy gazes at me with imperious subservience. It's a look signifying that while he may serve the people within these walls, most others who arrive on the doorstep are beneath him.

"May I help you?"

"I'd like to use your bathroom, if I may." I don't bother trying to fake an Australian accent. The country harbors its fair share of American expatriates, so it wouldn't be unusual to find one engaged in gainful employment.

The man looks at my uniform, the Green Gardens logo on the shirt pocket.

"As I am sure you are aware, there are facilities available in the garden house."

I can hear Esperanza coming up behind me, and I make an attempt to fill the doorway. "I know. But I imagine the ones in here are a lot nicer."

That takes the man by surprise and he arches an eyebrow. Esperanza is close enough now for me to make my move. I take a step that puts me over the threshold, forcing the man to back away. Espy follows me with a quick step, and then we're inside and she's closing the door.

My gun is out as he's opening his mouth in shock. His eyes widen at the sight of the gun and his words go unspoken. I do a quick check for interior cameras, but my gut tells me I won't find any. People like Manheim love cameras—as long as they're pointed elsewhere.

"How many people are in here?" I ask the man.

My captive studies me for a while and then crosses his arms.

"If you are intent on robbing the house, you will have to do so without my cooperation."

"Robbing?" I look at Esperanza. "Did either of us mention anything about a robbing?"

"No."

"What's your name?" When he doesn't answer, I add, "If you don't tell me, I'll have to call you Geeves, and that will be demeaning for both of us."

I can see that Espy is growing anxious. The longer we stay

in one place, the greater the chances that someone will stumble on this little one-act play unwinding in a setting suitable for an Ibsen performance. I take Geeves by the arm, placing the gun just above his right kidney. Even as I do so, I find it difficult to remain in my own skin. Less than a month ago, no one could have convinced me that I would soon force my way into someone's home and threaten an innocent person with a gun. It flies in the face of everything I thought I knew about myself.

I propel Geeves through a doorway to the left, then through a small greeting room and out an exit along the right wall. Now we're in a narrow, dimly lit hallway, lined with three doors, all on the left side. If I were able to see through the wall on the right, I would be looking back into the foyer we just vacated.

I reach for the knob of the nearest door. It's a coat closet, empty save for a pair of black shoes on the floor. Not only is it inadequately supplied, it's too shallow for what I have in mind. I close it and try the next door, which turns out to be a much better choice. It's a utility closet, and about eight feet deep. An assortment of brooms and mops, a shop vac, various cleaning solutions, and two rolled carpets fill the space, and there's a large sink mounted on the back wall. Looking over the room's contents, I notice there's a thin layer of dust covering everything. It suggests that this is a secondary storage area, one not often used by the staff. It's perfect.

I guide Geeves into the room, forcing him far enough in so that both Espy and I can join. I find the light switch and then close the door. I hand my partner the gun and, though we haven't rehearsed this part, she takes it with only a minimum of fumbling. Once she has it pointed in the right direction, I push Geeves face-first against the wall, slip my hand behind his coat, and search his back pockets. I'm rewarded with a rectangular wallet-sized bulge. Flipping through the wallet's contents, I find the man's license, pull it out and then hand the wallet back to him. I check the name.

"I really am sorry about all this, Mr. Stemple," I say. "I usually don't do this sort of thing."

He is unmoved.

I step past him and unroll one of the carpets, pleased with our good fortune. It's heavy and thick, and I'm confident the aged man will find it an unbeatable foe.

I gesture at the rug. "If you'd be so kind."

He responds with a snort and focuses his eyes on some point on the ceiling.

"We don't have time for this," Esperanza says. "If you don't move now, I'm going to put a bullet in that geriatric kneecap of yours."

There's no way of knowing if it's the tone of Espy's voice that does the trick, or the look of surprise on my face, which forces Stemple into motion. I don't blame him for the crack in his resolve. Espy even has me believing that she will indeed shoot this man.

I direct Stemple to lie down at one end of the unfurled rug. When he's in position I take the edge and fold it over him, then gently roll him along the floor, wrapping him in the thick material. There's enough length to get three complete revolutions. I take a roll of duct tape from one of the pockets of my work pants and proceed to seal him in. Stemple is now cocooned. A last length of tape serves to mute him.

I stand back and review my handiwork. I'd bet a year's salary that he couldn't budge more than an inch. Espy hands me back the gun—perhaps a bit reluctantly—and after I lock the door from the inside, we slip out into the hallway.

Juggling competing urgencies can lead to an ulcer, if the rumbling in my midsection is any indication. Espy and I are balancing two nearly incompatible realities as we navigate our way through the mansion: the necessity of conducting a search, and a keen understanding that time is not our ally. It takes us fifteen minutes to go through the first floor and I can hear the clock ticking in my head. It's only a matter of time before someone finds the old man in the closet, or wonders why there's a landscaping van parked outside but no workers in sight. The professional part of me—the one that can spend hours studying a single room in minute detail—thinks we're moving too quickly, perhaps missing something important. I have to force myself to remember that we're not searching for the bones; rather, we're hunting a person, and so a quick check of each room is all that's needed.

And I'm beginning to suspect that, besides the unfortunate Mr. Stemple, we might be the only ones here. The mansion's atmosphere is decidedly creepy. It's as if this vast estate were really a museum, and Stemple its curator. But, according to what I've been able to find out, Victor Manheim's father, George, is the lord of the estate. His signature is on the work orders received at Green Gardens. Is it possible that the family patriarch is the sole resident of the home?

A darker floor spreads out in front of us as we reach the top of a staircase. The silence here is that of a tomb. We're at the start of a hallway carpeted in a red so deep that it borders on black. It absorbs the sound of our footfalls. The décor is in the minimalist fashion: three paintings and a Renaissance-style sculpture. I try to stay focused on the six doors that open off this hallway—what turn out to be guest rooms—and yet I'm drawn to the sculpture. On closer study, it appears to be a genuine Raphael. Two men embracing each other as a loving father would hold his son. The primary figure is rendered thick, strong and well-muscled, with a long beard. But it's the secondary figure that most catches the eye, perhaps because it's grotesque—with half the body malformed, the other half perfect and beautiful. He is being succored, wept over. I can feel the emotion the artist felt as he coaxed it from the stone. It amazes me an object of such priceless value occupies a precarious position in the hallway. One clumsy move and this masterwork could be severely damaged. I reach out to touch the sculpture and have to force my hand back. I release a sigh and turn away and it's at that instant when another of the statue's features comes into view. I lean in closer to examine the cloak of the primary figure. It's easy to miss—near the cloak's midsection, near the beltline: the oblong *S*.

Espy doesn't see it, so I point at the discovery and find that my hand is trembling. We share a look, which is all we can do right now, and then we leave it behind. It's another piece in a puzzle that's growing more and more intricate.

We emerge from the hallway onto a balcony overlooking the foyer below. Turning and looking through the windows along the upper wall, I can make out the grounds in the back of the estate. We're in the narrow portion, where the front and back boundaries are separated by about fifty feet. The bulk of the mansion lies ahead, through a hall identical to the one we have just passed.

We conduct cursory inspections of the guest rooms, then walk through a small antechamber that allows us a choice of continuing through three different archways. I don't give the matter much consideration before selecting the one on the left. I lose track of time as we search the mansion, and the feeling that we're alone—that only ghosts occupy the place with us—increases with each passing minute. If Mr. Stemple is the only other living soul here, then everything we've done over the last five days has been pointless. Unless we just happen to stumble upon the bones themselves.

Esperanza, who has been walking in silence with me for what has to be forty-five minutes, touches my elbow.

"Jack, there's no one here."

I'm inclined to agree when, rounding a corner that I think will take us back to the antechamber, I see a shaft of light coming from a room halfway down the corridor. The door of the room stands partly open. Espy sees the light too and goes silent.

Up to now, I've paid little attention to the gun in my hand, mostly pointing it at the floor. Now my hand snaps up and the weapon points straight ahead. Slowly, the two of us close the distance to the light source. Reaching a point where I can risk a peek into the room, I see three upholstered chairs, a fireplace, and the end of a bookcase. Just as I decide to take a step closer to see more, I'm startled by a voice.

"Please come in, Dr. Hawthorne. And bring Ms. Habilla, won't you?"

CHAPTER 23

"There's no point in keeping the man waiting," I say to Esperanza with a smile that is half genuine. The bad news is that this meeting will not occur on the terms I would have preferred, but it will happen, and that's something of a victory. With the gun ready, I walk into the room, Esperanza close behind me.

My first impression of George Manheim is that, unlike the pattern in most families, the apple that is Victor fell well away from the tree and then rolled downhill a considerable distance. He's in a chair, a book in hand. I find I have to remind myself why I'm here—what George Manheim and his agents have done to those close to me.

"How did you know I was here?" I ask him.

"Please, Dr. Hawthorne. What kind of man doesn't know what's going on in his own home?" He gestures to the chairs by the fireplace. "Would you care to sit down?"

"Not really."

I look around the room, not certain what I'm searching for. This is all too simple, too cordial. Surely he's pressed an alarm of some sort, and we'll be surrounded by police, or worse, his own private security, in a matter of seconds.

"I can assure you that we won't be interrupted," Manheim says.

"You'll have to forgive me if I'm not comforted by your assurances."

Esperanza has taken a spot just inside the room, from which she can look out and see much of the hallway. She seems to have a knack for knowing the best way to handle this kind of situation, which is something I find disturbing.

"For good reason, I suppose," Manheim answers. "I heard about that nasty business in Laverton."

"Heard about it? You mean planned it." A flash of anger rushes through me, and my hand tightens on the gun. I can almost see myself pulling the trigger. The memory of what I saw in Jim's home is fresh. Manheim endures my anger without changing anything about his relaxed demeanor. I may even see some measure of sympathy in his eyes—the emotional resonance of a man for whom the bigger picture might necessitate casualties and for whom mourning those sacrificed is appropriate.

"I had nothing to do with that event, Dr. Hawthorne, other than bearing responsibility for bringing into the world the man who is to blame." He sighs. "Victor has shown extreme impulsiveness over the last few years."

"Even if that were true, in my book that's enough."

"Enough to what? Shoot me in cold blood?" Manheim sets his book on an end table and shifts forward in his chair. "No. I don't think so. There are two reasons you're not going to kill me, Jack. May I call you Jack? The first is that you're not that sort of man."

"Don't count on it. Some of your employees—or your son's employees—found that out." It's false bravado. I know it and Manheim knows it.

"Necessity makes animals of us all."

"What's the second reason?"

"You want answers, and you can't get them if I'm dead."

It's a baited hook. And exactly the right thing to say. I shake my head as if to chase away the siren song of information, of answers. I gesture with the gun, indicating the whole of the estate. "Where is everyone? Family, security? It can't be just you and Stemple here."

At the mention of Stemple's name, Manheim's eyes darken a shade. "I trust that Andrew is unharmed?"

I answer with silence, feeling a bit smug that I've said something to upset him. It's not a fair fight if only one of us is on the slippery slope.

But Manheim only smiles and says, "I'll have to assume that he's fine, Jack. I honestly don't believe you'd hurt someone simply for being difficult."

He starts to get up and I raise the gun back to level, just now realizing that I'd let it slip.

He waves me off. "I'm just going to pour myself a drink. Would you care for one?"

He gives Esperanza a wink, then crosses the room to the bar. He chooses a scotch and decants a generous amount into a glass. His back to me, he takes a sip, his hand on the bar.

"There's nothing here, Dr. Hawthorne." When I don't answer, he turns to face me. "You asked why there is no one here. No security. No family. The truth is that Victor is all the family I have left." He takes another drink and returns to his chair, placing his free hand on the chair's back. "There's no security because there's nothing left to protect."

I absorb the words. "The bones . . ."

"Are gone. Transitioned." He gives a short laugh. "Our time is finished, Jack. There are new caretakers now."

I work hard to process what he's said. There's a part of

me—the part that has sought validation for the sacrifices I've endured—which is exuberant at having this confirmation. Regardless of whether or not the bones have any power, Manheim has corroborated their existence. Yet the skeptic in me remains. I need to see them for myself, perhaps touch them. And Manheim has robbed me of that hope.

"Why?" I ask.

"Because that's the way it's always been. I'm certain your research has established that fact. I'm only surprised you've made it this far at a time that coincides with the bones' relocation." He indulges in another drink, draining most of the contents of the glass. "You should be proud, Jack. Few have learned of their existence, much less been this successful in their inquiries."

"*Proud* isn't the word I'd use."

"And you, Ms. Habilla. Do you not feel some satisfaction for being involved in one of the greatest coups in the science of antiquities?"

"With all due respect, Mr. Manheim, coming away empty-handed is hardly a coup," Esperanza says.

"Let's call it a triumph of the human spirit, then."

"You can call it whatever you want," I interject, "but we have to face the reality that my brother and several of my friends are dead, along with two men on the Manheim payroll."

"And thousands of men before them, and who knows how many to come. Even I don't know the number of all those who have lost their lives because of the bones, which is ironic when you think about it." He shakes his head and downs the rest of the scotch. "They have the power to heal—to raise the dead—yet they have been the cause of more death than any holy relic apart from the grail."

"Do you really believe that?"

"There is no room for doubt. They are as real as this chair." He brings a wrinkled hand down on the seat.

It's a forceful statement, and my gut counsels me against challenging it, so I try another tack.

"Why are you telling me this?"

"Because you won't find them. And because I think I owe you at least this much."

"That doesn't make any sense. If Elisha's bones exist, and if there has been some grand conspiracy to keep them hidden, why risk it? Aren't you concerned that I'll leave here and divulge your secret?"

"I'm not risking much. Whether or not you're willing to admit it to yourself, you were convinced of their existence before I said a word. As for revealing the secret to the world, well, let's just say that better men than you have tried."

"The Raphael," Espy says.

Manheim gives her an appreciative look. "Among others."

I run a hand through my hair, trying to dispel disbelief. I set the safety on the gun and slip it in my pocket. Manheim offers a knowing smile.

"The *S* on the sculpture, the same symbol on the carvings in the temple . . ."

"Identifying an organization, one as old as the bones themselves," Manheim says. "The first incarnation were Hebrew priests. Over the centuries, that dynamic has changed somewhat."

"The church in Ethiopia," I say, but Manheim ignores the conjecture.

"They're the ones who select the families, who facilitate the transitions and keep a watchful eye on those who would seize the bones for their own use."

"The brokers."

Manheim laughs. "I suppose that's as good a name as any."

"But . . ."

"Why transition the bones at all?" he finishes for me. "Why not just keep them within the organization?"

I nod.

"For the same reason there is more than one branch to your government. It's a check against misuse. They can concentrate on protecting the bones while avoiding the politics that invariably creep into any organization."

I don't have an immediate response. I'm in the strange position of having too many questions to ask them in a logical fashion. But then the one question I should have asked first, the one I've harbored for years, suddenly rises to the surface.

"What was at KV65? What did my brother die for?"

"Like the Raphael," Manheim says, "the tomb held unauthorized information about the brokers. A good deal more detailed than the symbol on the sculpture." He gives me a sympathetic look. "I wish I could say your brother died for the bones, Jack."

While it's not the answer I wanted, there is some closure. Yet there's something else I need to know.

"Did you order it?"

Manheim shakes his head. "Actually, Victor was tasked with handling the matter. I would have been more subtle."

I feel the anger returning now.

"Why a conspiracy at all? If the bones can do what you say they can, why not use them?"

"Gordon Reese," is Manheim's grim response. "And men like him. Reese has been after the bones for a very long time.

He has finally succeeded in tracking them to me, which is why they've been moved. Should he ever succeed in acquiring them, we both know what would happen. What if they had wound up in the hands of someone like Caligula, or Genghis Khan, or any one of a thousand other powerful despots? The reason that no individual tyrant can take the world to a place from which it could never recover is because people die. It's something of a safety mechanism, I suppose."

"So why keep them around at all? If they're that dangerous, why weren't they destroyed centuries ago?"

Manheim releases a heavy sigh and it makes him look even older. He steps around the chair, his hand trailing along the back, the arm, and he sinks into it.

"One should tread carefully when considering what to do with something God has vested with great power. It's been the dilemma of every incarnation of your brokers, ever since the original Hebrew priests took them from the men who removed them from the burial site. Do you know, Jack, that the priests killed those men? Not only that, they killed the man who had been raised from the dead. They were so fearful of what these bones meant that they murdered a person who was touched by the hand of God."

"And they still kill for them." It is not a question.

"When necessary." Manheim pauses, then gives me a wink. "I trust that Gregory Hardy is no longer a problem?"

"That one was handled by them, and I suspect Reese will be next."

I'm enthralled, like a schoolboy who has been shown something fantastic in a science lab. Every word of it might be a lie, but there's something eminently believable about the tale. I find myself drawn to this man, to the knowledge he possesses. I want to know what he knows. It's a need that has defined my life.

Esperanza has taken a seat in one of the chairs by the fireplace. Before joining her, I pour myself a drink from the bar. In the space of a few minutes, the confrontational nature of this audience has been replaced by a meeting of kindred minds.

"And what about Victor?" I ask.

"Victor will not see the bones pass into his possession."

"Why?" Espy asks.

"For the same reason that Mr. Reese cannot have them. Neither of them would be suited to the task."

I'm about to press the matter when a concussive sound all but deafens me. It seems to happen in slow motion, the red stain that appears on Manheim's white shirt. It spreads in a flower pattern, a deadly orchid. Both Esperanza and I are out of our seats before the ringing stops.

And there, standing in the doorway, is Victor, his gun now aiming at me. "Please sit down, Dr. Hawthorne." His voice is almost pleasant, as if shooting one's father is something of no great consequence.

There's a pain in my skull that I can only associate with hatred, and with having something hard-won snatched away. I watch the life bleed away from my link to the ancient secrets.

"Why?" I practically spit.

"Because he would give them away rather than entrust them to me. Now take a seat."

It's a good suggestion because my legs feel weak. Esperanza has already complied and sat down. I reach a hand back for the chair while slipping my other hand into my coat pocket, where I feel cold metal. Victor is less than five feet away, so when I fire the gun through the coat fabric, the bullet strikes true. He's propelled backward, his free hand clutching his shoulder. But when he lands, he's still holding the gun.

I'm across the room in a second, jumping on top of him, pressing my own piece behind his ear. It's all I can do to keep from blowing his head off. This is the culmination of everything I've experienced since leaving Evanston; this man is the embodiment of my own personal devil. The pain in my temple is stronger now, a pulsing sensation that fires the nerve endings behind my eyes.

"Jack." Esperanza's voice is soft but insistent.

I shut my eyes against the pain and concentrate on breathing. I force the anger to a place further back, where it can simmer instead of boil. And still I want to kill this man. Instead, I push myself up and then bring the butt of the gun down on his head. Breathing heavily, I turn and find Espy staring at me.

She puts a hand on my shoulder. "Are you all right?"

I nod, then point at Victor. "Can you do something with him?"

The front of George's shirt is covered red, a trickle of blood still flowing from the wound. When I reach the chair, I see that the old man's hand is moving. I bend down toward him and he grabs my forearm. It startles me so that I almost pull away. His lips are moving as tiny bubbles of frothy blood pool in the corners. I bring my ear close to his mouth.

". . . keep them from Reese." The next bit is incomprehensible. His eyes are closed, and I can see him fading, yet his hand on my arm remains strong. "They're still here."

"What?"

"The bones are here. . . ."

Chapter 24

I've always wanted a wine cellar. Not the brightly lit, modern, temperature-controlled variety favored by the upper middle class, the kind that exists solely so they can hold dinner parties and tell their guests they have to pop down to the wine cellar to select a nice Beaujolais. No, I fancy having a wine cellar like this one: the dark, dank, moldy kind lifted directly from a Poe story, with casks labeled by region, year, and vintner, and bottles of all kinds arranged in rows and columns crafted from wood dating back to the time of Columbus. To say that I am surrounded by a fortune in processed grapes would be a gross understatement. And such is my preoccupation that the wine goes mostly unnoticed.

My hand trembles as I run a finger along a cedar shelving unit well into the cellar against the south wall. The chamber was cut from the bedrock with such skill and care that the shelf structure abuts the wall with seamless precision. I push a thick layer of dust aside with my finger, and it falls from the wood like gray snow. I don't feel anything, but I'm certain this is the place. Manheim said it twice, and I absorbed his words. If I live to be a hundred, I'll still be able to repeat each and every syllable the dying man uttered. I take slow steps across the stone floor, letting my finger glide along the wood. I'm about to stop, retrace my steps, and try again, when I feel a hole in the frame.

I smile at Esperanza, who accompanies me with eagerness equal to my own. I reach into my pocket and pull out a ring, the one Manheim instructed me to remove from his finger. I hold it up to the light and it glints in the yellowish glow: the Manheim crest emblazoned in opal. I fumble for a moment until I can slip the ring's gem into the hole, which accepts it as if it had been machined to the proper size.

I'm not sure what I was expecting, but it was more than the nothing that follows.

"So you're going to be difficult," I mutter, releasing the ring, allowing it to remain seated in the hole.

"What's wrong?" Espy asks.

Hands on hips, I look around the room, searching for anything that might make this easier. "Nothing. Nothing's the matter."

Except that the room is clean. There's not even a piece of wood lying around that I can jam into the seam—provided I can locate the seam. I move to the right and start to run my hand over the bedrock. Although likely hidden, there remains a seam somewhere along this length of wall, probably within eight inches of the shelving. That would have been common to any work done during the time period in which the cellar was built. The problem is that master craftsmen were hired for this job, and they hid the seam well. I close my eyes, relying on the sensitivity of my fingertips. I feel every stone, every rising and sinking of the surface, though nothing with the constancy of a seam. I open my eyes and step back.

"Come here," I say over my shoulder. I scan the hundred or so bottles set into their nooks and select the dozen that, according to my limited knowledge, are the rarest, the most expensive. I pull these from the shelves and begin handing them to Espy.

"What are you doing?" she asks as she accepts two bottles.

"We're not animals, are we?"

"I suppose not."

There is still an element of time that dictates our actions, even if I buy in to George's insistence that we're alone here. Who knows what the younger Manheim has orchestrated. It's this uncertainty that makes me willing to sacrifice. Once the dozen bottles are safe, I go to the left of the shelving unit, wrap my fingers around the column board, and pull. At first, nothing happens. I tug hard and can detect no give, nothing to indicate any movement. I let go, rub my hands together, take hold of the wood again, and pull.

Passages like this one, even though constructed with weighty materials such as stone, would have been designed so a single person could manipulate them—the magic of hinges and rollers. I'm not sure, then, what's making this so difficult, especially considering that Manheim could not have left the bones unobserved for decades. I wonder if there's another entrance that he didn't have time to make known to me. Sweat is beading on my forehead, and I'm about to release, when I hear a cracking noise and watch as a thousand-pound slab of rock detaches from the wall and swings open. At least half of the remaining wine bottles are upset by the motion and tumble from their perches in a deafening cacophony. But the commingling of expensive wine into a pool does not mar my excitement as the dim electric lighting reveals the first few feet of a roughhewn passage, one that disappears into darkness.

This moment is the personal crucible for any archaeologist worth his or her salt. It's the point at which the thrill of discovery—the desire to jump in—is tempered by the sobering knowledge that one false move could destroy months of work.

While this is an unusual case—a well-preserved passage, new in archaeological terms, and cared for by acolytes—there is still the unknown that's encountered at any dig, where you can never know what lies down a corridor, what sort of condition any artifacts might be in, or if one ill-conceived step could upset some weight-bearing balance and bring a ton of solid rock down on what you've come to discover.

And for the first time in my professional life, I find that I don't care.

I turn on a flashlight we borrowed from the electrical room on the first floor—after securing Victor, who is still unconscious. I shine the beam of light into the passage. It curves slightly for about twenty feet and slopes downward until I can see nothing but rock and dust, then darkness.

"Ready?"

Espy nods and we step in. It's an entirely different atmosphere than when we entered Quetzl-Quezo. There's a heightened energy, a sense of expectation, and a healthy dose of respect for the unknown. If I were back in South America, or even Egypt, and this was a standard tomb, thousands of years old and filled with debris and rubble, I would feel less concerned about our safety than I do right now. Despite what one sees in movies, ancient tombs were not places in which ingenious priests devised complex defense mechanisms to deal with intruders. Those that do hold wards—beyond the standard curse carved above the main entryway or outside the burial chamber—seldom include anything beyond concealed pits or garroting wires. What concerns me here is that this is not an ancient tomb, but a relatively modern one, built in a time when people harbored fantasies about the ancients of the pyramid age. It's possible the builders might have included traps based on popular fiction—amateurs attempting something that the masters would not have tried.

We proceed slowly, taking short steps, allowing the flashlight to illuminate every inch of a corridor that looks to have been carved from the rock by heavy machinery. I lead the way, following the curve and the downward slope, and stopping when I see that the passage transitions to a brick-lined hallway less than a dozen feet ahead. I aim the light along the border, looking for potential threats, traps, anything hinting of danger. It looks clean so I move forward, trailing my hand along the old brick. Up ahead, the light disperses, indicating the hall opening up to something larger.

When Espy and I reach the end of the hall, we look out over a chamber of shapes and shadows. It's too large for me to get a true feel for it; the flashlight reveals a box here, a display case there, a wall hanging opposite us, but too far away to identify. The beam of light refuses to remain on anything and I realize that I'm shaking. My arm is shaking with the rush of discovery, the defining moment when the heart quickens, when the chest knots in some strangled emotion that's impossible to identify, except to know that it's good.

"We need more light," Espy says, stepping down into the chamber.

"Stop." I croak the word, transfixed somewhere between elation and fright. If there are any traps built into this place, there's a good chance they would manifest themselves here. I shine the light in her direction and find that she's taken a single step down to the chamber floor, which I see is cement, but she has gone no farther. I play the beam in small circles away from her position. More of the same. I step down and take her elbow in my hand.

"Don't go anywhere or touch anything unless I say so, got it?" I don't expect an answer, and she doesn't provide one other than to disengage her arm from my grasp.

I turn around and start to search along the entry wall, because Espy has a point about us needing more light. And there should be a source of artificial light for this room. I see that the wall itself is brick, giving the place a bunker feel rather than a tomb. Since there's nothing to the right of the entrance, I go to checking the left side. It's there, almost within arm's reach, and it seems an incongruous thing when I'm thinking of this event as another Tutankhamen discovery. Somehow a light switch doesn't fit. With a chuckle I step over and flood the chamber with light.

Almost before the deed is done, I see the small hole below the switch, just the right size to accept the ring's gem, but I can't stop the switch from completing its arc. There's a rumbling beneath our feet, like a subway car racing under a pedestrian walkway. I hear the grind of old gears and register movement at the entrance. I grab Esperanza and pull her down, stretching myself to cover her as a mixture of dust and stone and pieces of brick rains down on us. When it's over, Espy and I are coughing from the debris that wants to nest in our lungs. Finally the dust clears enough to see again, and all I can do is purse my lips and silently curse my own idiocy. Our exit is gone, blocked by a massive stone plug. What irritates me is that this is one of the traps the Egyptians used.

Esperanza, after taking in what has just happened, fixes me with a withering look.

"At least we have light," I try. And we do. Half a dozen three-bulb fixtures hang from the ceiling, bringing the room to life, and the repository of secret knowledge they reveal forces our dilemma from my mind.

The room is all bricks and concrete, a few sparse wall hangings, a long bookshelf lining one of the walls, and four display cases staggered in the center. Maybe it's because my experience is in crumbling structures, layers of sediment, and treasures teased from hiding, but I find it all a bit odd.

I stand and help Esperanza to her feet. I begin searching again, propelled toward the nearest display—a hardwood box unit, shallow, with a two-paneled glass top secured with a lever lock. Inside is a tattered scroll, unrolled and tacked on to chemically neutral hard plastic. The writing is faded, virtually gone in some places, but I can read enough to understand that it's a portion of an early copy of the Bible story that Reese quoted to me. There's no way to tell for certain its age, but if I had to guess I'd date it back to the fourth century B.C. I run my hand along the case, wishing I could touch the fragile parchment. It takes a moment before I realize that Esperanza is not with me. I spot her over by the bookshelf, paging through one of its wares.

I step over to the next display and what I find makes little sense to me. It's a collection of symbols on different mediums: cloth, wood, metal, clay. From what I can see, they bear no resemblance to the family crests at Quetzl-Quezo. If I were conducting a typical dig, this is something I would photograph, catalog, and later spend several happy months investigating. Today, however, I can only sigh before moving on.

"Jack, you've got to see this."

What she places in front of me is not a book but a series of hand-bound pages. I take it from her and flip through the pages, noting there are perhaps eight photos, individuals of historical importance, and a few pages of text for each one. The text is written in German.

"Since I don't speak German, you'll have to tell me what I'm looking at." I stop at a picture of Albert Einstein, the most recognizable of the subjects.

"Wait a minute . . ." Espy reaches across and points a finger at what's printed below Einstein's photo: *1879–1936*.

"Dates of birth and death," I say. "So?"

"Einstein died in 1955."

I feel a numbness run up my legs as I realize I don't need to be able to read German to understand what the pages say.

"How did he die the first time?"

Espy scans the page. "Car accident."

Two deaths, only one of them official. For all of his caution about using them, it seems those of Manheim's ilk have not been above drawing on the power of the items in their charge. I shake my head. Stalin's picture was also among the pages.

With new eyes, I look out over the treasure trove of antiquities; of things I could spend the rest of my life researching. And none of it matters. Only one thing is important, and I won't find it in this room.

I walk away from Espy, past the display case with the odd symbols, and around a trio of crates that look as if they hold the contents of an empty display. At least the elder Manheim was honest about one thing: this circus is soon to travel. I suppose I'm the caretaker now—at least until the brokers come to collect.

I saw the door when the lights came on, but like a person who enjoys the anticipation of Christmas more than the day itself, I ignored it. I wanted to soak in the atmosphere, prepare myself before facing this portal. That silliness is gone now, stripped away by a feeling of disgust that I'm not even certain I could name a cause for. All of a sudden, I just want this to end.

I stop a few feet away and study it. It's a nondescript metal door with a simple handle. There is not even a visible lock. I suppose that Manheim's forefathers, the ones who would have accepted the bones into their care, assumed that if someone made it this far, they belonged here.

I don't belong here. But I open the door anyway.

CHAPTER 25

I stand in the threshold and let my eyes take in everything before I allow my other senses to muddle the experience. Esperanza has joined me but I register her presence in some peripheral way, as if she were a phantom. There is something about the smallness of the room, the lack of anything ornate, that I find appropriate. After all I've gone through to find them, it seems fitting they should be as stripped of accoutrements as I am.

The room is less than ten feet square, and the ossuary is the only thing in it. I suppose I thought the bones would be housed in some grand display, a lavish container for items of divine power. Instead, the ossuary is plain, and I'd date the period as first century A.D. In fact, with the exception of the lack of carvings on the exterior, it looks like the Ossuary of Caiaphas unearthed in Jerusalem in the early 1990s.

I walk in and place my hand on the box. It's cold. I begin to feel along the lid, searching for a handhold, and when I find my grip I push the old stone with all my strength. In a rush, Espy is there, adding her strength to mine until the lid moves, scraping stone on stone until we've produced a gap sufficient to peer inside. Esperanza backs away a half step, as if she is granting me dibs to the experience.

They are gathered and wrapped in purple cloth. I reach in and lift away a corner until I see them, yellow and white and brown. I release the cloth and, after a pause as my hand hangs in the air above, I touch them with the tips of my fingers. And while there's no static, no transfer of divine power from them to me, I am still satisfied. I wish I had a cigar with which to mark the moment, but the last Cuban went to ash in Lalibela.

Replacing the cloth, I pull the bones out of their nest. I turn to Esperanza. "Do you have any tape left?" She shakes her head, so I secure the bones as well as I can in their own fabric.

Espy stands back, allowing me to savor the moment awhile longer before bringing me back to the matter at hand.

"How are we going to get out of here?"

Instead of answering, I set our precious cargo to the side, crouch down, and place my shoulder against the ossuary.

"Care to give me a hand?"

The two of us strain against the weight of the box and it seems like forever before it moves, just a hair at first, but then a few inches, then a few more. Finally we push the ossuary from its dais, revealing a two-foot-wide hole with a depth of less than four feet.

"Tomb building 101," I say. "Always have two exits."

My back hurts as I straighten, and I'm breathing heavily as I scoop up the bones.

"Ladies first?"

"Not on your life."

The flashlight is worthless, most of its glass parts smashing to pieces on the floor of the larger chamber when I threw myself onto Espy. I hate the thought of entering this exit passage without a light, but this is one of those occasions when complaining accomplishes nothing.

I sit on the edge and then lower myself down, and my head and shoulders are still in the room when my feet touch bottom.

It's cold in here, but at least it's dry. I crouch and step deeper into the tunnel so that Espy can join me. As we start moving, it doesn't take long before the light is lost behind us. I feel my way along with one hand, the other holding the treasure we've crossed the world to find and are now ferrying with what is probably an inappropriate lack of ceremony.

While shuffling forward, bent at the waist, my foot hits a rough spot and I'm forced to slow down. This far into the tunnel, the darkness is as complete as it's going to be, and Espy, unaware that I've slowed my pace, walks into me just hard enough to send me to my knees.

"Watch where you're going," I say.

"Funny."

Deeper into the tunnel the air is stale and still and I feel sweat beading on the back of my neck, making my shirt stick to my body.

It goes unnoticed at first, but when I recognize that the tunnel is constricting I realize it's been happening for some time. It's not much, maybe six inches, yet enough to slow us down.

Stopping, I say, "Keep your hands on the wall."

"What's wrong?"

"Nothing." I start off again, content that I've not really told a lie because it could very well be the truth. By my foot count, we've traveled about fifty yards, and since this passage almost certainly comes up somewhere within the house, it has to reach an end soon. At the rate the tunnel is narrowing, we should be out before it becomes impassable.

A moment later I'm sitting on the tunnel floor and my face feels as if George Foreman hit me, then held me down and rubbed the tender spots with a scouring pad. White dots dance in front of me and I try to blink them away, but they hang tauntingly out of reach. I touch my forehead and wince as fire spreads out from my fingers. It's sticky, but it doesn't feel deep. Similar sensations run along my nose and right cheek.

"What happened?" Espy asks.

"I hit something."

"What?"

What, indeed. I put my legs under me and feel along the ground until I find the bones, still wrapped securely in the cloth. Once I have them I stand and, with my hand straight out in front and at head level, I take a tentative step forward until I'm stopped by solid rock. Like a blind man, I search around for meaning, for shape, and determine that the tunnel has become a crawl space. In the darkness it's hard to tell the exact dimensions but it's enough to go in headfirst and shimmy along on my elbows. I release an explosive breath and turn, placing my back against one of the walls.

"There's a little problem."

"I'm turning around and going back."

"The tunnel shrinks just past me. It's large enough to get through in an army crawl."

Espy doesn't respond. After several seconds, I wonder if she was serious and is now making her way back the way we came. I reach out for her.

"Watch it," she says and slaps my hand away.

"We have to be near the end," I say in my most reassuring voice.

"You're going first, and you're bigger than me. So as long as you don't get stuck, I guess I'll be fine."

"Thanks."

I feel my way back to the start of the crawl space. After a few deep breaths, I slip in, clutching my cargo like a football.

Here, the heat is stifling, and fresh beads of sweat run down my face and my arms as I shimmy forward, scraping my knees and elbows.

I hear Espy following close behind me. I talk to her, to calm her, when my voice catches and I can no longer speak. Before I know what's happening, the walls of the crawl space close in on me, pinning me within the rock. The stone is like a living, breathing organism, compressing and holding me in its grip. In the dark, fear is a physical thing, with long fingers that can wrap around the heart, an insidious voice that whispers terrible things—hot breath on the ear. I can't move, can't even feel where my limbs end and the stone begins. Somewhere deep in my chest is a need that manifests as pain, and it occurs to me that I'm not breathing.

My world is made up of darkness and silence, a sensory deprivation chamber that keeps me from counting the seconds or feeling the pain in my knee. My mind gropes around for an anchor, and I seize on the only image I can conjure: my brother. He's sunburned, covered with sand, and flashing a raffish grin—the same one he wore when I last saw him alive.

I feel a sob somewhere in my throat, but it won't come up because I'm locked down and it's choking me. I think I hear someone calling to me, and I think it might be Esperanza. Yet the sound is fighting a fierce wind to reach me and I lose it on the gusts. I'm buried in sand, pawing at the stuff as it gets in my mouth and in my eyes. I'm calling for help, and I think I hear someone talking to me from above me but it's unclear. All I know is sand, and that the people up above will not reach me in time.

Whatever this is, it's killing me. So, with as much effort as I can muster, I force Will from my mind. I push him out, knowing the Will in my head is nothing more than guilt. Guilt is killing me. I seize on the only thing that makes sense; and while my grasp of the idea of God is not a firm one—a tenuous handhold—it's something that feels safe.

Somewhere along the line, I come to believe that fear has brought its best game. It is roaring like an ocean in my ears and I take as deep a breath as I can and force the sound of waves crashing on rocks to fade. The icy fingers of fear still threaten to wrap around my heart, but I can exercise some control over the air entering and leaving my lungs.

Sweat covers me and I'm shivering. I focus on the idea of God, something I have never latched on to before, and yet it's all I have right now. I force my hand to move. A small thing.

I hear Esperanza's voice.

Before I pop the grate up and push it aside, I'm sucking fresher air into my body. The light hurts my eyes, but I refuse to squint against it. Instead, I let it hurt. With leaden arms I pull myself up until I'm sitting on the edge, then swing my legs over and lie on my stomach to help Espy. Once she is out, we both collapse on the dirt.

It's like a rebirth, this emerging from the hole, and I soak in every sensation.

"What happened in there?" She's raised herself onto her arm, her face close to mine.

I appreciate the concern in her eyes but we don't have the time I would need to answer that question. Back in the tunnel, once I could move, it was only a dozen hard-fought yards before the straightaway ended and forced us up. Had I concentrated, before the fear took hold, I would have noticed that the darkness was turning to gray, a subterranean sunrise. But those last yards seemed like a marathon as I processed what happened, this episode that mirrored the one in Quetzl-Quezo. It's too similar for me to dismiss the claustrophobia theory so easily this time around, yet I know there's so much more to it than that. Grief, disbelief, anger—too much to think about just now. I wonder, though, at how I latched on to God. Maybe I have more in common with my father than I realize.

My only answer to Esperanza is to lift my head and kiss her, a drive-by. I roll to the side, climb to my feet, and extend my hand. With something between a smile and a look of irritation, she takes it and I pull her up.

I make a mental note to always try to emerge from a scary tunnel into what amounts to a pruned jungle. Exotic flowers, thick vines, and verdant shrubs surround us, and medium-sized trees whose topmost branches brush against the glass ceiling of a greenhouse.

We came out of what must double as a drainage hole. Before we pushed the grate aside, I noticed a trio of smaller drains beneath my feet, to keep water from pooling and trickling back down the tunnel.

We have to be somewhere on the northeast corner of the building, which puts us at the back of the estate. We will have to either cut through it or go around to make it back to the van, assuming the vehicle is still there. I opt for outside, principally because there should be fewer opportunities for someone or something to surprise us.

"Ready to go?"

I clutch the bones to my chest and head out, not waiting for an answer. When I reach a solid wall, I realize we're not in a true greenhouse, set off from the estate, but a section built into the existing frame, the glass ceiling providing the only light for the thriving plants. I move north along the wall, passing a line of orchids in full bloom. I hear a small gasp from behind me as Espy sees the plants, and I toss a glance over my shoulder to make certain she hasn't stopped to investigate.

I hit the door at the end with a firm thrust of my forearm, and the controlled air of the estate replaces the warm, humid air of the greenhouse. To the left is a set of double doors and I angle in that direction and push them open. Just as I suspected, we're in the back, stepping out onto the terrace. I turn right and start running toward the wing on this side. Reaching the far edge, we round the corner on our way to the van. The bones, still wrapped in the purple cloth, thump against my chest as I lope along in the heavy work boots.

When we reach the front, I am cheered to see the van still in its spot. We run toward it, and I feel as light as I can remember feeling, which is a state that comes from achieving the impossible. I'm holding the bones of a biblical prophet, having liberated them from something more daunting than dirt and time.

It's when I turn my head to smile at Esperanza, to share the conspirator's nod, that I see the figure emerge from the front door. He has his good arm raised, and he's sprinting across the stone toward the stairs. We are almost at the van before Victor fires the gun; I hear bullets slam into the side of the vehicle in uniform sequence. I lunge for the passenger door and yank the handle hard enough that I can feel my fingernail start to rip away, and then a mist of blood hits the paint. Espy crumples next to me, her hand slipping from the handle of the sliding door. When I look down, only half registering that Victor is still shooting, I see a small, neat hole in the back of Esperanza's head.

Time seems to slow and I can almost see each individual cavity appear on the side of the van as the Aussie fires another salvo, but the odd thing is that I can't hear the shots, or the impacts. A growing rumble fills my ears like an angry white noise.

I am a statue, frozen by weariness, and horror, and grief anew. She's come to rest against the side of the van, her eyes hidden by strands of dark hair. The bullets pop into the van—a staccato death song. Without thinking, my hand goes to the pocket of the borrowed work pants, to the gun that felt uncomfortable beneath me as I crawled through the tunnel.

Turning toward Victor, I see him as he reaches the bottom of the steps. There's a look on his face that, if I make it out of here, I will never forget. It's a look of malevolence on a scale of which I wouldn't have thought another human being capable. I pull the gun from my pocket as Victor raises the one in his hand, and I pull the trigger, knowing I want this man dead, knowing I'm firing with malice equal to his.

My shot misses, but Victor's is true. The bullet enters my much-abused leg; it burrows through the soft tissue and shatters my kneecap. The impact staggers me back against the van, almost blinds me. Shock is a swift worker, so I don't feel it when another bullet hits me in the chest. I can see a shadow of Victor coming toward me, and as I drop to my knees I level the gun and squeeze the trigger. The kickback sends the piece falling from my fingers, clattering on the stones.

I must black out then, because I open my eyes at some point and Victor has been dead for at least a few minutes, judging by the pool of blood beneath him. A fire burns somewhere deep in my body as I bleed out, as some vital organ succumbs to the second bullet. I cry out as I try to push away from the van. I catch a glimpse of Esperanza, her face pressed against the van door, blood congealing around the wound that killed her. She's almost within reach, but I find that I can't move my legs. Although it's growing harder to draw breath, there's enough left in me to release the strangled noise that has gathered in my chest.

A wave of grief strikes me, a hot and curdling feeling that wrenches my muscles and makes my stomach roil. I feel as if I'm going to throw up. The bones lie on the ground, somewhere on the stones, but I can't look away from Espy. All at once I am hit with a range of emotions I cannot hope to decipher, except to understand that the prong of anger is sharpest. I embrace the emotion, let it wash over me, and it shoots to the surface with such force that I know it's been with me for a long time—an old friend that I've known under an assumed name.

Esperanza's face is ashen white, growing cold. I want to pull her to me but it's an impotent desire, and for the first time in my adult life I begin to cry. For the immensity of loss. For the anger that is like a second flesh. For never holding on to anything so tightly that it would kill me to lose it.

I did not cry at Will's funeral. I've carried that guilt around with me.

I'm crying not just for Espy but for Will, too. And, to be honest, I'm also crying for myself.

I spot a blur of purple not far away, half under the van between Espy and me, one of the bones poking out from a separation in the cloth. The bundle draws my attention—a magnet for emotions running wild. I field a sudden urge to destroy them, to vent my anger on the ancient, brittle relics. And I feel brave enough, or maybe despondent enough, to recognize that it would be as close to punching God in the nose as I can get. Maybe the reason I accepted this job—this task that could only result in either the proof that He is a figment of human rationalization, or that He truly exists—is because of the opportunity it offered for a moment of reckoning. Either He steps up to the plate, or I am justified in giving Him no thought whatsoever. Or maybe it was so that I could stoke an anger I never thought possible, from which I could rail against a capricious being that revels in the misfortunes of others—who would take first a father, then a brother, then a friend, and now a woman I once loved so much I had to leave her.

My strength is going as I reach for the bones. My fingers brush the fabric and then fall away. I strain again, my pointer finger almost hooking the cloth. When it slips off, a curse leaves my lips. It's vehement and ugly and aimed straight toward heaven. It's a dare of sorts, uttered by a man who is maddened by the presence of these bones, and his inability to secure something so tantalizingly close.

With one last wrench of my body, I fall away from the van, coming down on my side. I stretch out my arm, and my fingers come to rest on the purple fabric, the bones held safely within. I'm not sure what I'm thinking, but there's a small part of my fading mind that clings to some kind of newfound faith—a belief system espoused in earnest by my father—and the person of a God whom I've never wholly forgotten.

I'm falling into a dark tunnel. With my dying breath, and with a faint sound that is neither a curse nor a prayer, I nudge the bundle until the exposed bone—yellowed with age, its marrow dried and dead—touches Esperanza's lifeless hand.

Chapter 26

I wish I could have watched as life returned to Espy. She's tried to describe what it was like when she returned the favor, but she hasn't been able to find the right words; only that there was nothing overtly magical, like bright lights or music or angels—just an absolute knowledge that she witnessed something other-worldly.

That was two weeks ago. Two weeks of trying to clean up the messes we've made.

When Espy and I walked into the office of the consulate general of the United States in Melbourne, I was convinced that we were bound for long jail terms. We'd left a trail of bodies behind us, two of them prominent members of the business and political communities. We had little going for us, beyond the fact that the two men killed at Jim's house would eventually be identified as drawing from the Manheim payroll. That, and the discovery that the younger Manheim had powder burns on his hands, and the gun found with his body was determined to be the one used on the father. Still, I thought the odds were good that I would have a long tenure within the Australian penal system. About all I could hope for was that our respective embassies would provide gratis legal assistance, and a way to shield us from at least a portion of the punishment we were sure to receive.

We decided, together, that we could not tell anyone about the bones—no matter the cost.

Then it just went away. One day the Australian Federal Police were interviewing us, for the twentieth time, and the next day we were free to go. No explanation. I would find, days later, that none of it had wound up in the press. Not a single mention, beyond the murder/suicide that killed a prominent family in Ballarat, and the death of an elderly couple in a house fire near Laverton. I am angered that the story surrounding Jim and Meredith was spun to be a lie; I have my suspicions about who made it happen. I wonder when the people of the oblong *S* will come calling—looking for the bones to hand over to the next caretakers.

Espy sits next to me in the Humvee. She's quiet. She has been this way since the police let us go. I think, though, that it's not a bad quiet as she's going over in her mind everything that has happened, and I imagine it will take some time. I know how she feels. There is much that I need to ponder in the coming days, much of it related to responding to a God who has proven himself to be something other than fiction. For the first time in years, maybe I can do it without artifice, without cynicism. But I sincerely hope that's not a spiritual prerequisite, because I might be sunk.

Right now that's not important. There's only one thing that is.

The wind feels warm against my cheek and I squint to keep the sand from entering my eyes. The sun is in that place just above the horizon where it seems to hang forever before beginning a grudging descent, as if having second thoughts about allowing the moon to replace it in the sky. For a few moments I stand and watch the dunes form and then re-form themselves, the grains of sand as fluid as water, making the desert an inconstant thing.

The Humvee is behind me, packed with enough water and food to last two weeks, along with extra gas, a radio, a tent, and anything else I could think to add to the manifest. But the most important item is the shovel, which I hold in my hands. It's old, pitted and worn, and seems appropriate to the task.

While the sun disappears, I dig a hole in the solid ground beneath the sand cover. It is hard work, but I don't mind. It's a penance of sorts. I dig it deep, each shovelful of earth like an offering. And when I've finished, when the desert air has turned cool and sweat runs down my body, I pick up the bones, wrapped in burlap, and drop them in the hole. And as the disturbed dirt falls back on them, I do not feel any guilt, no sense of loss. I work until the earth is packed down.

When I return to the truck, I toss the shovel into the back and then take Espy's hand in mine, and we stay there until the light is gone.

ACKNOWLEDGMENTS

Many people deserve my heartfelt thanks for helping to make *Elisha's Bones* a reality. But I'm going to start with those who have the power to say yes or no to more books! I'm grateful that Dave Long decided to bring *Elisha's Bones* to Bethany House, and especially thankful for all the hard work he did to make it a better book. Luke Hinrichs did the same—editing this thing until it became respectable. Thanks, Dave and Luke, and everyone else at Bethany House, for all the effort you put in. I'm looking forward to doing it again!

I signed with my agent, Les Stobbe, in 2004, and he spent the next four years sending out one manuscript after another. Thanks, Les, for sending that last one out, and for your constant encouragement through the process.

Almost fourteen years ago I wrote a book with my friend Rob Heidel and, while that one never found a publisher, working with Rob taught me a lot. Thanks, Rob. It's quite possible I wouldn't be sitting here typing up an acknowledgments list if we hadn't written that first page.

Back in 2004, Michael Snyder all but dragged me to a writers' conference, where I met and signed with my agent. A year or so later, he introduced me to a little online community called Faith in Fiction, where I first met Dave Long. So I guess it's fair to say that if you don't like the book, Mike bears almost as much blame for that as I do. Thanks, Mike—especially for the countless critiques I've asked of you over the years.

If anyone has waded through more of my writing than Mike, it's Ryan Burkholder. Ryan has slogged through one manuscript or short story after another and has offered needed encouragement, advice, and a literary perspective. Thanks, Ryan.

Sarah Wood, Angela Fox, Jerry Fox, and Chris Ude have also been helpful critics over the last few years. Thanks, all, for reading the pre-published stuff.

Thanks to the Laufer clan—Chris, Patty, Matt, Lisa, Bill, Kathy, and Tim—and Russ Gullekson, and Dave and Mary Ferrini, for late nights and much laughter.

Thanks to author par excellence Jeanette Windle, who was kind enough to say some nice things about a very poorly written book of mine (not this one!) years ago. Encouragement like that can make a guy keep writing until he gets it right.

Mike Rajczak was the first person who encouraged me to become a writer, way back in middle school. Thanks, Mike.

Thanks to Mandy Peitz for contributing to the cover artwork.

Finally, to Alyssa and Aidan—thanks, kids, for making it a whole lot of fun to be a dad. I love you.

About the Author

Don Hoesel, when not writing, works in the communications department of a large company. He holds a B.A. in Mass Communication from Taylor University and has published short fiction in *Relief Journal*. Don lives in Spring Hill, Tennessee, with his wife and two children. *Elisha's Bones* is his first novel.

If You Enjoyed *Elisha's Bones*, You May Also Like:

NEW!
Lured by the promise of restitution, disgraced FBI agent Greg Cayhill accepts an offer to work on a high-profile terrorist case. Yet he suspects not all is as it seems, and soon he finds himself fleeing for his life in a desperate cross-country pursuit. Racing against the clock—and would be assassins—the lives of millions depend on his survival.

Ulterior Motives by Mark Andrew Olsen

As the lives of Abby Sherman and her would-be killer collide, they are caught in a globe-circling adventure with the survival of an ancient spiritual society in their hands. From California to Nigeria, the war is never what they thought it would be.

The Watchers by Mark Andrew Olsen

Once again Abby Sherman and Dylan Hatfield must team up in the face of an evil onslaught. As they race to find an age-old secret, they rouse the Church's Warriors to action—and find themselves in the center of the fiercest spiritual battle of their time.

The Warriors by Mark Andrew Olsen

Grant Borrows has been Shifted: there's another man wearing his face; the man in his own mirror is a stranger. As his ordinary life ends, he learns he's connected to an ancient prophecy—and the central figure in a web of global conspiracy. He's now in a race—both for the truth of his identity and ultimately for the survival of the world he's known.

Relentless, Fearless, Merciless by Robin Parrish
DOMINION TRILOGY